Eagles' Crag

Ethel Carnie Holdsworth Series

*Edited by Jenny Harper,
with critical introductions*

Miss Nobody (1913)
Helen of Four Gates (1917)
The Taming of Nan (1919)
The Marriage of Elizabeth (1920)
The House that Jill Built (1920)
Down Poverty Street (1921)
The Great Experiment (1923)
General Belinda (1924)
Equality Island (1925)
This Slavery (1925)
The Quest of the Golden Garter (1927)
Barbara Dennison (1928)
Eagles' Crag (1931)

Collected Poems:
    Rhymes from the Factory (1907),
    Songs of a Factory Girl (1911),
    Voices of Womanhood (1914)

Cotton Factory Shorts (1906-20)
Barbara Roster Weymouth and
       Other Stories (1913-35)

Collected Original Fairy Tales (1911-1914)

Eagles' Crag

Ethel Carnie Holdsworth

with an Introduction
by Jenny Harper

Kennedy & Boyd,
an imprint of
Zeticula Ltd,
Unit 13,
44-46 Morningside Road,
Edinburgh,
EH10 4BF
Scotland.

http://www.kennedyandboyd.co.uk
admin@kennedyandboyd.co.uk

Frst published in 1931
This edition published 2025
Reprinted 2025
Copyright © Estate of Ethel Carnie Holdsworth 2025
Cover photograph © Helen Brown 2025

Paperback ISBN 978-1-84921-249-6

Contents

Introduction

'O brotherhood of world-wide clan of humanity- wert thou
only a dream in the hearts of poets, idealists, thinkers?'

Ethel Carnie Holdsworth was a rare example of an
early twentieth century female working-class novelist.
Born in Oswaldtwistle, Lancashire in January 1886,
she died in December 1962, having written three books
of poetry, eleven novels, a prolific amount of serialised
newspaper stories and a wealth of journalism. She was
a socialist, a pacifist, an anti-fascist, a feminist and
an indefatigable campaigner supporting the causes of
workers' rights and social justice. The volume of her
literary output was driven by a practical need to earn
money, given her working-class status. She could
write in two hours 'an impossible tale in a mediocre
journal' which could earn her three guineas, whilst
full time work as a winder in Great Harwood only
brought in between thirteen and nineteen shillings.
The content of Carnie Holdsworth's writing however
was fundamentally inspired by her fiercely held
social and political ideologies. She was an ethical
socialist, and although her work was informed by a
host of literary figures (Percy Bysshe Shelley, Omar
Khayyam, Thomas Hardy), it was the American
Romanticists, particularly Walt Whitman, who had
the most influence upon her personal spiritual creed.
The British ethical socialists included members of the

Bolton Whitman Fellowship, Katharine Bruce Glasier and Edward Carpenter. They saw within Whitman's pantheistic nature writing a new model of society which seemed inherently socialist, given its central tenets of comradeship, egalitarianism and inclusivity. Carnie Holdsworth envisaged a possibility of a new life, just as Bruce Glasier had in an 1894 letter to her Fellowship comrades. "Look up, cry aloud!' Bruce Glasier had written, 'Your long travail is over: a new life is born in the land of the sun; a life of fruition, of lore and of colour — full, free and sufficing — for all or for none.'

Carnie Holdsworth's 1917 bestseller *Helen of Four Gates* can be interpreted as an example of the author exploring the vibrant possibilities of this socialist ideal. Although the plot of the novel was a tale of bitter revenge, its main protagonist Helen, whom Carnie Holdsworth described as representative of 'Life and Love', triumphs against the forces of 'Hatred, Greed and Cowardice', symbolised by the main male characters in the book. *Helen of Four Gates* was written between 1914 and 1916 during the early years of WW1; however, it was a time of relative optimism in Carnie Holdsworth's life. She had married Alfred Holdsworth on the 3rd of April 1916 and finished the final chapters of *Helen* with her first-born daughter Margaret on her knee, writing 'by aid of a honey pot.' *Helen of Four Gates* was a novel in which the natural world was brought to life in a pantheistic vision of vibrant colour, woods shone 'opal and gold', and glowed a 'brighter emerald', bluebells were 'sapphire' and flowers 'danced in a richer pomp'. In comparison, the landscape in *Eagles' Crag* seems eerily bleached, like a photo negative; it is often 'colourless [...] A great pencil-sketch, in moorland black and silver of moonlight.'

In a stark contrast to *Helen of Four Gates, Eagles' Crag* was written in 1929 or 1930, in the wake of her marriage breakdown. She left Alfred in 1927 — her mother Louisa had been advised by her daughter's doctor to 'take her away from her husband if she wanted to keep her health (sanity).' Carnie Holdsworth had also ploughed all of the money she had earned from the best-selling *Helen of Four Gates* into the anti-fascist publication *The Clear Light*, which she and her husband had edited. Through their work on *The Clear Light* the couple had sought to rouse the British people to action against the rise of fascism and the repressions of a capitalist system. They saw the fight again fascism as closely intertwined with the struggle against capitalism, believing that both ideologies exerted a hegemonic control over the labouring classes, effectively chloroforming them against the truth of the prevailing socio-political landscape and turning them into apathetic and compliant citizens.

By 1926 however, it had become clear that their political activism had failed to contribute to the kind of ideological socialist revolution that Carnie Holdsworth had envisaged and instead she and her husband were left facing intimidatory threats from the British Fascisti and financial destitution. Carnie Holdsworth became 'very ill' and in a later 3rd March 1937 *Blackburn Times* article revealed that she had experienced a 'nervous breakdown', which had left her unwell for two years. The nature of Carnie Holdsworth's literary output shifted markedly at this time and her writing became far less agitatory – her biographer Roger Smalley noted that the novels she produced after 1927, *Barbara Dennison* and *Eagles' Crag*, showed very little of the activist propaganda displayed in 1925's *This Slavery* and he believed them to be less 'successfully realised'. While it is true that the nature of the texts differs significantly from her earlier works, an analysis of the more muted complexities of meaning in *Eagles' Crag* can cast valuable light upon an almost entirely overlooked and important transitory stage of Carnie Holdsworth's life and literary output.

In a Christmas 1936 *Blackburn Times* article, Carnie Holdsworth reflected upon the turbulence of this interwar period both for herself personally and for wider society. For a fleeting moment her ethical socialist vision emerged once more as she invoked the Christmas spirit of goodwill, and urged her readers to 'come, [...] follow the Christmas sprite – and dream forwards to the sun of the unborn years.' However, she also recognised the continuing evil effects of capitalism in the article, observing 'how still the old world fights its worldly battle for place, and pride, and possessions [...] for a strip of land, or a pot of gold.' Her sense of disillusionment is apparent as she asks herself, in words that reflect the deep loss of faith conveyed in *Eagles' Crag*, 'O brotherhood of world-wide clan of humanity — wert thou only a dream in the hearts of poets, idealists, thinkers?'

Eagles' Crag therefore invites an analysis which considers it as antithetical to her earlier vision — hollow, lonely, unmoored and at times, conveying an uncanny type of crystallised lifelessness. It presents an alternative imaginary, a world of alienation in which the connection to an animated life-giving nature is disrupted and problematised.

Eagles' Crag is a gothic horror, set like *Helen of Four Gates* on an isolated farm, though this time the location has shifted from the brooding Pendle Hill with its associated history of witchcraft, to West Yorkshire. Eagle's (singular) Crag is the name of a rocky promontory high above a steep-sided valley, about one mile west of Todmorden. In profile it resembles an eagle, its wings partly outstretched and its beak jutting skyward. Rarely marked on modern maps, it is familiar to rock climbers in the area and also to locals because of a supernatural legend associated with the landmark. It seems clear that Carnie Holdsworth knew of the legend given the similarities in theme and plot between the story and her own text; she was very familiar with this area of West Yorkshire having lived at Slack Top, Heptonstall from 1922 to 1927. It is easy to see why Carnie Holdsworth made good use of the fable, since it provided an excellent narrative bridge between *Helen of Four Gates* and *Eagles' Crag*. John Roby in his 1829 text *Traditions of Lancashire* provides the definitive version of the Eagle's Crag tale. He opens his re-telling by taking the reader back to the 1600s, describing how the 'infamy, of witchcraft, [had] infested this once peaceful and sequestered district.' To 'simple-hearted' peasant folk in the area, Eagle's Crag was 'no doubt [...] oft visited by the unhallowed feet of weirds and witches pluming themselves for flight to the great rendezvous at Malkin Tower, by the side of "the mighty Pendle"', he wrote.

Pendle Hill was a landmark freighted with meaning, embedded as it was in the cultural memory as a place deeply associated with the supernatural practice of witchcraft and the persecution of transgressive, 'outcast' women. For Carnie Holdsworth, this had made it an ideal location upon which to site *Helen of Four Gates*. The traditional fable of Eagle's Crag, its close association with the folklore of the Pendle witches, its portrayal of the ghostly and the supernatural and its inclusion of a non-conforming, subjugated female figure provided the inspiration for Carnie Holdsworth's novel. In *Eagles' Crag* she was able to build on the themes first explored in *Helen of Four Gates*, and beyond this, she was able to effectively reframe and reimagine them through mining the narrative of this local folklore.

The fable of Eagle's Crag centres on a fictitious beautiful heiress, Lady Sybil of Bernshaw Tower, who once lived in the shadow of the Crag. Lady Sybil was 'celebrated for her wealth and beauty, was intellectual beyond most of her sex and frequently visited the Eagle's Crag in order to study nature and to admire the [...] surrounding landscape.' Lady Sybil desired supernatural powers and made a blood bond with the devil so that she might join in with 'the nightly revelries of the then famous Lancashire Witches.' She had an admirer locally called Lord William, who pursued her and proposed marriage; however, she rebuffed his advances. Undeterred, Lord William persuaded another local witch, Mother Helston, to assist him in his endeavour. On the next Hallow's Eve, Lord William set out hunting; upon drawing close to Eagle's Crag he startled a milk-white doe (a shape-shifting Lady Sybil), who he then chased with his hounds, in the company of a strange dog that had materialised beside him (Mother Helston's familiar). The hound seized the doe by the throat which allowed Lord William to throw an enchanted silk leash about its neck. He then led the animal to his home. By morning, the captured doe had transformed back into the fair heiress and the couple were married. However, within a year, Lady Sybil has returned to the practice of witchcraft and whilst in the form of a beautiful white cat a local manservant cut off her paw. Lord William, though angered by his wife's actions, reconciled with her and by 'some diabolical process' Lady Sybil's hand was restored. Sadly however, the experience had mortally weakened the Lady and shortly after she died. Local tradition holds that Lady Sybil was buried just beneath the pinnacle of Eagle's Crag and that on All-Hallows, the ghostly figures of a hound, a milk-white doe and a spectral huntsman can be seen in full chase as they speed across the crag.

Elements of the fable of Eagle's Crag can be traced into Carnie Holdsworth's story. Burl, the gipsy woman in the novel, is an unorthodox figure with a great love of nature just as in the case of Lady Sybil. She too becomes entangled in a doomed love affair and Burl, like Lady Sybil, dies buried beneath the rocks of Eagle's Crag. Bernshaw Tower did exist and was a small, fortified farmhouse with turrets close to Eagle's Crag. It collapsed in 1860. The tower occupied a 'commanding eminence overlooking the [...] valley and almost under the shadow of Eagle Cragg,' and was positioned exactly where Carnie Holdsworth sited the farmhouse of Eagles' Crag in her novel. The turret walls of the shadowy farmhouse which Burl prowls in the novel clearly owe much to the original historic tower and Carnie Holdsworth deftly keyed into the folklore connected to the landmark in order to build a sense of atmosphere and place.

Eagles' Crag is a dark tale of doomed love between a journeyman farm labourer from France named Henri d'Gasconne and an enigmatic gipsy woman, Burl. Henri is employed by the deranged owner of the farm, the ninety-year-old Miss Havisham-like character, Jane Mowbray, who is struck by Henri's mysterious resemblance to her one true love, a man who abandoned her and whose spirit she believes lives on in Henri. Luke, Jane's sixty-year-old 'idiot' farmhand son also lives on the farm. Jane is intent on keeping the loving couple apart in an echo of the malicious Abel in *Helen of Four Gates*. However, she is murdered under mysterious circumstances, leading to the imprisonment of Henri and Burl. Seemingly destined for the hangman's noose, the pair are sensationally freed at the last minute by the testimonies of Luke, who confesses to the deed, and a fellow gipsy who claims to have witnessed it. Upon being granted freedom, Henri craves a return to his native land and intends to leave Burl; however, in a dramatic finale she lures him back to Eagles' Crag.

She reveals that it was he who had murdered Jane in a drunken stupor and that Luke had only confessed to the crime in order to ensure Burl's release. Angered, Henri runs Burl through with a sword. As she dies, her torch falls to the ground, setting light to the farmhouse; as if in a great psychic shock, the crags above the house quake and tumble downwards into the gorge, entombing the couple beneath them.

Carnie Holdsworth revealed in the *Hepworth Magazine* that Emily Bronte's 1846 poem, 'The Stoic' had inspired her portrayal of Helen in *Helen of Four Gates*. Another poem, Oscar Wilde's 1885 'The Harlot's House' though quoted fleetingly in the text, has a significant influence upon *Eagles' Crag* and its signature portrayal of ideas of the uncanny, of the 'half human, half other' and of the eerily animate, a notion which also owes much to Sigmund Freud's later conception of the term.

Helen of Four Gates was set in a kind of hinterland in which alternative social orders could be explored because temporal and spatial normalities had been suspended. In *Eagles' Crag* this sense of dislocation is even greater, there is an even more significant shift in perspective which is expressed via the landscape of the novel, a sense of being entirely unmoored from temporal and spatial markers as bearings are lost. In Wilde's poem he gestured to a natural world which was similarly inanimate and lifeless ('black leaves') to the one often described, without colour, in *Eagles' Crag*. The unsettling and uncanny strangeness of the landscape in the novel is further expressed through Carnie Holdsworth's description of bodily figures and persona. In Wilde's verse, he depicted skeletal figures who moved in a *danse macabre*, appearing like effigies, half-living and half-dead. Carnie Holdsworth's portrayal of Jayne Mowbray, echoes this imagery, she has a 'skeleton-like countenance,' and her palsied shaking also gives her 'something of the ridiculous look of an automatic figure,' a visual image that featured in Wilde's poem, in which he described 'wire-pulled automatons.' Novelists such as Charles Dickens and Henry James had previously used such notions of the uncanny in their texts. Some of Dickens's ghost stories for instance featured apparitions and effigies who were 'supposedly inanimate but uncanny mimeses of the human,' (*A Christmas Carol, The Signalman*), and Carnie Holdsworth can be regarded as following in this literary tradition. Carnie Holdsworth presented characters as dehumanised in this way in order to make a social comment about the evils of capitalist society, in a manner which was far more subtle than in her 1925 novel *This Slavery*, but which however can be traced back via a fine thread to her earlier journalism in *The Woman Worker*.

In *Eagles' Crag* then, Carnie Holdsworth was able to build on previously explored ideas, of an animated/ unanimated landscape, of the supernatural, and of the witchlike. The notion of the uncanny fitted well within these themes and allowed her to explore and adapt them in different ways in order to present an imaginary which was profoundly unsettling, disrupted and distorted. The physical and psychic world of *Eagles' Crag* stood as antithetical to the ethical socialist vision of a new utopian life, full of colour, fruition and a seamless sense of harmony between all things.

Endnotes

1 Ethel Carnie Holdsworth, 'A Wayfarer's Diary,' *The Blackburn Times*, 26th December 1936. P. 6.

2 Working Class Movement Library, Typescripts of article/ lecture(s?) by Ruth and Eddie including list of references, notes and correspondence connected to above item, Ethel Carnie Collection, PP/CARNIE.WCML

2 Bolton Whitman Fellowship Archive, Bolton Whitman Fellowship Papers, 23rd February 1894, ZWN, 45.

4 Mrs E. Holdsworth, 'Helen of Four Gates,' *The Hepworth Magazine*, February 1921, p. 112.

I am indebted to Chris Lynch for providing me with this article, copies of these issues are extremely rare and Chris suspects his bound set may have belonged to Cecil Hepworth, the director of the *Helen of Four Gates* film, himself.

5 'The Poverty Blockade,' *Cotton Factory Times*, 14th November 1917, p. 1.

6 Ibid.

7 Carnie Holdsworth, *Eagles' Crag*, (Stanley Paul, 1928), p. 27.

8 *Eagles' Crag* was written by Carnie Holdsworth whilst living with her children and parents at 51 Rainhall Road, Barnoldswick. Roger Smalley's biography.

9 Oral testimony provided by Margaret Holdsworth, Working Class Movement Library, Typescripts of article/lecture(s?) by Ruth and Eddie including list of references, notes and correspondence connected to above item, Ethel Carnie Collection, PP/CARNIE.WCML.

10 *The Clear Light* staff was infiltrated by a member of the British Fascisti led by Rotha Lintorn Orman. In 1923 the same organisation threatened to bomb the office of the journal's publisher William Ackroyd.

11 Ethel Carnie Holdsworth, 'A Wayfarer's Diary,' *The Blackburn Times*, 3rd March 1937, p. 4.

12 WCML Margaret Holdsworth oral testimony.

13 Roger Smalley, 'The Life and Work of Ethel Carnie Holdsworth, with Particular Reference to the Period 1907 to 1931' (unpublished doctoral thesis, The University of Central Lancashire, 2006), p.322.

14 Carnie Holdsworth, 'A Wayfarer's Diary,' 26th December 1936. P. 6.

15 Ibid.

16 It's likely that she was also referring to Germany's military advances into Rhineland here which had occurred earlier that year in March 1936. These actions were in contravention of the 1919 Treaty of Versailles and caused great concern within the British Government. The Rhineland was a demilitarised area, a 'strip of land' as Carnie Holdsworth described it here, between Germany and the nations of France, Belgium and the Netherlands, and contravening it was a clear act of aggression by Hitler's Germany. Carnie Holdsworth equates the hegemony of capitalist systems with those of aggressive militaristic nations in this article, which had been a common line of argument in *The Clear Light*. https://www.nationalarchives.gov.uk/education/resources/german-occupation/

17 Ibid.

18 As noted previously, Carnie Holdsworth spoke in a 1919 *Cotton Factory Times* interview of how *Helen of Four Gates* had been 'written chiefly [...] against the crystallised lifelessness of the eugenic idea.'

19 I am indebted to members of the Pendle Radicals research group for their local knowledge and for informing me of the Eagle's Crag fable, particularly Irene Vince and relative of Alfred Holdsworth, David Rycroft.

20 Carnie Holdsworth delivered a lecture at Cornholme Labour Club near Todmorden which is less than a mile from the Eagle's Crag landmark on the 17[th of] January 1926, providing further evidence that she knew this area particularly well. I am grateful to David Rycroft for this information. Todmorden Advertiser, 22nd January 1926, p. 5, *Hypocrites*.

21 John Roby, 'Traditions of Lancashire,' https://www.gutenberg.org/ebooks/15271 [accessed 10th December 2024]

22 Malkin Tower was the reputed meeting place of the 'Pendle Witches' and home of Elizabeth Southerns (known as Demdike) and her granddaughter Alizon Device. Both were central figures in the subsequent trials. Many historians believe that the group of women gathered there to practice their Catholic faith (repressed by James I at the time) and to celebrate a Good Friday mass.

23 John Harland and T.T. Wilkinson, 'Lancashire Legends,' https://archive.org/details/cu31924028040057/page/n47/mode/2up?view=theater [accessed 10th December 2024]

24 Lady Sybil continued the literary motif employed by Carnie Holdsworth in *Helen of Four Gates*. Like the bricked-up nuns and the figure of Joan of Arc in her first novel, the fictional Lady Sybil represented a historical woman who had challenged societal and gender norms. Lady Sybil's wealth, intelligence and resistance to marriage made her a transgressive female and she is castigated much like these previous representations. Carnie Holdsworth utilised such figures as devices which enabled her to explore issues of gender prejudice and social injustice.

25 Ibid.

26 The story makes use of the folkloric superstitions associated with All Hallows Eve (or Halloween). The Celts believed that the dates of Beltane (on May 1st) and of Samhain (November 1st) were important liminal points of the year when deities and ghostly spirits could cross from the Otherworld more easily and when supernatural powers and spells were more powerful. In *Helen of Four Gates*, Carnie Holdsworth brought ghoulish beings and other figures from nature to life at the time of Beltane, indicating that she was aware of the Pagan Wheel of the Year.

27 The imagery of a white cat as a witch's familiar also appears in *Helen of Four Gates*. Sue Marsh's companion was a blind white cat in the novel and Helen drew supernatural strength from the feline before battling for the love of Martin in a pivotal scene.

28 Ibid.

29 The tower's foundations were damaged when locals dug them up in the belief that there was a pot of gold beneath them. Unfortunately, this was a local folktale which proved untrue.
Leslie Irving Gibson, '*Lancashire Castles and Towers,*' https://www.gatehouse-gazetteer.info/English%20sites/120.html [accessed 10th December 2024]

30 The Tower dated from at least 1626 and was likely to have been much older. In the Manor Survey of 1626, it was noted as being held by the Lomax family. Its existence at the time of the Pendle Witch Trials (1612), allowed the fable of Lady Sybil as a witch and the folklore surrounding the Pendle Witches to be easily associated in the early 1600s.
Anon, '*Beamshaw Tower,*' https://www.gatehouse-gazetteer.info/English%20sites/120.html [accessed 10th December 2024]

31 Jayne Mowbray also bears a strong resemblance to the character of Sue Marsh in *Helen of Four Gates*, although Jane is portrayed as a far more malevolent figure. Both women become embittered and 'withered up' having been cruelly abandoned by their male lovers. There is also a suggestion that Jane was a 'fallen woman' since she is unmarried and has a sixty-year-old son in Luke, making her even more marginalised as an 'outcast' woman.

32 Mrs E. Holdsworth, 'Helen of Four Gates,' *The Hepworth Magazine*, February 1921, p. 112.

33 Carnie Holdsworth was familiar with Oscar Wilde's work. She read Wilde's *Fairy Tales* whilst travelling in Germany in 1910 and her later children's story *The Blind Prince*, (published in *The Lamp Girl and other Stories* in 1913), was clearly influenced by Wilde.

Ethel Carnie, 'From One Girl to Another,' *Women Folk*, 11th May 1910, p. 755.

Dr. Kathleen Bell, 'An Assessment of Ethel Carnie,' https://www.cottontown.org/Culture%20and%20Leisure/Literature/Pages/Ethel-Carnie.aspx [accessed 10th December 2024]

34 Oscar Wilde, 'The Harlot's House,' https://allpoetry.com/The-Harlot's-House, [accessed 10th December 2024]

35 Carnie Holdsworth refers to Wilde's poem towards the end of the novel. As Henri and Burl take shelter in an isolated cave, she describes the arrival of morning as if 'on silver-sandalled feet,' a line from the verse.

36 Ibid.

37 Carnie Holdsworth, *Eagles' Crag,* p. 110.

38 Ibid.

39 Simon J. James, *Spectral Dickens: The Uncanny Forms of Novelistic Characterisations* by Alexander Bove, Victorian Studies, Volume 65, Number 3, Spring 2023, pp. 504-506. https://muse.jhu.edu/pub/3/article/922748/pdf?casa_token=MFXFKDEXniIAAAAA:YUCINXM-Es3HqJibOGW4sggOBbf1UbsucA8z3LXbSnddre7JVP6Hk_toatIAY3lZ1bE4e5lG9w [accessed 10th December 2024]

Book One

Chapter One

The sighing of the wind, s-s-ss-ough, s-ss-sough, like
a muffled dirge, went through the dim Clough. Over the
grey pebbles on the winding footpath; over the sheets of
stagnant water a hundred feet below; through the ivy and
lichen-trailed old trees, trees so ancient they seemed to
be ossifying, sough-sough, went that melancholy wind,
its martial music spent on the heights, spent on the wide
black moorlands, on the hill-ridges which through this day
of gloom had stood loomingly and crushingly in their mist-
magnified bulk.

The Clough echoed back that melancholy dirge. From
its tree-tops lost in the lost sky came answering dolorous
music. The wind seemed to drop down from the black
boughs, with their heavy mist-dews, and run sobbing
along the heavy grass.

The dams, once reservoirs, but now scummed over with
green slime almost to the edges of the sheer, black banks,
had that lifeless, mournful aspect all stagnant water has.
In this spot, at this hour, the gloom and oppressiveness of
them was beyond description. A sensitive beholder would
immediately have likened them to gloomy lakes in some
scene of Dante's Inferno.

The darkness of the mist-blotted sky, which, had it been
brighter, could scarce have shed more than a twilight
through the thickly intertwined black boughs—the banks
of mist only rifting to show the green and black gloom of
the scummed dams—the shadows which fell as without
the accompaniment of light, gave to the Clough, an
uncanniness which oozed from it at every turn. The dams
looked not unlike those places against which northern
mothers warn their children that if they go too near them,

"Old Jinny Green Teeth" will rise and drag them under. The old trees, many of which had forgotten the meaning of spring, many of which, lightning-split, leaned their shattered boughs together, boughs which pierced through the murk like broken spears, looked less like trees than ancient prophets, made prisoners in a vale of melancholy. Particularly was this analogy true where they stood in heavy ivy cloaks, which waved and flapped in funereal gloom. From out the deep shadows, here and there, fungi bleached with a ghostly whiteness the dampest hollows.

Gloaming.

That pleasant hour between night and day, when the beauty of sunset spreads its pomp opposite a sky where the stars rise like silver canoes floating to the fathomless canons of blue-green evening. Gloaming, that hour of which bards sing. In Mirley Clough it came rather as the deepening of shade than the departing of light. Day had dawned on the heights above the Clough with the rising of a pale and spectral sun over Mirley Crag—a sun so wan through the vapours steaming from grey fields, with other vapours from low-dragging clouds down-falling to meet them, children newly going to school along the hilltop roads, and unused to being out on a morning of mist and cloud, had taken it for the moon.

The day had gone from "bad to waur".

Road-menders had left their stone-heaps at noon, laid off till the morrow, their clothes wet clouts, their bodies chilled to the marrow with raw wind and penetrating, clammy mist. There had not been one bright glint in the whole long day. Inured as the hill-toppers were to this flowing in of winter's first waves of greyness, several ancient cronies had assured each other, with genial satire, that to-day "had been a reight un!"

On the tops, indeed, the murk had been terrible. The grey mist had only been lifted, even there, by a bleak, fierce wind, cold as a wet knife. In the lulls between its cutting gusts, like a torn and tattered curtain of mist and cloud the gloom had fallen again, trailing over a land wide and grey land sodden with four days of rain—the dykes yet being almost brimful, the dead grasses standing there half-drowned, whilst above, in the dark hedges, the last few lingering leaves of the year looked like unmoving birds.

Natives with most forethought had, on looking from their windows that morning, footed it to town for winter medicine supplies, lest frost should follow rain and mist, turning the roads to glass, and making the last steep brow which slid into town "like a bottle". But dree as the day had been, and though the way through Mirley was a short cut to town, none had taken it, preferring the way along the top road, with its cutting wind, and the fellowship of an occasional passerby. A dismal spot at any hour and season, on such a day as this, Mirley was best left alone, though the top road was longer by two miles.

Picture the desolate Clough, then, on the edge o' dark, on this the first day of winter-edge o' that darkness which towns know not, a darkness which flows in like a tide creeping and sweeping along from some ebony cistern, blotting out wall-top, gate, stile, hill, knoll, and fence, till from road underfoot to the topmost sky blackness is so opaque in its un-lamped grimness that the phrase, "you could not cut it with a knife", gives only a weak impression of its solid effect, when the metaphor that comes anywhere near the reality is as of the solid earth having arisen and filled the bowl of the sky, so that groping along, the traveller expects to bump at each step into a wall of solidified night.

High above the Clough, on the tops, moorland dwellers had, many of them, stacked up a week's firing, from boughs snapped and tossed down on the roads by the raging wind. In the little grey stone houses, built of the stone of the neighbourhood, hewn from quarry pits edged with bents and heather (stone which, in a few years takes on the hue of winter clouds on grey days) fires halfway up the chimneys strove to banish the fine mist which crept into the houses through keyhole, door-hinge, and window-sash, mist which poured in like smoke from the outer world, when anyone opened the door, making lamps burn dimly. And the lamps had been lit almost all the day.

The storm was spent.

Over the upland fields, and on the slacks between, sullen, dark and rain-sodden, lay a sea of mist, torn here and there whenever the wind tried to blow again—giving momentary glimpses of the rough, wild land, its dark, humped knolls, where, the village children avowed, men and horses had been buried in old battles. It lay, too, over the stone walls growing more bleak with each moment. It veiled the hill-ridges, which, on clear days, could be seen, running round like some immemorial wall, shutting in the northern shire. If for a moment the mist lifted, showing the hills like black city walls, the weary wind, its force spent would drop to silence. The mist curtains would close. All would again be grey mist, grey silence over a wide grey land, lost earth one with the lost sky.

Great drifts of dead leaves, which during the gale had blown about like brown and yellow birds, now lay in heaps by the wayside. When the wind stirred now they did not move. The mist-moisture had made them too heavy for this tired wind's blowing.

Bright fires and lighted lamps in the little grey houses on the tops, and, upon the walls within, rosy in the fire-glow, shadows of clothes mist-clouted, hanging to drip from beam-hooks or from "winter-hedges" around the fire, steam going up between lamp-shine and fire-flame. And for miles along the moorland "tops" this picture an extended one, from village to village, the only breaks being made by bleak, dark fell, glowering moorland, pitch black hill, and stretches of peat-beds soaked with rain under misted sky.

Past these houses, though it was not yet night as the natives reckoned it by the clock, an occasional storm-lamp straggled its topaz-hued gleaming through the ghostly air. Telegraph poles, black, elongated shadows in the mist, shot up as to a sky under-drawn by mist, their tops lost in it, like the masts of ships in spume. Winter coughs sounded hollowly and reverberatingly, from shadow figures going by like wraiths. As the lanterns they carried illumined for a brief moment some stone wall sheeted with mist, across it skipped, as on a grey screen, their magnified black silhouettes, half on wall, half on sky. They became, for a moment, on that screen of mist, black giants, with giant lanterns, dwarfing the huge landscape so that it looked as though they could have stridden across miles of it at a few steps.

Wild and dree enough here on the tops.

But compared with the Clough, this was a bright picture. For here, whenever the wind thinned the mist a little, making it diaphanous, lights of scattered hillside forms shone through it, though but for a moment. Then it was as though the dark and sombre North wore over her face a fire-specked veil.

From the Clough nothing of this could be seen.

A dark trench in the earth, with the ever-darkening dams, the ever-blackening trees, filled with the eternal sighing of the wind spilled from the heights, sighing, sighing, as though having got into the Clough it could not get out, Mirley presented with each moment nearer nightfall an ever more forbidding aspect.

Yet, along its winding and uncertain path, where sinuous tree-roots from old trees had struck, and lay like black serpents, walked a traveller. At intervals, he stopped, a dark figure against the drear landscape, stopped in the attitude of one trying to find out where the path would run up to the road, and for the test as though the dark spell of the scene about him froze his blood.

Then his steps would go on again, waking hollow echoes, which, to the ears, seemed to roll through the Clough, falling into its deep and sombre silence.

Once he stopped for quite a while, bending down, under the shadow of a huge tree, to examine his feet, his boots and socks cast on the grass below. His voice, speaking as though to reassure himself that he was a living human being, and not a spectre lost for ever in this gloomy place, fell on the heavy air, which threw the words back again, from across the dams, to where he still leaned down, drawing on his socks once more.

"Twenty miles in Curdy's boots," sounded his voice, in speech which whilst good English had in its accent something foreign—a musical liquidity very different from the burr of the North.

The silence following the echoes his words had awakened, seemed deeper as they died away. Our traveller went on again. Dark and vague as everything now was, his figure, even in the gloom, would have conveyed to anyone meeting him, lithe and vigorous youth, though not early youth. The bundle swung on the end of a stick he carried over his shoulder made lively movement, as did his swinging figure, in a scene where all else seemed lifeless. Even in that gloom, too, he would have been seen to be taller than the average native of these wilds, where burliness rather than height is the general rule, as though a strong broadness had been caught from the hills. There was an almost wild grace in his walk, despite the care he had to take not to stumble over the black serpent-like tree roots on the path, and be hurled headlong into the dams below.

If Henri d'Gasconne had expected to find some thinning of, or opening in the trees which would allow the dim sky to filter enough light to show where the path ran up to the road, he was disappointed. At the darkest and grimmest part of the Clough, as though the utter silence all about him were too much to be borne, his voice rang out in song, rang out in clear resonance that gibed at the melancholy scenery, even as the scenery, its gloomy echoes waking to the gay tune and words, mocked at the fitful gaiety of the singer.

"Sur le pont d'Avignon
L'on y danse l'on y danse,
Sur le pont d'Avignon
L'on y danse, tout en rond."

The song died away.

So weirdly had the echoes come back, from the black banks on the other side the dams, from the ghostly trees, from the mists, Henri sung no more.

He amused himself by picturing Curdy's chagrin, by hearing in imagination Curdy's string of heavy English oaths, when he found his new boots gone, and his left in their stead. It was through Curdy he had been discharged at Labrador. In some ways he regretted having had to leave Labrador. He had got used to the great tree which stood at that farm's gable-ends. The plough was almost new, easier to drive through the soil than many of the old, worn machines he had had to put up with on other farms. There had been no stint of buttermilk, saving in farrowing times, and after the litter came. Alice, the farmer's daughter, had made delicious "afterings" puddings and cakes. There had only been low hills to be seen from his bedroom window, so that the sky had not been shut out as much, and the colour of many a dawn and sunset, coming up over those, had compensated him for their being there. Though he would rather it had been all sky. And he had just begun to think seriously of "saving up", as Curdy phrased it, ceasing to be a rolling stone, going from farm to farm, of staying at Labrador till he had got enough saved to take him to France, with six months' living in his pockets. Now, that dream became as far off as ever. Through Curdy's cunning, he was having to seek work, journeying through this hellish landscape.

When would the path run up to the road? No sign of it doing so yet.

And, "On the bridge of Avignon people dance, people dance."

The tune and words ran in silent melody and poetry through his mind, lightening it from the gloom the Clough was weighing it with. Avignon! Some day he would go there. He would see the bridge, the water below, the people dancing. Avignon! The light and joyous euphony of the name singing itself over in his mind, was cheering. Often amidst the bleak, black lands of this dreadful North, in winter, his mind, catching hold of some name-place of the southern lands, had forgotten the bitter roughness of this wind-swept, barren country.

It was so even now, as the name, Avignon, sung itself in his mind. Whilst his material senses were guiding his steps through this, the most savage bit of northern England he had ever sampled, his imagination was away in Avignon, where people danced. He saw them dancing. He also was there, dancing with them. Sunlight, burning sunlight, like golden wine, made the blood leap. The sky was very blue. It had not one cloud. All blue from one rim of it to the other. The women's dresses were of gay, butterfly colours. Their laughter rippled. Their speech was like the singing of birds. He danced with the prettiest. Her little hands were on his shoulders, he swung her round, faster and faster, to her rippling laughter. Her little feet twinkled, on the bridge of Avignon. She spoke his name, Henri, with the "i" sound sighing in it, spoke it not as these flat northern women spoke it, heavily, and stumblingly, and with the "r" rolling in it—an ugly burr, which made one wonder if they had caught it from the curlews, or the curlews had caught it from them. It became a song on her lips. And she loved him. That made it twice a song. What must it be like to be loved? To hear the lilt of love in a woman's voice, to see its ray in her eyes, to hear its laughter on her lips, feel its touch in her fingers.

He stopped suddenly, on the night-darkening path.

A bitter laugh—stifled even as it sounded, fell upon the melancholy air.

Dreamer! Fool! Madman!

He stood, soul an-ache at the vision imagination had conjured before him, and threw stones at that dreaming portion of himself. He came back from Avignon.

He stood looking at the gloomy Clough. He was here, night-beset, with but three shillings between him and what Curdy called "the wide". He was journeying on his way which seemed inauspicious in its iron-cold gloom, to Eagles' Crag. Eagles' Crag. How like an ill-omened vulture-croak the name of the farm he was journeying to, sounded to his mind, as he thought of it.

The path veered suddenly, sharply. He went on looking over the edge of it. Even the dams could scarcely be seen now. The vacuum over them was thicker with mist. To look down was like looking into a great cauldron full of mist. He had to feel with his feet, at every step, lest he should catch them in the tree roots, so dark it was now. True, it would be as Curdy styled it, "sudden death, sudden glory" if he fell over into those gloomy stretches of water. But it was the glory of life here and now he ached for, not the glory of a beyond which might not be there. Thus musing, and going much more slowly than hitherto, he made his way along, becoming more impatient as the path seemed more and more endless.

Suddenly, a sound came to his ears which was so surprising, issuing from the gloom about him, that he almost dropped bundle and stick. He stood, staring upwards at the boughs of a tree, its top lost in mist.

Doves, wood-doves, in this wild o' the earth, or he was much mistaken. Doves, which should flash white wings silvernly in the sunshine, beating across a blue sky to green tree-tops. Or flutter in some old grey courtyard, with dragoned fountains spouting and guggling crystalline water-music on the radiant air. Or walk by pools of translucent water, on a path lozenged with moss growing in the flag-niches, their irised bosoms reflected in the clear depths below. And they were here, prisoned in this North, moaning in this winter wood. Poor doves!

Thus mused Henri, his grouche against his own lot forgotten. He stood staring upwards, whence that beat of wings, those faint sounds had come. Thus mused the man standing with bundle and stick over his shoulder, only three shillings between himself and "the wide", what he stood up in, and Curdy's boots. So passes many a man of imagination through the gloomy wilderness of reality, tormented ever by what is and what he would have life be, not only for himself, but for all living creatures. As Henri stood there, anger fierce and fine made his heart burn in the intensity which seldom flashed forth, balanced as it was by Gallic gaiety, the ability to quickly forget anything which had moved him to anger. He hated the North, in that moment, as he stood there, thinking of the doves. He hated it from one end to the other; the grey skies over it, the heavy black soil underfoot. He shook his fist at the mist, the dreary shadows of the winter trees, at the gloom about him, as though challenging and defying the spirit of the place, challenging and defying the North, which in its heavy lack of imagination had had doves brought to this spot more suited for ravens. It was the anger that whitens the cheek, brings a still glint like a grey sword's sheen to the eye, whilst all the being else looks more calm.

Then he cooled down, laughed shortly, wondering how much of his sympathy had been for the doves, how much for himself, who felt doubtless very much as they did. English, mere English, he realized, was a cold language to express just what he had felt for a moment. His emotional heart had heard in the cry of the doves, in the beat of their wings from one leafless, grim tree to another, pain and protest, such as his own sun-loving spirit had often felt, but stifled, pushing the feelings down deeper and deeper, into the fastnesses of his being, as he had travelled from one grey farm to another, looking out in winter over the mist-trailed black lands when he pined for glowing skies, for music, skies unbroken by savage hills, for flowers, for the Athenian beauty, not the Spartan rigors of life. The call of the blood. He knew it was only that. The call from the land where his birth had not been, but whose fires were in his being—sun-wild, passionate, laughing land, which called louder and louder to him each year.

Depression gripped him as he fared on. Doves! Here in this dreary valley, where winter reigned six months in every year, where the heavy soil riddled with stones, encroached on by couch-grass, dragged slowly and stubbornly past the plough. Louring fells, black moors, mist-wrapped hills. Flat women, bumpy land. Crushing, wild hills. People who rarely fought, who had to be driven to anger, cold and heavy as their own land. Broth, which they called "soup" when he asked for soup so thick the spoon would stand up in it. Balls of suet cast into it. Their laughter heavy, too.

He walked on, brooding on it all. Endless as this path. And once more the worst time of the year was coming. Six months of this before the slow spring came. May and June, very far away, those, the only two months in which it was fit to live in England. The doves would wait for it. He would wait for it. And—yes—it could be so they and he might die, waiting year after year for just two months of the year—for their life— the rest of the year endured.

Then, with a swift change of mood, with the nonchalance which had often stood him in good stead for his lack of English stoicism, he sang again, of Avignon, his thoughts running to the tune of the ballad.

He had written that he would arrive at Eagles' Crag by seven in the evening. *Vive la France!* Would he ever arrive? Moreover, did he wish to arrive? Eagles' Crag. The name of the farm, as he had deciphered it, written in poor ink, on cheap paper, in a sprawling, illiterate handwriting, had sent a shiver down his back. Eagles' Crag. Another prison to which he was journeying, to be sold as much as any farm-horse was sold, bone, sinew, and muscle, exerted to its last capacity, bringing little more than sufficed to keep him alive.

The harsh, wild-bounding names of some of these farms. Grey Wain, his first farm. Red Syke, the next. In between them and Labrador all the others, lonesome, awful in winter, work-filled in the spring and summer. Labrador had been a very ice-refrigerator. And, by the sound of its name, Eagles' Crag was at an high altitude, another grey box amongst the rolling clouds, mists, and hurtling east winds. Eagles' Crag. The very sight of the name, as it had met his eyes, had felt to curdle his blood. It had conveyed to him a sinister impression. Gloom and coldness had rushed over his mind as he had held the letter in his hand, reading it in the fading light by the window at Labrador. Only the sight of Curdy, back bent, as he toiled at a broken fence, working overtime for nothing, eager to get his place, the place he had schemed for, had decided him to apply for the situation. Now he was on his way to Eagles' Crag. Might not be too bad. Yet the very gloom of the Clough he was journeying through was not encouraging. He applied cold reason to his fears, even as he sung the ballad of Avignon.

Could Eagles' Crag, whatever it was like, be any worse than the rest of the farms he had sampled? What could befall him there any worse than had befallen him at the other farms? He would doubtless have the same heavy male companions. The same kind of flat-chested female would serve him broth in lieu of soup. And it was something to be getting away from Curdy, who had played hymns all day on Sunday on the concertina. One must be thankful for small mercies as the patient Alice had used to tell him. Alice had been very nice. Perhaps, if he found in a few years' time that he could not save enough to get to France, with six months' living in his pockets, he would marry a woman like Alice, provided she was not flat. Then he would have children who would look and laugh at him with his own eyes. Bah! And they would be miserable also. The more like him they were, the more miserable they would be, in this North. Best not have children. They and he would be like the doves in the grim, winter wood, beating their wings till they died. And the patient, flat woman he took—for most likely he would not find one that was not flat—she also would beat her wings, seeing he and they were not happy.

Weariness began to make both body and mind sag, as he went on. Oh, to get to Eagles' Crag, no matter what it was like. Would they, at Eagles' Crag, as at Grey Wain, boil the farm-dog when it died, and order him go feed the pigs on it? "Waste naught" had been the great cardinal point driven into Henri at Grey Wain. And, if he had missed a few meals, consequent on the training, that also had "saved summat".

Endless path, when would it run up to the road?

And, but for springing up at Curdy, who had given a yell at the sight of his angry look, little Alice would not have come running from the dairy, leaving fifty pounds of butter just as it was turning. The fifty pounds of butter had been spoiled. Which was why he was here, journeying to Eagles' Crag. And his French blood had been blamed, insulted, by Alice's father. But Curdy had grinned and said nothing of the provocation he had given. It had been the third time that week Curdy had knocked his book out of his hand. Twice he had stooped and picked it up, silently, smothering his wrath. The third time had been too much.

He left the path over the dams.

It broadened. There were trees on each side of him now. He guessed that to his right they hung over a sheer slope.

The path dwindled again. He was walking on grass. The soft feel of it eased his aching, blister-bleeding feet. He stumbled into a little copse. Darkness was almost as deep here as in the Clough. The trees, though, were thinner. Grey sky, watery glimmer of moon rays, shone through them. The scent of the damp mould of fallen leaves brought a freshness. He could feel the cold air of the uplands, blowing down. And, as pallid moon-rays, though but for a moment, anon glimmered through the trees, he could see a few leaves yet hanging on some of them. They stirred in a little wind. The sound, after the weird silence of the Clough brought pleasure, a sense of companionship. The grass was very long. A tree branch almost hit him in the face. Drops of moisture fell on his cheek. And still he might be far from a highroad. He listened now for that surest guide to the northern country roads—the bubbling of the wells that stand by them, whose voices, in the silence of evening, sound a long distance.

He groped his way, sometimes touching the mist-wet backs of trees.

The hoot of a motor sounded to him, coming to him like the cry of grouse, many times multiplied in volume. When the sound had died away, he listened once more for the sound of wayside wells. But all was still, save for the faint rustling of the grass, the drip of mist-dews down the grass-blades, as his steps brushed through them.

Then, just as he told himself that it would be nine by the time he reached Eagles' Crag, the copse ended.

Henri stood, overwhelmed, staring with grudging admiration at a panorama which might indeed have wrung praise from any not utterly insensate to beauty.

Cold—yes, it was certainly a cold and austere beauty which flashed upon him from the landscape stretching before him.

Yet, even he, with his love of colour, could not deny that the scene before him was wonderful breath-taking, almost uncanny in its sombre and majestic grandeur. Savage and wild. Yes. But the spell of it, bursting upon the sight suddenly. Colourless, as colour is thought of by vivid natures, by Turner-lovers, by those who on grey days dream of sun-blistered villas with poplars spiring the blue sky's haze.

A great pencil-sketch, in moorland black and silver of moonlight. The North! Austere and rugged, wide and wild, overpowering in its rocky strength, the soul of it flashed out on Henri, as it had often flashed out on him, unexpectedly at times—as when he had seen sunset on purple-heather, for the first time, or the tops at Grey Wain, every bell becoming a glowing pink-purple gem, and the whole of the heathery miles appearing to wear a flushed smile, which fading swiftly, had left all grey, but left also that memory of sunset afterglow on heather—a fadeless memory.

But this was different. The glowing colour of that scene on the tops at Grey Wain had been a paean of rich pomp, stirring sensuous beauty-loving senses, leaving a recollection of sun-glow on heather which he had often recalled on wet grey days of rain. The soul had leaped up, then, to see that the grey North held so much of splendid tintings. Before the scene stretching out now; under his awed gaze, it stood hushed and still. Nothing like this had he seen before. So said Henri, to himself, as he stood stock-still on the road, gazing with fascinated eyes at the North which not long ago he had told himself he hated. This great North. Misted, rain-filled, it was, he mused, as though only in rare moments she revealed the glory of her spirit.

He was standing on a white road sweeping between two moorland hills.

The mist had rolled away.

The moon, just emerged from a dark cloud, sailed large and white in the sky's calm deeps.

On one side of him lay moon-bathed bracken, its sere tops looked like tawny gold in the silvern light. On the other the hills, whose short green turf looked like antique bronze, rose solemnly; sheep on their heights moved slowly, crossing and recrossing the white disc of the moon.

To his right, beyond the rustling bracken, rose almost sheer hills, on whose summits crags and boulders bit blackly into the wide sweep of the moonshot steely blue of the night sky. Stars twinkled in the firmament with crystalline brightness. Each one was like a silver ship sailing through immeasurable, fathomless seas of space. The few clouds were pinnacles rising from broad bases of snowy whiteness into moon-gleaming spires, wonderful as ice peaks. A tree on one lofty height stood like a speck against such an ice-peak cloud, black, desolate against its glory. He looked at the shadows the great crags and boulders flung down the hills, where the ling and heather looked not black but brown under this moon. He moved slowly on and up the road, still staring. The stupendous glory of the scene awed him.

Was there, he wondered, as he moved over the road where his shadow fell on the limestone, some bond between him and the North, that, at every turn, when he had decided almost to leave it, once more it gripped him— its vast bulk, its gloom even, as though, sun-lover though he was, it refused to let him go? Vast, and cold as vast. It awed him. He hated it, but even as he hated it, it held him. If he went away, where there were no hills to shut out the sky, he knew that he could not, would not ever forget it. Musing thus, he reached the crest of the moorland road.

It dipped down. He saw a village, its mist-wet roofs pearled and silvered with moon-fire, down in the hollow.

And, as he realized that at last he could inquire where Eagles' Crag was, he came upon one of those gorges in the moorland hillsides common in the county of moors and mists. The thundering music of a torrent, leaping from crag to crag, made him stop once more. The past four days of rainfall had swollen it from a trickle of water, lost amongst sere bracken and rocks, into this dashing water-force. He watched it, its almost phosphorescent splendour thundering from one dark crag to another, on which it broke and flashed to the next. Rushing, roaring, tumbling, leaping with wild joy, it seemed like a living thing. Tons of water were coming down the gorge. What a swirl it must be where it broke over the topmost crag. For, looking up the gorge, he could see the great boulders and crags in the torrent's course dark and stark against its dazzling sheen. Bush, withered furze clumps stood dark also. To the left of the gorge, where no crags were, on the crest, the ragged fringe of heather-bushes blowing in the wind could be seen against the wide sky-like the almost imagined curves of a dark tide And surely—yes—

On a boulder which looked no larger than two feet across, from where he stood, but which must be a huge thing, was a human figure. The width of the sky behind it gave it that solitary aspect the distant human has, and also that curious dignity a background of loneliness gives.

Even as he stood, staring, the figure moved. It was gone.

The great moorlands which probably rolled miles beyond these crags, had swallowed it again. He experienced an odd sense of acute loneliness. For hours he had journeyed through gloom and mist. No human being had spoken to him. He had spoken to none. That small, far-off figure against the sky's solitudes had reminded him that others beside himself lived lonely lives.

He passed on towards the village.

Five minutes later he witnessed a spectacle so unusual it drove from his mind the almost wistful wondering as to whose had been that figure against the wide sky, what its lot, its joys and sorrows—what its need that in a world teeming with people, aloof, desolate, and wild, it stood on a boulder which seemed perched on the earth's edge, and found the best companionship in starry skies and a pagan earth. He forgot these thoughts as he stood watching a lunar rainbow.

Across the sky, faint, but growing ever more vivid with each second, a great arc of colour was appearing.

Some shower was falling in the valleys beyond these hills each side of him. The moon was shining through the rain-cloud. The bow of it began behind a great hill which stretched greyly and cloud-like. Over fields, fells, and a score of streams, it spread. The night sky was as though a path of flowers, misted with moon-rayed dew, were being woven across it. Henri looked for the other end of the arc. It rose from above the gorge, slowly swept over it. The sky was resplendent with the irised wonder. He stood staring up at it. As he looked, another bow was forming, fainter, but beautiful. He stood under the double arc, spanning the great bowl of the sky, everything else forgotten but this feast of colour. Slowly the hues faded. Moonlight, and thin grey mist falling again, wove a thousand tapestries on wayside grass, white road, and the moor sweep on each side of him. Then the moon went under a black cloud. All was dark once more. He remembered that he was on his way to Eagles' Crag.

If only there were someone he could ask where the outlandish place was.

He moved down the road.

It was in the process of being mended, littered with new flints, left for people to help get smooth with their feet. Henri, his feet feeling raw, moved to the strip of grass which ran into the moor stretches. Against the sky, he saw an opening in a stone wall. Standing there, quite motionless, was an old man carrying a lantern. The rays of the lantern lit up the yard of ground he stood on, the heavy grass, and the brown rushes by the wall. The lantern rays, some of them reaching his face, showed its leanness. A thin bush of a beard was on his chin, of a gingerish grey. His eyes were deep-set, small. His attire was shabbily nondescript, black cloth which long wear and all weathers was turning to green. This was the impression Henri got from his brief survey in the uncertain light.

"A grand rainbow, that was, dad," Henri greeted him.

"Eh?"

He came back, as from some distant place in thought, jerkily, to the sight of a stranger speaking to him.

"I said it was a grand sight—that rainbow," Henri repeated.

"Never saw it," the old man answered.

Henri stared at him.

"Never seen it?" he asked in wonderment. "Why, dad, where were you looking?"

There was silence for a moment. The old man's eyes had become ferret-keen. They narrowed till they looked like bright specks in his thin-jowled face, not unlike a lantern itself, in shape. Evidently he was taking stock of Henri, realizing that this was no native, but an "off-comer", that equivalent for foreigner, though in these parts it applied equally to anyone coming more than ten miles away, as to those who had come thousands. Once more Henri felt the loneliness that dogged him wherever his steps went. He had become familiar with the way natives addressed each other. Always his accent told them he was not one of themselves. But even as he stood, not knowing whether to move on with a brief "good night", the old man left the gap in the wall where he had been standing, and moved towards him.

"I'd not seen't rainbow," he said, speaking as from the depths of thought. "Whilst I were stannin' there, lad, I'd seen naught nor nothing. I'd been—to Hell an' back."

There was something in his tone, restrained though it was, which sent a shudder through Henri. He stood silent, looking at his companion, over whose weather-beaten countenance, dimly though the lantern lit it up, were playing fierce emotions.

"I'm sorry to hear that," Henri said, at length. "But Hell's always a good place to get back from."

He had moved a few steps.

The old man moved also, by his side.

"Folk never does get back, nor away fro' it," he told Henri. "Not them that has bin thear right. Well, if they do—the flames has burnt in, to't bone. There's no forgettin' Hell, for them 'at's gradely fashioned—any moar nor thear's no forgettin' Heaven. They purtend to forget; But that's a'."

They walked slowly on together, side by side.

" 'Twere't anniversary my lad shot hissel'— through a woman—to-day," said the old man.

"That's a pity," Henri said. "Not many worth it, dad, are there?"

"There be'ant one," said the old man? "Not one worth it. For if they be'ant fause, then they're noodles. An' if they be'ant neither—they blows like't wind, now cold, now hot, an' all ways at once. God made man, an' was disappinted in't job. He started in to makes woman. That brak His heart. He gav' up to it. An' the devil came an' finished the task. Which is why when they're angels they weary us. An' why when they're devils they hold us, but wear us out. An' 't was for one o' these last mak' my lad shot hissel' down in't Clough yon, and when she heard on't, all shoo said were—"

His lips went on moving, as Henri saw by the lift of his beard. But no sound came from them. There was too much bitterness to be spoken, Henri assumed. The old man looked as though he were choking with it. He suddenly tore at his collar, ripped it loose, and walked on, with his lips moving, but no sound coming from them. Whilst Henri's curiosity was deeply stirred. He wished to hear what this unknown woman had said when a man shot himself through her.

"Shoo said, when they went up an' told her, at Eagles' Crag yon—"

He stopped again, his lips moving silently once more.

"Eagles' Crag!" gasped Henri.

But the old man did not hear him.

"Shoo said, stannin' in't door-hoyle, with her hands on her hips, an' her head thrown back, an' her black e'en laughin'—aye, lad, laughin'—'Am I responsible for the manufacture of fools?' An' slamm't door to, reight in their faces. Most women would ha' dropped a tear, for pity's sake. For he were a farrantly lad. But all shoo said were— well, as good as that shoo weren't his mother, so the fool-part o' him wasn't her blame. An' sin then—look, that's Eagles' Crag, over yon."

Henri turned round. The old man's grip on his arm was like steel. He could feel every bony finger through his sleeve.

"Thear! Noa, not where tha'rt lookin'. Furrer on. Past that tree. Ay. That's nigher. But furrer yet. Where that stane sticks up—"

"There?" inquired Henri, tensely.

But the old man did not notice his excitement. For the stone being pointed out to him as near Eagles' Crag, was the rock on which he had seen that lonely human figure standing, as he had passed the hillside gorge. Could it be that that figure was "shoo" who had slammed the door on those come to acquaint her with the fact that a man had killed himself through her?

He pointed into the mist, which had thinned a little, so that the hill-tops and the boulders stood out fairly clearly.

"Ay. It's ower thear," said the old man, with vicious energy in his voice. "Eagles' Crag enough. An' my curse is on it. An' on a' inside it. On a' as breathes the air shoo breathes. On the black roof of it, to the stanes they walk ower. On th' yeth under it, an' the sky over't top of it. Day an' neet it broods ower't place, an' shall e'en when I'm deyd, till the last stane on it stands, an' Burl Furber can slive no moor looks at men, but lies wi' the worms creepin' in and out her e'en-sockets."

Henri's flesh felt to starken on his bones.

But all he said was: "She has not an English name."

The old man left off muttering and chewing his beard.

"Shoo's a gipsy," he told Henri. "Shoo's half-gipsy, sohowbeit. Her feyther tir't o' the gipsy life, got some brass somehow, and took a bit o' land hereabouts. Wed wi' an off-comer, fro' somewhere or other. Italian, most like, for they ate that stuff they ca'—hang-it—well, it's like white worms."

"Macaroni," prompted Henri.

"Ay. That's it."

They walked on in silence. Henri was walking farther from Eagles' Crag, just to be companion to this fiercely bitter old man. The latter appeared suddenly to become aware of the unspoken sympathy Henri was feeling. With a superhuman effort he pulled himself together.

"An' whear art for, lad?" he inquired.

"Eagles' Crag," answered Henri.

"Eagles' Crag!" almost screeched the old man. He stood still, in the middle of the road, his lantern lifted to survey the intrepid individual who would go up to Eagles' Crag, where Burl Furber lived, and over which his curse stretched night and day.

Once more his hand gripped Henri's arm.

"Turn back, lad," he advised.

"I'm no coward," Henri told him.

"Cowards live, an' courage folk gets killed," the northerner told him tersely. "Cowards has common sense. Courage folk don't like runnin' fro' a fear. Them's um this world kills, mon, either in one way or't other. Turn thee round, an' go back to whear thee came fro'. Doan't go to Eagles' Crag."

When the old man saw he could not turn him from his purpose, he said "good neet", brusquely, and left him. Henri turned round. He had come a mile past the place. He would have to climb up to it along the gorge. A curious excitement was upon him. His first forebodings as he had read the name of the place to which he was to journey, were gone. Eagles' Crag; And eagle-like people, from what he had gathered from his companion. Was there, not also something of the eagle in his nature, too, though it was the wildness of a sun-loving eagle? In this eyrie to which he was going, there were eagles, also, withal eagles homed amidst the black rocks, desolate grey skies, and dragging, rain-filled clouds.

When he stood, almost exhausted by his climb up the gorge, on a rock set round with the moon-flickering water of the torrent, he looked up to the heights. He could just make out dark chimneys, a portion of the house roof. Above it curved great overhanging rocks, which doubtless had been the nesting-places of eagles, before the wild, majestic birds had been exterminated. Moonlight and mist and clouds gave the view of the farm an uncanny look. It hung, under the shadows of the rocks, just set back a little way from the edge of the gorge. One of those old baronial halls, one of the many in this North, now turned into a farm. He stood looking up at it. As he climbed farther up, the windows appeared. There were no lights. Only the misted moon cast a glimmering radiance into the panes, as shining upon black pools.

"Another eagle is coming to Eagles' Crag," thought Henri. "Hear me, you shall hear me, you wild eagle-woman. You shall come out to meet me. You shall be looking for me."

He infused all the will in his being into that thought.

Then set himself to clamber up the last and wildest part of the gorge.

Chapter Two

Where through the solitudes of dim grey sky
The lonely eagles once were wont to fly,
Amidst the storms which rolled around grim rocks,
The cloud-burst's fury, and the land-slide's shocks.
Where roaring winds made music's thunderous chord,
And each loud raindrop was creation's word
Swelling the torrents and the winding streams—
A mighty world of loneliness and dreams.

Henri stood at the head of the gorge, panting, dishevelled, his heart thumping against his ribs with the fatigue of the ascent along its rock-strewn way. Almost impossible as the climb had seemed to him, at times, looking down on the way he had come along, it seemed quite impossible that he could have reached the rock at the top, safe and sound. The spray was tossed about the stone he stood on, that stone on which "shoo" might have stood, little more than an hour ago. The stone was black and slippery with water streaming over it. He turned from his survey of the torrent, glistening in spray, mist, and moonlight, the dark rocks around which it boiled and frothed, the dim shape of the moor-slopes on each side it, widening up to the sky, which was clearer here of mist. The mists indeed were rolling down the moor-sides, leaving the tops now. Their waving and ever-changing films, shot with the pallid moon-rays, gave to his imagination the impression of wraiths gliding over the moor-slopes—wraiths of dead moorland dwellers who had once lived at this dark farm which stood before him.

His feet were on a path through heather, ling, and bracken. In this unmisted blue-black darkness he discerned the farm, some fifty yards back from the edge of the gorge. He wondered why all the land in front of it had not been cleared and cultivated. This path on which he was walking was overgrown by coarse bents, which were visible to him even in the gloom, having been whitened by the beating winds of who knew how many aeons of years? Stones rolled under his steps, once pebbles in deep, cold fathoms of unsunned sea-water. The wild and weird atmosphere of the spot terrorized even whilst it fascinated him. As he drew nearer to Eagles' Crag, his sight becoming accustomed both to the darkness, as to the vague uncertainty of the half-light which streamed and wavered over it, whenever the moon came from under heavy clouds, he guessed why that cold, wild name had been given to it.

Towering above the building which was now looming up, a black bulk, its unlighted windows at intervals shone on by the moon. High above it, and curved over it were giant rocks, which even through this darkness gave the impression of the place being a wild eyrie, set high above the world. When the moon glided across some gulf of sky between clouds, and her light shone for a moment on these rocks, their smooth portions of surface showed her light in them as polished ebony shows a moving lamp; their rough surfaces stood in inky gloom, ponderous, overwhelming in their savage weight.

Swooping shadows from these rocks filled the space between them and the roof of the farm, also dark with their shade, as were the walls down to the moorland soil. Even on the brightest days of summer those rocks would shadow the place, even as the rooms behind it must be very dark, their walls not far from the soil and rocks, and only such light as filtered between house and that wall of earth, able to dimly light them. Nearer and nearer approached Henri, the gloom of the place growing ever more upon him. Yet even as the vague terror increasingly oppressed him, like the powerful attraction of some dark magnet, the house felt to be drawing him towards it, against his will. As it grew less shadowy, he dimly made out the black outlines of a turret against the black rock-shadows. The rocks which had seemed close down to the house, he now perceived, had enough space between them and the highest chimney to allow a six-foot man to stand upright on the turret wall, and just clear the rock above.

But the wild eagle-woman, where was she?

Was she compound all of courage and savage strength, all eagle, that for twelve months out of every year, she could abide in this fastness of the hills, moving from one rock-shadowed room to another, in an atmosphere of perpetual twilight, and feel within her no desire for strong flight across world-skies?

Was she so strong that his thought, though it had reached her, was being resisted, with lonely eagle-strength? Or was thought, and its force, a chimera to those who lived in places like these, unsicklied by books—living ever a life of strenuous action even as the birds, the passing clouds, the heather drawing its sustenance from the ground, fighting so keenly for physical continuance that the culture and aestheticism of the world beyond could not beat past this pure oxygenated air—the life of simple people? Henri could not make up his mind. But even as Eagles' Crag was drawing him step by step, with its magnetism of gloom, nearer, ever nearer its threshold, so he could not abandon the thought that thought of his, intense as he had poured it out, as he had clambered up the gorge, should penetrate even those thick walls, and reach her, bringing her out to meet him.

The house stood somewhat to the left of the gorge. Even now, when so near to it that the thundering force of the torrent was like a sullen, muted roar, when so near to it that he could dimly see a black porch with black pillars and hear the whip of a dead black creeper blowing against the black walls, he still felt, along with the fearful magnetism of the place, a desire to turn round make his way back down the gorge and take the road, sleeping in some sheltered nook throughout the night until dawn came, when by its light he could journey on and find some other farm where he might get work. The thought struck him that she might know he was here, outside, under this night, and even as she was resisting his thought that she should come out and meet him, be making him unable to carry out his desire to escape from the spell of this grim house. If that was so——

He turned to walk backwards along this path which had almost brought him to the steps of the farm, steps sunk into the earth, steps which by the feel of the first one under his boot, were moss-grown and never used by those who lived at Eagles' Crag.

The next moment something happened which arrested his first hesitant step backwards along the way he had come—a step which had felt to necessitate the full impetus of his will, as though already Eagles' Crag had claimed him as its own, and striving with all its gloomy eyriness to bring him within its dark walls.

Surely, upon the top of that turret-wall a light was moving.

Yet how could light shine through the overhanging rock-shelf above it? It was impossible. He knew it, as he stood there. But a tiny disc of light was certainly playing on the turret wall. It danced along from turret-square to turret-square, whilst Henri stood, unable to move backwards or forwards, watching it. The texture of the rough stone leaped out from the surrounding gloom as that light danced over it like a will-o'-the-wisp's lantern. Cold sweat began to ooze from Henri's brow. Was the place haunted? Or was this uncanny speck of light, on this turret wall, the effect of some natural phenomena, a phosphorescence rising from the dampness of the rocks above the house, consequent on the past four days of rainfall? He could not tell. He only knew that his very blood stood chilled and as cold lead within his veins, as he watched that light gliding along the darkness of the turret. But move he must. So he told himself, even whilst his heart stood still in his breast, clay-cold to anything but terror.

Then from the heights above him floated a voice, northern in its accents, but of so peculiar a timbre it reminded him of flame travelling along a silver wire. Its effect upon him was to quell the fear that he was witnessing something supernatural, even whilst its words, which might almost be symbolic, when he recalled the thought he had sent out, whilst climbing the last part of the gorge, sent a shuddering and fearful rapture through the blood, rushing pell-pell through his veins, released from that awful icy fear that this could be no natural phenomena; that the dark house, the dark rocks above it, the eyrie glow creeping from turret-square to turret-square was cast by some evil demon, from some phantom house on a phantom height, with phantom crags above it, and a phantom silence lapping it all about, darkly and weirdly.

"You're late," said the eagle-woman's voice. "But better late than never. You'd best stay there till I come down and guide you to the door. Otherwise, the hounds might make a meal of you."

"Where shall I wait?" inquired Henri.

He hoped his voice did not reveal the tension of his nerves, but feared it did. And was that the echo of a silvery, mocking laugh, blown down to him from the turret-wall, as the light travelled back along each square, black stone, finally disappearing, and leaving him in the darkness, waiting. But before its disappearance into the black gloom, he had a vivid impression of a head crowned with coils of black hair, of a pair of fathomless black eyes looking down at him out of a long, pale face, and of the unearthly tinkling of—bells—bells ringing so faintly and echoingly the air scarce undulated to the sound, so that he told himself, standing there in the darkness: "No, it is imagination." Even as, so swiftly the face had looked at him, and gone, now that he was left alone in the darkness, he could almost believe that that also had been a supernatural vision, or some fantasy of his brain, overwrought by this scene of lonely gloom and melancholy eyriness.

Whilst he stood thus, he heard her footsteps.

How she had got down from the turret-wall, round the house, he could not guess. The light he had seen on the turret-tops was the light of an ordinary storm-lamp, such as he himself had often carried about on winter nights on previous farms. Its light played now on her dress, on the path before her, and dimly, upon her countenance.

She reached him on swift feet, swinging along to him with a long stride almost masculine in its freedom of movement, its great vigour. But the most surprising thing was—she was attired in gipsy dress. Bright pins fastened the heavy coils of raven black hair. A long dark cloak, slashed with crimson, came almost to her feet. The open cloak revealed a green bodice and a tambourine slung over the shoulder by a long ribbon explained the ghostly and echoing jingle of distant bells.

Henri tried not to stare at her.

But her appearance in this festive dress of the gipsy races was so strange in this setting of dark wildness, he was even yet not sure but that she was an apparition. She had lifted up the lantern, and was scrutinizing him with almost anxious keenness. Then, apparently reading his wonder upon his face, she remarked: "On the day of the year when my father came North I wear this dress, in honour of my gipsy blood. I stand on that turret and mourn that I am a gipsy living with Georgios. I hear all the winds calling to me, and think of my rugged people, whose ceiling is the sky, whose floor the wide earth. Hence this dress."

Henri bent his head.

Such savage splendour had leaped up in her eyes, so wild a light had lit up her pale features it had been for a few moments, whilst she was speaking, as though the souls of all her wild, sun-loving ancestors had leaped up in her. It died away, as her voice ceased, leaving a pallid mournfulness of aspect. He guessed that to speak out from the depths of her being was rare. She was amongst Georgios who did not understand the nomad spirit, even as he, with his dream of sunlit lands and the Latins to whom he belonged was "that Frenchman", or, even in most tolerant affection, where he had won it, "Froggie".

She was moving on, to lead him to Eagles' Crag. It seemed to him that as she glanced towards it, its dark gloom and lowering bulk, that what of radiance yet lingered in her countenance flickered out, leaving in its stead a stony fortitude.

"And when you come down from the turret?" asked Henri.

It was a woman all of the North—its cold granite, who answered him.

"When I come down from the turret," she answered, walking slowly over the uneven ground littered with stones, "I come down from the turret. I am a Georgio amongst Georgios. Else, how could one live? I set that one day of all the year apart—to mourn."

He followed her slowly, perforce, since she was moving slowly. She wheeled round upon him suddenly, all at once, so suddenly that he was taken aback. Her face was but a few inches from him. The raven hair with its bright pins, the face with its clear pallor, those eyes with their fathomless darkness which, as she had spoken of her gipsy blood had looked like black tarns with the sun on them, was close to his face. Her eager breath was warm upon his cheek.

"You are not English?" she inquired.

"French. Born in England, though," Henri told her.

Burl Furber laughed.

Her laughter rippled out into the darkness and silence. The rocks echoed it, with a note that sounded as though they defied glad laughter to defeat the gloom they threw about Eagles' Crag.

Once more her face lit up.

Then she turned, dropping the lantern from where she had stood lifting it down by her side, and swung on. Henri scarce knew if she was speaking to him, or speaking aloud, half to herself, when she broke the silence again, whilst still leading him over the rough ground.

"Blessed be the sun!" said Burl. "Not English. Where one is born matters nothing. As old Jane says: 'If't cat kittles in't o'on that doesn't make 'em loaves.' Blessed be the sun for that."

He followed her in silence, walking on the rays her lantern threw on the ground. The strange pagan thanksgiving of the phrase she had used, blessing the sun that he was not English, had given him an odd sensation, a weird premonition of the sunless, wild life on these shadowy heights. He knew little about gipsies. Probably she knew as little, beyond dim memories. But as he followed her, the lantern-rays making the surrounding darkness yet more eyrie, more black, beyond them he sensed a spirit he could imagine having behind it long lines of ancient people who had worshipped the sun in the days when England was an uninhabited waste. What life must be to one like that, life in so grim and dark a place, shrouded half the year with mists and storms—above all, for one young— for she could be no more than twenty—chained amongst

Georgios, chained to this rock-shadowed house, gave him a feeling of compassion.

Yet the fact that she but mourned on one day of the year—setting apart one day of the three hundred and sixty-five for wild grief—calmly bearing herself through all the others with stoicism told that she was also very much of the North; that its life and climate and unemotional hardness had made her largely its own. Even whilst he felt compassion he knew it would only infuriate that part of her nature to know he pitied her. So much the North had taught him, in his experience of it.

But whither was she leading him?

So engrossed had he been in the encounter of their meeting, it was only as he found himself standing once more before that great door with its black pillars and porch, and heard again the thin, melancholy sound of the creeper whipping the black walls, that he knew they had turned on their steps and were in front of the house. Moreover, he was beginning by this time to feel like one drunk with physical weariness. The excitement of seeing those lantern-rays travelling along the turret, followed by a strange ecstasy which had filled his being at finding that there would be one within the walls of Eagles' Crag who would know and understand his antipathy to the North and English people, had come on the top of a day in which he had trudged twenty-five miles, of which the last five, in their rough, ever-ascending blackness, had taken as much strength as fifteen ordinary miles.

"Why—" he began.

"Yes. We will go in by this door," Burl told him.

Henri lurched after her.

The light from the lantern was now falling on the steps. Glancing down he saw that he had been right in assuming that they were moss-covered. The black steps were half-covered with moss an inch thick. In the lantern's light, staring dizzily upwards, he saw long cobwebs blowing in the wind, hung from the porch. A couple of owls, their yellow eyes alone gleaming, so that in the darkness they looked like flying eyes of fire, rushed out from the blackness and away into the darkness with an echoing hoot, which the rocks towering over the place flung back.

Half-dead for sleep Henri felt like one in the grip of nightmare. He stared up at Burl. She stood two steps above, the lantern uplifted, smile lifting the corners of her mouth.

"You'll not ha' to be so skeered, if you're coming to bide at Eagles' Crag," she told him, dropping into the vernacular.

He gave no answer. The sullen roar of the gorge-torrent was in his ears. It felt to gather and surge there. As he mounted the steps and stood by Burl, he noticed that she was breathing quickly. He could hear that rapid breathing. And staring down from her, he saw that the door was half-overgrown with long grasses, nettles, and thorns.

With lantern uplifted in one hand, with the other she lifted up the heavy knocker, letting it fall with such force that it seemed to Henri the door must split. The sound of the iron knocker falling on the iron plate under it, rolled like thunder on the silence. The rocks threw back sullen, grim echoes. Whilst from Eagles' Crag also came back the echoes of that terrific bang, as from some black vault. Even whilst he was pondering why this door should be opened, since it was evidently never used, and whilst to his imagination, Burl, for all the boldness with which she had let that knocker fall, showed some small signs of fear, there came to his ears, from behind that massive, nail-studded door, the sound of approaching footsteps. The nearer they came, the paler grew Burl Furber. Yet she stood, with head proudly thrown back, though her eyes looked like the eyes of some wild thing returning to a cage.

Nearer and nearer came the footsteps.

A glint of light shone through the keyhole of the door.

"Burl!" came in a savage female voice.

"Ay," Burl answered.

"Is it—?" asked the voice.

"Ay. It's him," Burl told the owner of the voice.

"Well, take him round," came the voice, angrily. "Hast gone mad to bring him to this door?"

The footsteps were retreating once more.

Once more Burl let the knocker fall. The same gloomy, desolate echoes awakened once more within that dark house, and rushed to the two standing on the mossy steps.

Henri heard the sound of a fierce imprecation. The footsteps which had approached the door and retreated had been the feeble, slow steps of one evidently far advanced in age. But Burl's persistence in again knocking for admittance had given them what he could only assume to be the strength of fury. They came with almost a rush to the door. Rusty bars shot back in their sockets. Their scraping awoke weird echoes. The door was flung back as though it had been of match-wood, rather than massive oak. A mouldy air rushed out. To his utter astonishment Henri saw that upon the flags beyond the door was white mould. He felt rather than saw the trembling of his companion.

Then, beyond the rays of Burl's lantern, he saw, holding in her hand a flickering candle, a dim yet terrible figure, an old woman, straightened by rage from the decrepancy of age—a woman with Medusan locks, grizzled and grey, curling round a face livid with some intense emotion. It was a face which even without that rage upon it he felt would be terrible to gaze on, in its cold cynicism. She gave Burl a look as she advanced upon them, which Henri felt would have caused her to fall lifeless—if a look could have killed. They were in the shadow of the porch. Involuntarily his hand touched Burl's shoulder.

She was close to them now, still upheld by that rage, six feet if she was an inch, a woman unkempt in attire, and with the shadow of those Medusan locks thrown upon a skin of yellow deadness, her eyes glaring at them, her thin lips writhing as to find words to express her ire.

What she would have said was never spoken.

"Look!" came from her lips suddenly. "Look! Th' Eagle!"

Her skinny forefinger was pointing beyond them. The rage had died out of her eyes. She had shrunk in stature and was almost cowering. "Th' Eagle! Th' Eagle!" she moaned. "Th' Eagle of Eagles' Crag."

Henri heard Burl's breath catch.

She had turned to stare out into the darkness, into which the old woman was pointing that skinny finger. He turned also, staring out into the gloom. He could see nothing. Even the dim rays of the lantern and the glim of light from the old woman's flickering candle had made darkness more blinding now he stared back into it. But, was it imagination, or did he not hear the beat of rushing wings, striking through the gloomy silence, sounding nearer with each moment? As he stared, the moon sailed from under a great bank of clouds. The light brightened. He saw the rough ground littered with stones, the dead bracken waving ghost-like beyond, the blowing tops of the black heather. The rushing of great wings came ever nearer. The old woman, her wrath forgotten, was cowering abjectly against the wall, the candle dripping its hot wax unheeded down her skinny arm. He had turned to look at her, hearing her low cries of terror, cries that were all the more terrible for being half-suppressed.

"Th' Eagle!" she cried, over and over again between her chattering teeth.

He turned from her to the girl.

Burl Furber was leaning against one of the black pillars. She was staring straight out into the night.

Then he forgot her entirely, as across the moonlit spaces of the sky, sailed a great eagle. There was no mistaking that it was an eagle. So clear was the steely blue of the sky where the clouds were not banked, its mighty outstretched wings could be seen plainly outlined—its steady flight marked—and it was coming nearer, lower to earth. Henri held his breath. If it was an eagle, beating its way northwards to the sea, there was nothing to be afraid of. But so uncanny a spell had Eagles' Crag cast upon him, and so infectious is the sight of human terror, and he yet had in his mind the spectacle of that frightful old woman, a Medusa of fury, become a fear-shaken, puny creature, whimpering through her teeth, that the sight of the eagle cast upon him the fear he had felt in the darkness before Burl Furber had spoken to him from the turret.

The eagle grew larger.

It was now hovering, with a dreadful kind of stillness, conveyed from it to them.

Henri's brain was working.

One portion of the ground the eagle would pass over was the faded and tawny bracken.

If it were really an eagle on its way to the coast, and went over that lighter patch of moonlit ground, its shadow would fall there.

It was going in that direction.

He watched.

The great wings came steadily lower. They appeared to be motionless, sis it dropped nearer the ground. It was going over the bracken patch now. Would the shadow—

Then he saw that the wings were already over it. Quite over it now. But no shadow fell.

A deathly coldness spread through his limbs. They felt about to let him fall. His stick and bundle clattered from his hands, rattling where they struck the stones at the bottom of the steps. He turned to Burl. From behind he could hear the chattering sound of the old woman's teeth.

Burl lifted up her lantern, suddenly.

As he stood close by her, staring into her face, pallid as it was, almost bloodless, even her lips white at this strange occurrence which meant he knew not what, he saw her eyes, dilated though they were, leap with that radiance he had seen in them as she spoke of the gipsy folk.

"Hail, Eagle," said her trembling voice, travelling into the darkness and silence.

She had lifted the lantern up higher, as though it were a sun, for that mighty bird to see. The great eagle still hovered over the bracken patch.

"Hail, Eagle," repeated Burl, more loudly and with the tremor going out of her voice. "Bring doom and disaster if you will, but bring Love. Hail, Eagle—"

Out from the mouldy darkness of the great hall, down the steps rushed the old woman. She clutched at Burl's cloak with her talon-like hands, "Fool! Fool! Fool!" she almost screamed, in a thin, high voice.

Burl shook her off, fiercely.

She was standing with the lantern held aloft, its light streamed on her pale, wild face, with its dark eyes staring out into the night.

"Hail, Eagle!" she called once more, in a clear, high voice.

With a little moan the old woman tottered, and sank down on the steps, leaning her head against one of the black pillars. Yet Henri knew she was still watching that eagle shape—that eagle beating its way to the seas, or that spirit of an eagle which was the premonitory symbol of some dire thing to be.

Then, through the night silence came the unmistakable sound of that majestic bird—a whistling sound—the call of an eagle to its mate. And whilst Henri stared, his breath held; the great shape was gone. The sky was a clear, steely blue, with banks of clouds travelling slowly once more to the edges of the moon. Her white disc was blotted out. All was darkness.

Burl was stooping over the old woman. She threw her arm about her shoulders. He followed them up the steps. Burl closed the door, drew the rusted bolts. The footsteps of all three passed over the flagged hall, with its white mould. And in a distant doorway, leaning heavily upon a stick, Henri saw a man of some sixty years. He was coming towards them, on slinking steps. His whole form seemed to slink. At his approach, the old woman Burl was upholding almost with her young strength, roused. She began to rate him.

"I only wonder't what 'at din was about," he said.

His voice had a slinking note which matched his whole appearance.

"It wer't Eagle, Luke," said the old woman.

"Th' Eagle! Th' Eagle o' Eagles' Crag!" said the old man. "Th' Lord ha' mercy. What's comin' on us now?"

As though the old woman so much enjoyed the sight of his fear that she forgot her own, her laughter cackled through the echoing, mouldy hall.

"Ay. It'll come for thee, one o' these neets," she told him. "It'll carry thee away ower't rocks an' drop thee into a shak-bog, tha gurt loon. Luke, get out an' see if a's fastened oop."

Her eyes looked malicious enjoyment at his terror.

"Nay, if a's not fastened oop, it mun stop unfastened," expostulated Luke.

"Do as I bid thee," she bade him, "or I'll hide thee well."

Henri almost gasped.

She must be almost ninety. The old man looked over sixty. She addressed him as though he were a child. And by the way he retreated before her, gazing with angry fear upon the menace in her countenance, it was plain that her words were no idle threat.

Muttering and lamenting by turns, Luke retreated through the doorway where Henri had first seen him standing. Whilst, as though her passage-at-arms with the old man had quite broken the spell of supernatural fears which had so lately made her Medusan spirit quail, she turned to Henri.

As that gaze fell on his face Henri felt a curious shudder run through him. There is nothing more beautiful than the face of an old woman, however age has peaked and puckered it, when a great old soul looks through it. There is nothing more hideous than its opposite. Jane Mowbray's face was that of such an opposite. She looked like a death's head grinning at the spectacle of life. But her greeting was quite commonplace.

"Tha's brought a wild neet wi' thee, lad," she began.

Then she stopped abruptly.

Into her dim-sighted eyes came a spark of incredulous terror and hatred.

She crept nearer to him. Her mouth opened.

She stood "gaupin'" at him. Perplexed, embarrassed by this scrutiny, Henri glanced from her to Burl. The latter was standing, holding the lantern which alone lit the great hall.

"Nigher," commanded old Jane.

Burl obediently lifted the lantern so that the rays fell on Henri's face. He stood almost blinded in the light. Yet upon Burl's face he thought he saw an expression of mockery as she looked at the old woman, though there was something of sadness in it too.

"So that were why tha brought him to that dur?" she exclaimed, flashing a vindictive look at Burl. "Ay. He's like. Varra like. Varra like."

Then, muttering to herself, her chin drooped towards her breast. She stood, having forgotten Henri, Burl, and even the Eagle of Eagles' Crag, a softened look upon that face which had so appalled him. It became the face of a human being, with human feelings. And even whilst the decrepancy of age was more strongly evidenced, as those softer emotions trembled across it, like pale sunlight over a wintry landscape, the softening of those hard features lent to them a certain strange beauty as though a beam from youth's long distant land threw its reflected warmth upon them. The softer expression died as suddenly as it had come. When it had gone, her face looked more grisly in its utter hideousness than before, the coarse curling locks about it more like coils of pale snakes, whilst the eyelashes, such as were left around her eyes, set round with inflamed flesh, might have been made from the white mould on which they were standing.

"Ah. Tha's brought a wild neet wi' thee," she told Henri, withdrawing her gaze from his face, "But wi'se mayhap see wilder afore tha leaves Eagles' Crag."

She tottered a little.

Burl made a movement towards her.

Henri forestalled her.

With the courteousness towards women which was part of his nature, he offered the old woman his arm.

She glanced at him, derision blazing over her face.

"Though I be ninety—ay, though I should live to be nine hundred," she almost hissed, "I would not lean on a chap's arm. Gan it to her."

Henri looked at Burl. His experience of women had taught him that they were either like cats or mice. To his astonishment the girl, with a countenance unchanged from its calm by the insult, moved quietly towards the old woman who was obviously spent with the excitement of the evening. She threw her arm around the old woman's shoulders, supporting the now tottering frame with her young strength. And despite the savagery of that fierce nature, he saw the old woman lean upon that strength, so heavily that she must have been a dead weight. Involuntarily, he made a step to assist her. Buri shook her head at him, glancing at him mutely. They travelled very slowly towards the doorway through which Luke had gone. Swift as was Burl's usual pace, she went slowly along, no sign of impatience on her face.

As they came to the glow of the kitchen, Henri saw Burl's face, as she still guided the old woman's faltering steps. So tender an affection shone from her look, it seemed to him that in this dark house it was like the gentle radiance of an unquenchable star, lighting its black gloom.

"That'll do. I'm a' reight now," was the old woman's querulous thanks.

She sat in her chair, staring into the fire.

And as Henri sat down also, recalling as he did so, that he had dropped his stick and bundle and left them outside, the full weariness of bodily fatigue made itself felt. The kitchen, like most farm kitchens, saving that it was twice as big as the biggest he had seen, swam before his sight for a moment. He sat, trying to shake off not only physical fatigue, but that weirdest of all sensations, the feeling that had suddenly gripped his mind in the hall—the weird impression that he had seen it before, with the grey rusted swords that hung upon it, the grinning, grotesque heads on its corniced carving, the groined roof of it, with the black shadows.

"Imagination," said reason. "It could not be. You have never been here before."

Burl made supper when Luke came in, bringing a bucket of eggs, which he set down by the old woman's chair.

She cut thick slices of home-made bread, scalded tea in four pint pots, which she stood by the plates. Then into the fire, a red blazeless fire, she dropped eight eggs, in their shells. She raked and lifted them from the glowing cinders with a long-handled iron ladle, and set them, their shells mahogany-coloured, on the plates.

Luke drew up to the table silently.

He began to peel the eggs with his fingers.

Burl motioned Henri to draw up a chair also, Then she sat down too. The old woman drew her chair along also.

"Get summat down thee, lad," she said, glancing across the table at him. "Tha'll need to be strang here. Baith strang in't arm, an' strang i' th' yed."

Then they ate in unbroken silence, saving for the heavy ticking of the great clock, and the hoarser blowing of the wind outside which was growing louder with every moment.

"Time for bed, Luke," she told the old man, at the conclusion of the meal.

He scraped his chair back from the table. Then bending down began to unlace his clogs—clogs made from boots, the soles being wooden with the usual irons, the tops made from cast-off Sunday boots. He cast a furtive glance at the old woman, as hazarding whether to say "good neet", and finally ventured to say it.

"Good neet," she told him. "If there's anny difference in neets when folk are owd. An' tak' this mon up an' show him whear he's to sleep."

Henri followed Luke up the stairs.

As though the surprise of the old woman saying "good neet" had affected him to senile hilarity, the old man climbed the stairs. Henri heard him mumbling an old northern nursery rhyme:
"Up wooden hill,
To Blanket Fair,
To see how they sell
Sheets a-pair."

The old man, half-singing, half-humming this over and over on the slow ascent up two flights of wooden stairs, paused finally on the threshold of a room whose door stood ajar.

"In thear," said the old man.

Henri nodded.

He was tumbling to the fact that the old man was in his dotage. Was he the old woman's son? He looked at him. There was certainly some resemblance. But it ended with physical likeness. "Good night," Henri told the old man.

"'Neet," he said. Then, in a stealthy whisper: "Fasten a' oop afore she cooms down. I didn't. I dossen't. I went no furrer nor't barn-dur. Net when't Eagle had been seen. Noa. I'm noan goin' to be carried ower't rocks nor dropped in't shak-bogs."

He slunk away, the glim of the candle he carried growing fainter. His slinking footsteps seemed to awaken all the echoes of the place. Henri dived into the blackness of the chamber which was his sleeping-room. He eventually found matches, and lit the inch of candle stuck on a saucer. The light would just last him long enough, to enable him to undress and have a smoke. Then he recalled that his pipe and tobacco was in his bundle outside. It was a grievous disappointment after a hard day, and a nerve-racking evening. From feeling overpowered with sleep he became wide awake.

Chapter Three

Henri lay in the big four-poster bed in the barn-like room whose roof was not underdrawn. The candle, its feeble light flickering in draughts which blew from every point of the compass, added to the gloom, rather than decreased it. The few pieces of old, dark furniture, heavy though they were, emphasized the hugeness of the chamber in which he lay. The pictures, weird etchings in ebony frames, left great deserts of cold, whitewashed wall-space, ghostly in this dim light. Brocaded curtains at the windows, heavy as they were, swung in the draught of the wind howling up the gorge and blowing through the loose-fitting sashes. The high sloping ceiling, going up to a point just over the bed, was deeply shadowed on each side the big "bawk" that was just an unplaned tree-trunk whitewashed over.

From behind the house came the sound of one of the farm dogs howling. The wolf-like sound, the rattling of its heavy chain, came to him even above the roar and racket of the wind, which was shouting like demons let loose. An unfastened gate banged at intervals, adding to the pandemonium of noises raging outside in the black night. Since he had ascended the stairs this storm had sprung up, as to keep him from the sleep he sorely needed.

The bed was piled up with clothes, yet he felt frozen. The long hard day, he told himself, should have induced sleep. He had never felt more awake in his life. The cold, the largeness of the room, the strangeness of the place, felt to have brought every sense into abnormal activity. The many shadows, shifting and changing as the now almost guttering candle-flame was blown in the draughts; the barbarity of the curtains, blood-red and bordered with a valance whose heavy tassels, once of gold thread, were now

42

turned black with age; the bed-hangings, fully a hundred years behind present-day draperies; exorcized his mind with strange thoughts and fancies.

These things, following upon the weird atmosphere which he had felt existed between the tenants of Eagles' Crag, deepened the uncanny feeling he had had even before he had stepped into the place. It was a place to rise and flee from, with all possible speed. It was a place wherein it was best not to linger another hour. Something told him this. But he continued to lie there, trying to reason away his fears.

"Rise and flee whilst there is time." Like a voice speaking, clearly and distinctly, he heard those words. Did they come from the ghostly walls, the blood-red curtains, from the spirit of the place? Or from some deeps within him, which had known this lonely, rocky height before, these two women, that slinking old man? He could not tell. But it was indeed as though some actual, living voice had spoken, warning him not to wait even till the morrow, but to depart with all possible speed, before the spell of Eagles' Crag grew stronger than reason.

He lay in the great bed, staring fearfully round the room.

"Rise and flee whilst there is time," came the words again.

Henri sprang out of bed.

He crossed the bare boarded floor noiselessly and opening the door of his room, looked into the unlighted gloom of the corridor. All was silent darkness. No human being had approached the door to whisper that warning. When he got back into bed, satisfied on that point, the candle was guttering. But there was all the more cause to fear since it was no human being who had spoken that warning. The candle, its flames blown wildly, as its light caught the hot fat in the saucer, sent great flares of light over the huge walls. Then the light would almost go out. Its spluttering sounded loud in the echoing, gloomy room. The next moment the light would leap up again, making the heavy shadows move as though they were alive. Henri raised himself on his elbow, and blew out the light. Better the dark blankness than that fantastic movement of glaring light and succeeding darkness. He closed his eyes, and strove for sleep.

Finally, he dropped into restless slumber.

How long he slept he could not tell, when some movement within the room startled him into wide wakefulness, every nerve on edge. He sat up, in the dead blackness of the room, sure that some person was moving cautiously about it.

From outside came the shouting of the wind in the hollows of the rocks above, the sullen roar of the torrent, the howling of the wolf-hound.

His impression that someone was within the room grew ever more strong. Surely that was a stealthy footstep sounding now from the middle of the chamber?

Noiselessly, he lay down and feigned sleep.

And as he lay, after a time, he felt a hand touch his head; a cold, dry hand at whose touch his whole being shuddered.

"Asleep!"

He caught the ghostly whisper.

His blood curdled.

He could see nothing but the blank darkness of the room.

But the hand was lifted from his head now. He felt no more that palsied caress, like ice, on his brow.

He had been right in thinking the place was haunted. This was probably what the old woman had meant when she had said they needed to be "strang in't yed" who lived at Eagles' Crag.

"Asleep!" came the ghostly ejaculation once more.

The cold hand was stroking his face now.

He wanted to leap up, give one wild yell, and rush from this place, undressed as he was, away, away, into the big, clean night. Why, oh, why had he ever come to this rock-shadowed, ghoul-haunted eyrie of the wilderness?

"Varra like," sounded to his ears, in a muted breath, as he thought thus. "Varra like. That were why't Eagle came— th' Eagle o' Eagles' Crag. But it weren't a red Eagle. Noa."

Henri held his breath. His marrow curdled as well as his blood, now. It was no ghost whose icy touch he had felt upon his face. It was that old woman's. She was bending over him. And as she bent, she was talking to herself, living back in those years when life had been a joyous thing.

"Morns—when the yeth was Heaven," came her sighing words. "Noons when the sun warmed the blood warm enough bout it—ay, though the sun had gone out in't sky. Evenings, full o' th' twittering birds. An' neets full o' stars. Yeth beautiful, an' life beautiful, an' th' sorrow o' his gannin', an' th' rapture o' his comin's. An' I've to gae through it a' again—at ninety-three."

Henri lay as though he was dead.

He could hear in the distance the blowing of the wind, melancholy now as the old woman's sighing words, and the dismal howling of the wolf-hound. He could hear the rats scuttering in the walls. It was all a weird chorus to the old woman lamenting youth gone, and the grave waiting to receive her ancient bones. "Ay. That's why th' Eagle o' Eagles' Crag appeared unto us," she went on. "It knew I'd to gan through it a' again, at ninety an' three. An' Burl, shoo liked him. I see it in her e'en. But shoo shan't ha' him. I'm old, I know. But th' speerit n'er grows old. An' we'll feight for him."

Henri felt a sudden, irresistible impulse to laugh, Ninety and three were her years. She ought to have been toddling three times every Sunday to church, and praying for forgiveness for her sins, and getting her laying-out clothes ready. Instead—

But the touch of that clammy old hand, once more caressing his brow, killed his impulse to laugh; besides instinct telling him that if he laughed it might be his last laugh. And even whilst he lay, his flesh creeping with horror, as that icy hand stroked his eyelids again, what she had spoken of Burl liking him filled him with a quiet happiness, even whilst it disturbed him.

He breathed again, as that chill hand left his brow.

She was going.

He drew a full, deep breath of the air she was leaving him to breathe, purged of her ghastly yet majestic presence. For he had felt the majesty of that spirit which was not going to end life kneeling, ashamed of life, and its fires, but at ninety-three was feeling the flames rekindle—though they would go out as suddenly as the candle-glare before the last bit flickered. Had it been an omen, his snuffing out that candle-flame? Was that why he had come to Eagles' Crag, to flare a foolish and futile old woman, possibly in her dotage, into the idea that she loved him? Even as he wondered he heard the door close behind her. He lay back on his pillows, the full significance of her coming bursting in on his mind.

She had come to stroke his face, and find out if it was like some face she had known and loved in the dim past. Whose face? A face she must have often stroked—to have kept through seventy or more years, the memory of its shape. And, he had heard that women, unlike men, were incapable of the grande passion after thirty-five. She must be doting. But even as he told himself that she was doting, he knew this was no dotage. And the words: "Rise and flee whilst there is time," came back to him. He would leave Eagles' Crag on the morrow. Leave before they were up. For it would certainly be most unpleasant to have an aged beldame in love with him. Yes. He would leave the place at dawn.

So thinking he fell asleep.

He awoke to a loud knocking upon the room door. Sleep was yet so heavy upon him he did not feel that he had been long asleep. Through the heavy curtains the room was filling with light. Through the dark folds it came in lurid crimson.

He must have overslept.

"Time to get up, lad," said the old woman's voice. Then, after a pause: "But tha need n't hurry thysel', seein' its thy first mornin' here. Naught's spoilin'."

"I'll be down soon," Henri told her.

Her feeble steps went along the corridor.

And as she went, he realized that it was no dream, that recollection of her stroking his and saying she had to go through it all again— at ninety and three. She was "making a stir" of him, as Curdy would have phrased it. And, as he splashed at the wash-basin, he also remembered that he had promised old Luke to have fastened up, when she got down. And he had overslept. What would happen now? The old man would be in the hobble for not having faced the fear of the spectral eagle and gone farther than the barn-door to see that all was right for the night.

Even as Henri wondered, the echoes of the conflict came to him from below stairs.

When Henri entered the kitchen, he found old Luke blubbering like a big child. He was alone in the kitchen.

"S-shoo b-b-belted m-me," he bellowed. "A' through t-t-thee."

Henri did not know what to say.

"Is she your mother?" he finally ventured, whilst the bellowing burst out again.

Old Luke wiped his sleeve across his eyes.

"Noa," he managed to say. "Shoo isn't. For I axed her once. An' shoo said she'd foun' me under a wickan tree."

Henri wanted to laugh.

He had no longer any doubt that old Luke was old Jane's son. She had varied the old tale of the gooseberry bush to wickan tree, the tree which in this North was held to be a mystic tree. The old man's deficient intelligence was also beyond doubt. And Burl—how long had she lived, with this old tyrant and this slinking, cowering, blubbering slave?

Even as he mused on what her life must have been, Burl entered the kitchen.

She crossed over to the fireplace without looking at him.

The hair he had seen coiled round her head on the evening of his arrival hung down her back in two great plaits.

"Good morning," Henri greeted her.

"'Mornin'," she answered, with something in her voice which told she considered "good morning" an unnecessary irony in Eagles' Crag. And as they breakfasted, the gloom of the kitchen, shadowed by those great rocks, was matched by the view of the outside world. Grey rain misted the sky. The rough ground rising in a slope, stone-littered and bare, ran up to the bracken and black top of the heather. The world outside looked as ghostly as the world within.

Burl, when their plates were emptied, jumped up to serve them more "stirabout", a dish made of onions, fat, with handfuls of meal stirred into it. Like the supper of the night before, the meal was eaten in silence. And indeed Henri was not sure that it was not more pleasant, eating in that strange silence, than when it was broken by speech. For when old Jane said: "Well, let's get into work o't day," so weird were the echoes of the place, after that silence which had felt like the silence hung around some great rock, he had felt almost startled.

When he saw the old woman struggle into a leathern coat, and for all her age, go out into the mist and rain, to work, he was not surprised. She had left directions that Luke was to be "kept at it". Henri went to milk. He found the cattle fine, healthy animals in comparison with some of the cows he had found on other farms.

The milk swished into the pail.

The fresh dampness of the outside world came to him through the open doorway. Within the farm kitchen Burl was rolling the milk kits across the flagged floor. The rattling of them came to his ears. The coldness of the air had felt to take his breath, when first he had entered the shed. But after ten minutes he found he was getting accustomed to its sharply exhilarating keenness. None the less he was glad when the last cow stood over, to see Burl looking in at the shed door, a pint pot of steaming coffee in her hand.

"Thought you'd feel the cold," she said. "It's frosty this morn." And set the pint pot on the flagstone outside the shed door. The heat of it made the ice which thinly glassed it over begin to melt.

The last cow milked, the last pail full of creamy, frothing milk set where they could not kick it over, Henri left the shed, and standing outside the door, took up the coffee, and sipped it. Burl had boiled it. There was cream in it too. The thought flashed through his mind that she also was "making a stir" of him. The next moment he felt ashamed. She had come once more from the house, another pot of steaming coffee in her hand. She went through the misted greyness to where old Luke was sitting on a rock amidst the bracken, tawny under the pale mists. Henri was as sure that she was comforting the old man for the belting he had had that morning, as though he stood beside them, and could hear every word. When she had gone, leaving the old man alone, Henri went to have a chat with him. As he reached him, he saw the old man staring up at the brightest part of the misted sky.

"Th' clouds is goin' to break," he told Henri.

"Looks like it," Henri agreed.

But they allus close again, after," said old Luke, wearily. "Ay. They allus gather thick an' heavy again. That's life all through."

It was as though, free from the darkness of Eagles' Crag, out here where the width and light of the sky was over his head, he was no "loon" as the old Medusa had called him, but something of a rude philosopher. And when Henri left him to go back to the shed, and carry the milk-pails into the dairy for Burl to sieve the milk, looking back, he saw old Luke still staring at the brightest portion of the sky, even his poor old dulled brain responsive to the influence of light and air.

Burl helped him fill the milk kits.

He was to take them to the station.

She put the horse in the shafts of the cart, helped him to lift the kits into it. Then she went away into the house again, after pointing him out the road, a hairpin road which seemed to Henri to hang over a perilous ravine, a road which ran behind the house, winding up past the rock above it and away to town. Old Luke came to watch him off.

"Do we always have coffee at nine?" inquired Henri.

"Only when shoo's out buyin,'" old Luke told him.

"Oh," said Henri.

Chapter Four

Spring, those who call thee gay have never known
The cost of life;
Lo, every flower which sways besides a stone
Has had its strife,
Beating up through the dark and savage earth
Toward the sun,
Creation taking toll with every birth
As when the world begun.

Spring!

Never had Henri seen one so beautiful as this which
had danced down on Eagles' Crag. In mid-April all had
seemed winter still. In three short weeks the whole glory of
springtide had burst upon these heights. The gorge torrent
flowed gently past mossy stones. Ferns poked out from the
shale and great rocks: Daisy, blue bugle, and water-haven
grew in profusion, sunned into rapid life under this wide
sky; now the cold was gone. Rabbits and hares frisked
in the sunshine; Lying on the old bracken which winds
and rains of the dreariest winter he had ever experienced
had laid flat as straw to the ground, Henri had counted
twenty rabbits in the last half-hour. Two days of blazing
sunshine, of heat which would have been torrid saving for
the breeze on these heights, had made the bracken a dry
warm couch. Rocks were so hot food would have cooked
on them.

Spring! Sunshine! Flowers! Bird songs. Above all the
sunshine, floods of it in these past two days.

He lay with half-closed eyes, staring upward, into the
blue deeps of a cloudless sky. In all his remembrance
he could not recall more than half a dozen days in this
North when the sky had been of such deep, exquisite

blue. It was such blue as he had pictured over Avignon. The sunlight was like golden wine. Two days of it. He was drunk completely. He had forgotten the blackness of winter departed, the deluges of rain swirling down from the rocks over the window ledges, so that for weeks together it had been like looking through a moving curtain of grey water. He had forgotten rattle of hailstones on the rocks above the house. They had sounded like demonic drumsticks through the silent evenings in Eagles' Crag, those long dark evenings whose only consolation had been that sometimes at supper, when the old Medusa was too overpowered with sleep to be watchful, Burl who knew how the savage winter in this savage household without laughter or conversation was appalling him, would slyly rest her feet upon his.

And then the snow. They had had weeks of it to the end of March. Each bleak, raw dawn the cold white stuff had to be shovelled away before they could get to the outhouses. Every morning, from his window he had looked shiveringly out on the same white desolation—blowing snow-mists, or grey sky, white drifts, black rocks, fringe of the black heather. Burl had tried to make him see the beauty of it. When the old Medusa had gone buying cattle one day— gone despite the fact that a blizzard might rage before she got back, making old Luke drive the cart, he and Burl had been out from noon to milking-time. Henri had endured the shuddering cold for her sake. He had seen no beauty in the wind-swept waste of icicled rocks, frozen streams, snow-covered trees, hills lapped about in that silent whiteness. Burl had been disappointed. He had been laid up with a chill for a week. The old Medusa had tended him.

A "cawf" and cow had died through their being away that day. The old woman had wormed the fact from her son that they had been away. Loss of calf and cow—or was it that they two had been from under her eyes?—had made her half-demented for a time. But she had not sent Henri from Eagles' Crag. She would never send him from Eagles' Crag. He took full advantage of that fact in a score of ways, as now, lying indolently on the warm bracken, basking in the sunshine, waiting for Burl to come out to him and sit beside him. She had promised to do so. He would have felt very impatient, for since the calf and cow had died they had never had an hour together. But the air was too warm, the sky too blue, for one to feel even one grande passion saving lazily, as part of a dream in a world half-dream in its beauty.

These were the early days of their love. In the usual way of things it would have been expressed with all the innocent demonstrativeness of open loving, smiles at seeing each other after a night's sleep, sitting by each other's side in the evenings, reading from one book. But this, as Burl had told Henri, would drive old Jane Mowbray into her dotage. On the rare occasions when they could be together their meeting was as the meeting of two flames. They would post old Luke on the rocks above the house, to watch the road along which she would come, driving the cart at dusk on that road over the steep ravine, sitting bolt upright holding the reins with her almost skeleton-like hands, at an age when most old women would have gone to bed at seven, tucked in and tended like a child.

Yet despite her almost savage strength, Henri often felt that Jane Mowbray must be in her dotage. From those inflamed eye-sockets, with their scant eyelashes which reminded him of the white mould on the hall flagstones, she watched them with the keenness of ah old eagle, out of those sunken eyes. But for all that he was sure she was in her dotage, since Burl had told him that to old Jane Mowbray he was the reincarnated spirit of one she had loved nigh on seventy years ago.

And in that terrible concentration of watchfulness, since her visit to his bedside on that eyrie midnight, which had been the first he had spent at Eagles' Crag, there was all the abnormality of something like, if indeed it were not, madness, since it had been no carnal old woman, but one obsessed with the idea that his spirit was that of her old lover, who had stood bending over him in the darkness, the winds howling round the place.

For Burl's sake, no less than for the menace of peril he felt it would bring, were the Old Medusa to become aware of it, they hid their loving from those deep-set eyes, eyes like dark shadows holding a fiery spark, set round with those inflamed lids with their white lashes.

Once, when he had said "'Beryll", drawing the name out to its full beauty of expression, the old nomad had turned sharply, suspiciously upon him, saying: "Burl's good enow; We haven't time to give one another mouthfuls of name up here."

But the old Medusa was confined to her bed to-day. This heat which Henri was so enjoying had been too much for her. And fortunately her room was behind the house. She could not spy on them from the window.

But for how long their flesh and blood humanity could feel all the passionate gladness of each other's nearness day after day, enforcedly in each other's company, sharing as they did farm-tasks together, and repressing all token of it in voice, and in eye, was a question Henri had often asked himself during this last month. The old woman was tough. Ninety and three she might be. She cane or a race in which a hundred was quite a common age to live to. When she had sat in the kitchen, on the winter evenings, when he did not dare to look at Burl, nor she at him, and had been totting over all the members of her family who had lived to be over a hundred, she had made him feel half-crazy with despair and repressed love—love which could not even ease its crave by a look at the one beloved.

A hundred. If she lived to be a hundred. The maddening thought that she could do so—nay, that she would probably do so, would come to him in all kinds of places round the farm, when be was milking, when he was brushing the horses, when he was taking the milk in the cart along the path over the ravine. Even to-day, as he had flung himself down on the bracken, memory had mimicried her voice as it had drawled: "Ay. An' my feyther's sister, shoo lived to be a hundred an' five, an' shoo wouldn't ha' deed then; if shoo'd ha' ta'en reight care o' hersel'. Shoo'd ha' lived years after that." But he had thrust the maddening recollection of the longlivety of the Mowbrays out of his head, and after lying outside on this sun-warmed couch, under blue sky, breathing air that was like wine, winter, the old Medusa's tragic loving of him, Burl's and his tragic loving of each other, the gloom of Eagles' Crag, and that other enigma which disturbed him lately, old Luke's somewhat changed demeanour towards him, were all forgotten.

He lay, enjoying the delight of being, just being, of listening for Burl's step. It was with difficulty he could help himself from singing, singing so loud that his voice would reach the old Medusa, in that dim room where the lamp would be lit, despite all this sunshine outside, for the rocks and earth came so close to the window only a trickle of light could penetrate it. He had felt like doing so once—singing, so that she would hear him, revelling in her being bedfast, free from her tyrannical hold—which could send Burl away from Eagles' Crag, even though she would never let him go away. Then he had fallen to listening to the voice of the torrent in the gorge below. The golden hush of the moontide—still, very still, saving for the breeze in the heather, a distant sandpiper's thread of song, the dream-like murmur of the torrent that was now only a lively stream, the call of grouse, brought peace to heart and mind.

To-morrow the old Medusa would doubtless be up again.

The tragedy would tun on again.

To-day—blessed be the sun which had smitten her so that he and Burl could be together for an hour.

"Henri!"

Her eager breathing of his name came to him.

But before she had spoken, before her footfall had sounded, he had said: "She is coming now."

She came, and flung herself down on the bracken beside him.

They looked at each other in this silence on the heights—a silence so deep it laid its spell on them, tragic, passionate, frantic lovers who, long day after day, week after week, must give no sign of their loving. But of speech there was no need. They looked at each other with devouring eyes of joy—and all was said. Then leaning together, in silence, they listened to the same sounds, looked on the same greening heather, the same new growing tufts of rushes, stared into the same blue sky.

"But I cannot stay long. I am to be there with her. Perhaps she is afraid that we will be together. The air is stifling. The lamp is lit, burning up what there is of air in the room. And out here is the sun—and you."

Henri's cheek had grown pale.

"You have but just come, chérie he said, in pained protest.

"Yes. And I had so looked forward to it, for weeks, when we could be together. And old Luke now. Have you noticed the change? She has set him against us. You cannot depend on him any more, Henri, to stand on the rocks and give us warning. She has promised him barley sugar. You know how fond of it he is."

"Then we can never see each other again—?" asked Henri.

Burl's frantic gaze met his frantic gaze.

"We shall see each other every day," she told him, recovering at the sight of his wild look. "As we have done for the past weeks."

"With her there, or old Luke?" queried Henri.

"Yes. That is something, surely, Henri," Burl told him, almost pleadingly.

"That is worse than not seeing each other at all," said Henri, springing to his feet. "That is purgatory. Why, for weeks we have looked forward to one hour in which to be able to look the love we feel, and you are now to go in? Defy her. You need not go. Leave old Luke to attend to her. He is her son."

He dropped down in the bracken beside her once more, rebellion in his look.

"She is ill, and ninety-three. Quite helpless. Otherwise, the house might fall. I should sit here with you all this afternoon," Burl told him.

"She will not know how long you have been away—" he began.

"She had Luke's watch by the bedside," Burl told him.

"The old tyrant," said Henri, in a voice of still rage.

He sprang up from the heather.

"She will live," he told Burl, with bitter conviction, to be over a hundred. Winter after winter—Burl, you don't know how your northern winters eat into me—we shall be waiting. She will live deliberately, to keep us apart. Spring after spring, when the heart leaps as the trees leap, dances as the thorns dance—and she will be living. I believe she knows that she stands a barrier which only death will remove. *L'Diable!* She will live—for ever—for ever—for ever—I tell you."

From slow bitterness his voice had become like a rapidly rushing torrent—fierce, burning. The words tumbled over each other. He stamped backwards and forwards on the bracken, like a horse pawing the ground impatiently under its feet.

"Luke is calling," Burl told him, in a warning voice. "He is coming to see where we are."

Luke was not yet within earshot, but moving towards them, as fast as he could, which was not very fast.

"She will live to see our love flicker out—burnt away, futilely waiting, waiting through the long years," said Henri, prophetically. The dejection he had lost in these days of sunshine had come back like a black tide.

He was gazing into Burl's eyes as he spoke,

He saw them dilate suddenly, lose their northern calmness. A gipsy looked at him, the northern woman shed quite away.

"'Flicker out'," she repeated. "Love never flickers out. You are talking like—like a Georgio, Henri!"

It was her deepest expression of contempt.

They stood surveying each other with wide eyes of anger, such anger as only those who love can feel. The sharpness of foiled love was in their accents.

"Take that back," said Henri. "Almost—why did you not call me English, and have done with it?"

"Take back your stupid talk of love flickering out, then," Burl threw at him. "Those fires which for Georgios are taper-lights for us are deathless stars. Henri, take back about the flickering out—"

"There are no deathless stars," Henri declared sullenly and sombrely. "If love is a star, even stars need space and air to burn in. Eagles' Crag is a tomb—"

"There are stars that shine over tombs," she told him, passionately. "'Flicker out', you said, Henri. You love, then, like the bulls which have to be blessed, since all cows look alike to them? Eh, you love like that, Henri? You wish to go away, eh? You will forget? You will say 'that was yesterday'—eh? And I, a gipsy, have given my heart to a Georgio. Why was I born?"

"Hush—old Luke—he is almost here, now," Henri told her.

Calmness, some degree of it, had come back to him, as she had lost hers. He wished to use the half-minute before old Luke reached them, in making peace, but it was now a gipsy, stirred to the depths, who confronted him.

With hands on her hips, with her head thrown back, with the same mocking look she must have had in her eyes when they had come to acquaint her that a man had shot himself for love of her, he saw her standing before him, laughter in her eyes, like sunlight oil some still, dark tarn, fathomless—the same, yes, this was the same of whom the old man had talked as he had come up to Eagles' Crag. Gipsy, yes, she was all gipsy now.

"Eagles' Crag is dark," she gibed at him. Like a tomb, as you said. But we are eagles. Eagles, not meadow-pipits. What peace one loses through being an eagle, in a world full of tame things! And do not think I will ever wish old Jane to die. For why? She is an eagle. At ninety and three she loves a young man because he is like her lover of seventy years ago. For that I will bide with her, and tend her, though she live for ever, as you said she would. Yes. Though she divided us for ever, and it were possible to love you twice, thrice, ten times as much, I would not have one day taken off all the years she could live because she is an eagle. Ha, ha, ha! La, la, Henri! You will be an eagle also, before you leave Eagles' Crag!"

Her mocking laughter rippled out as she swept past him.

He scarcely heard the savage sob it ended in.

He was standing rooted to the ground, horrified.

He knew now she would never leave old Jane Mowbray. She loved the old tyrant, because she was an eagle in a tame world. And he had wished she would die. He started, noticing Luke's shadow on the bracken.

"Coming," he told Luke, who mumbled about some task or other to do. "How's shoo?"

"Shoo's gotten up," Luke told him. "Ay. Shoo's gotten up, though shoo was told she'd not to point her foot to't groun'. Shoo says shoo can't liy there, an' a' goin' to rack an' ruin. Shoo's gotten up. Shoo's sat in't chair. An' shoo's a devil. Ay, mon. Shoo's a devil, shoo is an' all, to-day. I tell't her th' Eagle'd be comin' again if shoo went on like shoo was gunnin' on—an' shoo said shoo felt it't Eagle had to come just now, shoo'd mak' it fain to pike some other place to hover ower. Ah. Shoo's a devil, to-day."

He hobbled away, laughing and chunnering to himself. It was quite plain that the old Medusa was keeping on the right side of old Luke. He and Burl were to be given no chance to be together at all. She knew. The old Medusa knew. She was going to enjoy the spectacle of their starving for each other, under those sunken eyes of hers. And Burl would never leave her. Henri knew it. In that savage burst of emotion she had revealed that she would stay with the old tyrant for ever—if she could have lived for ever—fanning that flame of life whenever it flickered, because—yes, she loved the old Medusa as fiercely as she loved him. He could leave Burl, though. And he could leave Eagles' Crag. He stood staring down at the bracken—then across at the dark house. Even on this bright spring day it looked like a black cloud.

Yes. He had feet. He could walk away.

But instead of walking away he walked towards the house.

Burl was stood by one of the windows.

Her face looked at him from the background of the shadowy gloom with agonized appeal. Her lips were moving, but he could not tell what she said.

Henri walked up to the window.

She stood pressing her mouth against the window-pane.

He placed his lips against the cold glass?

She smiled at him, and was gone.

This was their afternoon which they had planned together.

When he went into the kitchen from the outside world, it was indeed like entering a tomb. The light from the windows fell over two yards of floor space below them. The rest was dimness, which varied from twilight grey to black. The fire glimmered like the red eye of a demon, watching them all. The clock ticked with a slow, funereal sound. A couple of pigeons lay neck downwards on the edge of the wooden table. Blood dripped on the flagged floor from their beaks. Old Luke was washing his hands at the sink. He had just wrung the necks of two doves—in springtime. They were going to go into the pan, to help keep life in this old beldame who hung shivering over the fire, in the old tyrant who could part them even from the sight of each other.

"Pluck them, if tha's naught to do," croaked old Jane. "They'me varra nourishin'. An' whilst they're stewin', tha can cal wi' me. Thee's bin outside all't morn. An' thee, Burl tha can milk this day. Henri's goin' to sit an' cal with me. Isn'y ta, Henri?"

Henri began to pluck the doves, after nodding.

Added to the unpleasantness of the task of stripping these tender and graceful birds, was the irony of having to entertain with his conversation this old Medusa.

Burl came and took them from him when he had finished the task. She dressed and plopped them into the pan. The sordid ghoulish of existence, where all the animal kingdom yielded up its simple, beautiful life to feed humans oppressed him, as it had often done. The simmering of the doves stewing for a meal for the old woman, made him want to give one great curse against it all. And it was to keep life in her, to divide him and Burl in the springtime of their loving.

He entertained her, joked with her, all this stirring within him, in the cauldron of his mind.

For the first time since he had come to Eagles' Crag she appeared to him entirely a ghoul.

Already he seemed to have been at Eagles' Crag eternities. It was but a few months. Tick-tick, said the slow clock. Yes. She will live for years yet. Every one will be an eternity;. Every one will be more dark. Every one will have worn something of love away. But at last you will have Eagles' Crag and all she owns. Tick-tick. You can then go to Avignon. The bright beauty of springtime will have gone, waiting. Tick-tick, but you can go to Avignon and live the rest of life out with Burl. Tick-tick. Play up to her. Tick-

tick. Have Eagles' Crag for the sunlight of heart and mind it took, for the years dropping past, leaden and heavy with love's futile desires, rick-tick. Yes. That will be something. And in that last tick-tick of the old clock he heard the clay rattle on her coffin.

The old Medusa laughed, a dry, rattling laugh, at one of his *bon mots*. They talked on.

Then she ordered Burl take the pigeons out.

He must needs eat along with her; eat the tender doves, killed in the merry springtime. He gave an exclamation.

"French!" said the old Medusa, holding up her fork at him with an attempt at coquettish gaiety which made her look more ghoulish than ever. "French! What does it mean in the Yorkshire tongue?"

"There is no equivalent for it in your northern language," Henri told her, looking at her with some of her own devilish malice. "It is not translatable."

He had given expression to the most maledictory oath in the French language. It eased his feelings a little. But later, when she had gone to bed, making Burl go up to sit and read to her, and telling her she must not come down again, when Burl did come down, she found him standing by the window. Outside was a night of stars. He stood staring at them.

"*Chérie,*" he confessed, "I think if I stay here after next winter, I shall become a little mad. I find myself thinking the damnedest oddest things. Wicked things. Ghastly. Monstrous."

He broke off suddenly.

"Kiss them out of my mind," he said, and bent towards her. The almost wild solemnity of his look scared Burl.

"Yes, yes," she said, in her swift gipsy way.

She enfolded him in her arms. His head was against her breast, drooping there, heavily and wearily. She kissed him again and again.

"They are gone, now?" she asked.

"Yes. Quite gone. Stay a little—"

The slinking steps of old Luke were approaching. He had been to "Fasten oop".

"We must outwit her," Burl whispered. "We must buy him more barley sugar than she does. I cannot stay. If she wakes. Perhaps tomorrow—"

Henri was left by the window, staring out on a night of stars.

To-morrow.

And it would always be to-morrow. Every morn, every evening, it would be to-morrow. For years, long years, dropping slowly away. Tick-tick.

He cast an exasperated look at the old clock.

"I am going out, Luke," he told the old man, as he came in, his shoon slithering over the sanded floor.

"A' reight," said old Luke. "A' reight. Mind't Eagle. I'm tinkin' t'were a sign o' death when it gan ower't house t'other neet. Shoo's failin', be'ant shoo?"

Henri looked at him sharply.

"Ay. Shoo's failin'," said old Luke. "Failin' fast. I shall outlive her. Then Eagles' mine. Lots o' barley sugar, then."

Henri stood looking at him.

Was there another at Eagles' Crag, then, waiting for the old Medusa to die? It seemed so. The old man cringed under his stare. He slithered over to the cupboard, took out the barley sugar, and began to crunch it with his few yellow stumps of teeth. Her son. And he, too, was wishing her dead. The horror of it overcame Henri. He left the house hurriedly, went to stand on the stone above the gorge, on the stone where a far-off, lonely figure he had first seen Burl. It was a clear night. The stars seemed almost to touch the moorland hills on each side the gorge. He drew deep breaths of the air. For how long he stood, listening to the soft murmur of the torrent, he could not have told.

What was that? A sound not of the gorge, neither whisper of fern, rush of water around stone, blowing of the heather, transfixed him.

He stared up.

A great black shape was going over the sky.

The stars shone through its outstretched wings, pallid as through black smoke. There was no sound now. That faint rushing which he had taken at first for the wind's sighing, had ceased. It was the Eagle of Eagles' Crag. Terror took hold of him. He stepped back frond the stone upon the rough ground. Then he recalled Burl, lifting up her lantern and hailing the Eagle. Should man be less courageous than woman?

"Hail, Eagle!" called Henri.

His voice sounded weak as water. His bones felt soft in their sockets. She had gibed at his lack of hardiness, his gay sunshine-loving nature. He would be more valiant than she. He would be an eagle when he left Eagles' Crag, she had taunted him. *Très bon!* He would be one now, now.

"Hail, Eagle!" repeated Henri.

It seemed to him that the black shape stood still in the heavens.

"Bring death, swift death to the oldest eagle in Eagles' Crag," he cried, "and give me Burl— and Avignon."

He stood staring up into the sky, wildly.

Had the air been riven by the echo of a scream?

Through space, as from futurity, had a cry of dreadful terror sounded?

The sky was empty.

The stars were shining.

He was alone on the heights, listening to the wind in the crannies of the black rocks, the swaying of the ferns, the blowing of the heather. He turned and almost ran back into the house, the gloomy house, and sitting down, bowed his head in his hands. Was he Henri d'Gasconne—that same Henri who had swung along the path in the Clough six months ago? Or some other person? Or was it Eagles' Crag, which was changing him? Or could it be that the old Medusa was right, that he had been here before, that this rock-shadowed house held him whilst he hated it, kept him there when he would fain be away? Burl had hailed the Eagle asking it to bring love, whatever the cost of it. He had asked for possessions.

He crept upstairs to bed, stumbled into the dark room, and undressing by the light of the stars, tried to sleep. The once deep slumbers which had been his after hard days, were his no more. This night he slept not at all. The winds went round the bleak place with a soft, murmuring melancholy. He heard the heavy striking of the slow clock downstairs. At last it was time to get up.

Chapter Five

The spring had gone. The summer had gone. The days pulled in soon, as they styled it in these parts. The gorgeous colouring of the bracken was turning to one sere deadness. The hills no longer stood like blue clouds. They were turning to that grey-black under grey skies which fell chillingly on his very soul. The curlew's cry sounded through pale, trailing autumn mists over moors where the heather's purple was turning ash-white under winds and rains. The torrent had an angry, stormy surge in it, prelude to its sullen, winter roaring.

Yes. Winter was coming once more, black, bare winter, hellish in its gloom. And the old Medusa was as strong as ever. Almost it seemed as though, with diabolic cunning, she knew they were wishing her gone—he and Luke. The spark of life in those sunken, red-lidded eyes burned with a fiercer glow. Or was it the knowledge that she was keeping him and Burl in love's torment of unfulfilment which gave to her a fiercer zest in living? Or both? Possibly both. She was feeding on love and hate; on the sight of love famishing, on the hatred that would lure her hence, And in sheer spite, as it had seemed to Henri, she was for ever now going over the long list of the Mowbray family who had neared a hundred, and those who had gone over the hundred years, winding up always with: "And I'm hale and hearty yet. Ay. I'm hale and hearty."

Then she would lift her gaze to Burl's pale face and the spark would brighten, like life leaping up at the thought of all she was robbing them of. Or she would look at Henri. What his face revealed he did not know. But as she totted over all the long-lived Mowbrays he would find himself thinking in the ardent language of France thoughts which were indeed untranslatable in the cold northern tongue. Then, in very devilry, as not to be outdone by this demonic old eagle, he would make *bon mots* to make her laugh. It was some slight comfort to him that when she laughed, risibility took every atom of her strength, that for every gay jest he made, with his heart aboil with hatred, she paid with something of her remaining strength.

Lately, she had begun to hold up her skeleton of a hand, when he had been about to joke, saying: "Nay. I've not strength to laugh. I might brast a blood-vessel. Noan o' thy tomfoolery to-neet." And she was taking the greatest care of herself. Six pigeons a week went into the stew-pan. And as Luke wrung the burnished necks, Henri would mutter in French "Would that she had six necks and that they were all wrung." Without the least conception of what he had muttered, she would hold up the fork at him, and say: "Na, na, noan o' thy French. We'se Yorkshire here. Tha might be sayin' ill on us. An' French is one o' they flowery languages, isn't it? There's no strength to a language like that." Despite himself he had to laugh when she called the French language flowery on such occasions.

Yes. Winter was coming. Winter once more in Eagles' Crag. As the old Medusa had said at dinner, it would soon be the shortest day.

He pulled the blankets up around him, thinking of all this, the midnight autumn wind moaning round the bleak place. Already there was frost in the air. Bracing, they called that bite in the air, in this North. Bracing—when it went through one, as through a sieve, chilling the very marrow, freezing the blood, as one broke ice off the water before the provender could be got ready for cattle and hens. Oh, to sleep. And sleeping, to dream of sunlit acres in warm France, in the lead-coloured dawns, and a farm with rich-coloured shingles, and with fat Jersey cattle, their bells ringing as they moved slowly across lush pastures divided from each other by lines of blossomed fruit trees.

But even the conjuring up of such pictures were becoming now too tantalizing to be borne. The contrast between the pleasant dream, the grim, iron-cold reality, was too bitter. He would wake from dreaming to the stark cold gloom of

Eagles' Crag, which felt a thousand times darker for that dream having risen, mirage-like, in his mind. He paid with additional melancholy, or with bitter, burning ache for the gay little dream, as now he paid with heart's-blood for every look he stole at Burl. In the midnight house, all still as a tomb, dark as a tomb, and more tragic than a tomb— since it held the living—he thrust that dream away from him now and tried to sleep.

What was that?

He sat up in bed, listening.

Was not that the sound of a door opening? Yes.

As he listened, he heard it close. Then a footfall, Burl's footfall, the footfall of youth in this house where all was old, but their passionate ache of love.

Was the old Medusa ill?

Was Burl coming to call him?

Was that tenacious hold on life loosening at last? Was the black flood of death coming to bear the old eagless on its tide, to sweep her away where she could no longer sit in the black chimney-corner enjoying their pale, sad, hungry looks at each other—looks which of late they had often dreaded to look, lest already love should be a waning light, damped by the mould of this air where all was old, old, old; where even the echoes were hundreds of years old? Was she coming at last to tell him that the old Medusa was dying or dead?

He held his breath.

Burl's footsteps went softly, lightly past his door.

The glimmering ray of the candle she carried threw a flickering beam on his bedroom floor, the door being ajar.

Henri crept out of bed. His greatcoat being over the bedpost. He went down in it each morning now, so savage felt the sting of the cold. He groped his way to it, put it on, and followed that travelling light. When he reached the top of the stairs, Burl had almost reached the bottom of the first flight. He could see her black hair, a streaming silken cloud, almost to her knees; She was in her nightdress, a long trailing; nightdress of coarse cotton, bleached to the whiteness of snow. It trailed behind her. Her rounded arms looked like ivory in the candle-glow.

"Tick-tick," came her voice, in a shuddering sigh of utter sadness and weariness.

Burning tears sprung to Henri's eyes;

She was counting slow time, as he had often counted it.

She moved down the second flight of steps.

Henri followed.

She paused, reaching the last step, hesitantly, and stood leaning against the wall.

He moved down and past her, and stared into her face. Her eyes were open. They were full of tears. And she was asleep.

"Tick-tick," she murmured, fiercely.

She moved from the wall. Her bare feet moved over the gritty sand on the flags without its hardness awakening her. Down the long passage, down another. Henri followed. Where was she going?

She opened the oaken door that led to the hall.

Henri's hand held it back as she went through. He followed her.

She went straight to the wall whereon hung the many swords which were its sole decoration. Old Jane had had her and Henri polish them up but a few days ago.

She took down the longest, brightest, sharpest sword.

Then turned round and made her way back, Henri's heart stood still.

He knew he ought to awaken her. But he had heard it was dangerous to awaken anyone in somnambulistic state. And having got the sword, she was moving swiftly along the hall. How coldly the shadows flickered round her. Her hair swung like a black curtain with the speed of her now almost rushing form along the mouldy hall. He put out his hand once and touched that silken curtain of hair. But she kept ahead of him, though he was almost running. Up the first flight. Then the second. Along the corridor. She opened the door of the room she shared with old Jane, and leaving it open, moved towards the bed on which the old woman was lying.

What—

Henri's mind half-formed the question, then stumbled in horror.

His will felt paralysed.

Fascinated, he looked at Burl, who had set the candle down on a small table near the old woman's bed. Its yellow light fell over the yellow face, sharp, and with the skin stretched tight as the skin of a drum over the sharp bones. And the old woman's magnified shadow was on the wall. Her knees were hutched. Her shadow looked like the shadow of a humped witch. She gurgled and snorted as she breathed. He wanted to laugh suddenly, loudly. He wanted to dance and see Burl swing that sword high, and lunge it into her. Then she turned slightly in her sleep, and murmured: "Ay. Th' winter's comin'." And Henri found that his ever so momentary a desire to see her killed was gone, slain by that pathetic human lament. His paralysed will became active. Normality came back. He must awaken Burl.

Then, as he looked, still fascinatedly towards that humped shadow-shape on the wall, he saw the sword swing its shadow over the old woman.

He leaped forward, and caught Burl's wrist.

"*Chérie!*" he breathed, "*Chérie!*"

As if even that low whisper of endearment penetrated to her brain, she answered, "Henri."

She laid the sword down.

But she was still asleep.

He had to shake her before she awoke.

Then she flashed a look at him, at the room, at the old woman.

"What are you doing in here?" she asked, fiercely. "Get out. Get out—"

Henri retreated before that northern blaze of anger.

But half-way to the door, he saw her gaze fall on the sword. She picked it up, and following him, handed it to him silently.

"You came to kill her?" she asked in a horrified whisper. "Henri, you came to kill her?"

He had suffered much in this dark house.

There were times when even his love for Burl was tinged with something like hatred; For if he had never seen her, no place could have held him there against his will, and against reason.

"What if I did," asked Henri. "Would that kill your love for me?"

Burl shuddered.

It was the northern woman in her which shuddered. Then she said, looking at him with her gipsy look: "The only way a gipsy's love can be killed is to kill the gipsy."

He found himself standing thrust outside the door the sword in his hand. He could not bring himself to go along that echoing, mouldy hall again, to hang it up. He decided to leave it till morning's more cheerful light.

He slept at length.

And oddly enough, the dream of Avignon came to him, clear and bright. The waving meadows were beautiful in the sunshine. The radiant warmth of the air was almost luminous.

The sunshine, it was golden wine. His spirit felt to bathe in the glow of it. And the farm, with its rich-coloured shingles stood with the yellow ricks about it. Doves perched on the roof. The shadows of some poplars near, their leaves shimmering and dancing in the Warm wind, mellowed down the gay colour of it all. Burl came along a little path, sabots on her feet, a sunburnt baby in her arms. She called "Henri". She wore a blouse, two buttons of which were unfastened. Her neck and arms were golden-brown. The baby espied him, suddenly, and let go its clutch at her back hair. It guggled delight, clapped its podgy hands, which went together so funnily he began to laugh. Its ten bare brown toes began to wriggle with joy as he laughed. Its small brown face was a circle of smiles. Its dark eyes danced, like its toes. Its black curls were lifted by the warm wind. It stretched out its arms to him. Burl held it out for him to take. He strode forward. They were going away from him. They were growing dim.

He called to them loudly. His own voice calling awoke him.

The savage pain of it.

He was at Eagles' Crag. At Eagles' Crag. The dim light of a wet, grey dawn was flowing through the blood-red curtains. One of the wolf-hounds was baying at the moon, dropping down behind black hills as the sun came up. Avignon, the sunshine. Burl, that sunburnt baby—they were far, far away, as he had seen them. They would never be his. He sat, smoking his pipe, in the great red-canopied bed. How that wolf-hound bayed. In this superstition-haunted North it was held to be a sign of death. Would it were so, for the old eagless. Avignon, sunshine, Burl with that radiant, happy look on her face, and the baby with her hair and his eyes. Then, presto. It was far away. He watched the smoke wreaths from his pipe curl along the ceiling. Short dark days, soon. The weeks of rain. Snow on the bed when he awoke, blown through the ceiling which was not underdrawn. Breaking the ice in the lead-coloured dawns. Above all, the pain of frustrate love.

He got out of bed, thrusting back the heavy curtains.

A wild, stormy dawn was breaking over the hills.

He dressed, went down, hung up the sword in the hall, and passed into the outside world. The black rocks loomed up through the pale mists. They would be there for ever, and he also, watching them loom up through the eternal dawns. He was chained by unseen fetters to this savage height So he felt in the bitterness of that mood.

He could never leave Burl now. She had given him the greatest proof any woman could give any man of the fibre of her love. Her words came back to him, as he sat on the rocks, amidst the mists: "The only way a gipsy's love can be killed is to kill the gipsy." A strange sense of feat came to him. A titanic love is awesome as titanic hate. His own love for Burl was ardent. But he could not vow that whatever happened, whatever she did, no change would be wrought in it. He looked at the great rocks about him.' Her love was akin to them. His for her, like the mists that kissed them. Slowly he left the rock whereon he had sat, walking towards the house, her words yet ringing in his memory: "The only way to kill a gipsy's love is to kill the gipsy." And as he heard it again, in memory, almost that warm, wild speech of hers was like a challenge.

As he went over to the kitchen window, and stood looking through it a crow flew from one of the heavy trees which looked black in this dim dawn.

He crossed over to the fire, to stir it into flame, and stood looking down into grey ashes;

The fire was out.

Old Jane had told him the fire in Eagles' Crag had never been allowed to go out, since Eagles' Crag stood. Every night it was banked up. It had been banked up as usual last night. But it was out. The old pagan custom of keeping the fire in was kept up at many of these outlandish farms, without the inhabitants knowing that it was a custom come down from antiquity. It was held to be unlucky if it went out. This morning Henri wished he could have been absolutely superstitious. The fire going out meant the death of a descendant of the house where it went out.

Perhaps this next winter would be his last in Eagles' Crag.

Perhaps when the winter gales blew—

"Burl, the fire's out," Henri told her, as she came through the kitchen doorway.

She looked at him, incredulity on her face.

She bent down and stared at the fire, and then back at him.

"So it is," she said. "Don't tell her when she comes down. Shoo'd think it was perhaps a sign for her." As she re-lit the fire the crow went backwards and forwards across the window space, cawing. When the fire was lit, they stood in the chimney-corner, in each other's arms, but through the moment's heaven listening for old Luke or the old woman coming down. The crow went past the house again, cawing hoarsely.

"It's laughing, Henri," said Burl, pushing him away.

She took the blower from the top-bar where it was ledged. Something flew out of the fire. It fell on the chair in the chimney-corner's gloom, where the old Medusa sat so many hours, enjoying their misery, and thriving on the sight of it.

"A coffin,' said Burl. "Henri, it's shaped like a coffin. And it flew out on to her chair. Henri, don't be wishing her deyd. It may be soon."

And in her eyes, for all their pleading, he saw the answering desire of his own. They were all wishing her dead now.

Book Two

Chapter One

Only the wail of the curlews' crying,
Only the sob of the night wind's sighing,
The whisper of grey leaf's fall.
But from Love, a-dying,
No sound at all.

They walked on the flagstones by the black turret-wall. The winds hurtled over the black heather and grey bracken under the moonless, starless sky. It sent to them where they walked, a cold, wurthering lament. The blowing of the wind amongst the rocks under whose shelf they walked was another sound, like the sea beating through a pitch-dark cavern. The echoes of their steps, backwards and forwards, fifty paces each way, never one more, never one less, fell in with the hurtling of the wind, the blowing of the black heather, the sullen roaring of the torrent in the gorge.

"Four winters!"

Henri's voice had a sepulchral tone, a shuddering, hollow anguish in it.

Burl gave no answer.

What answer was there to give? None. None, repeated her heart, sick also with waiting. She pressed his arm with her hand, even whilst knowing that that token of affection might drive him into one of his raving fits or into bitter brooding melancholy which would last for long weeks. For the tidal ocean of desire for each other could no longer be appeased by little tokens of affection, a kiss snatched when the old Medusa was asleep worn from watchfulness by fatigue, or by Burl resting her feet upon his at supper-time.

A gentler passion in gentler hearts might have been sustained by them. They were eagles. In this eyrie of the hills, wild and primitive in its simplicity, with not one book in the house but those on farming, and an old magazine or two which the old Medusa had read over and over to her—to induce sleep—the intensity of desire could not be diverted into "sublimity", that modern sophistry for the translating of a simple, natural emotion into thought and intellectuality. Had they been cultured enough to know about sublimating what they were feeling, they would have held it a blasphemy to try and sublimate Love, the sublime, the immortal eagle of time, whose wings fly from the peak of one age bearing life on to the next, which would else be barren, a dead pinnacle set under the starry and sunrise spaces with no human eye to gaze upwards at them no human heart to throb at their splendour, no human mind to brood on their eternal mystery and boundlessness.

Love which feeds on light and warmth was perishing within them.

They felt it dying within them. With each caress it flapped its wild wings, mocking the double cage they kept it in, the cage of Eagles' Crag, the cage of their agonized breasts. "Let me fly. Let me nest. Let me build in this wild waste of a world," was its eternal song. They tired listening to its plaint, as it tired listening to their denials of its crave. They had chained its feet to the rock-shadowed house. But its wings had gone on beating wildly, restlessly. Now they must bind its wings, so that their wild beatings could distress them no more. They were doing that now. And wild eagle that it was, as they were eagles also, it dipped its beak into their hearts.

They tired of the long agony. Almost at times they wished it were dead, since old Jane did not die; wished it were dead, leaving them serenity of feeling and thought, wished they had never met, that each dawn might have been greeted without its crave waking with them, that each night might have come in sunset fires and silver starshine, a benison, without the agony of dreams, which waking them, brought the thought, "I wonder if she is sleeping," and "I wonder if he is sleeping."

They stood, pausing, at length, leaning over the turret wall, looking out into the darkness.

"Spring will soon be here. The shortest day will be here in a fortnight, now," Burl told Henri, laying her hand chill with the night's coldness on his, where it rested on the turret stone. No pulse leaped at those meeting hands. Cold dew dripped on them from the rock above.

"What is spring, without the spring o' the heart?" he asked her, with violent restraint. "To see all unfolding, a-bud, a-burst, a-flame, a-singing. And to hear from every dancing leaf, every new blade of grass, from every throstle on a white bough: "We never wait." I heard the thrushes sing that last spring. What comfort is there to me that I shall hear them sing the same thing again—this? Better that it were winter always. One grows torpid, then."

"Is it not the same for me also?" she asked, catching his irritable bitterness.

"Yes. But women are different."

Her laughter echoed into the night as to say. "What babes these men are." It had lost its joyous ripple. It had the sound of a stream flowing with effort, ice-checked.

"Are they not?" he inquired, peering at her through the darkness.

"We are just the same, but we must not acknowledge it," she told him. "Whilst it is bulls that are blessed, on farms, it is women who have to have their minds blessed throughout the ages. We are taught to think we are different, because you like to think us different. Then you turn on us and say: 'You are different. You do not know this or that.' We are just the same, Henri, when we love. But we must not say so!"

"Then why have you told me?" he asked.

"To make it easier," she answered. "That you may know you are not alone."

"The devil!" he ejaculated. "Why, you have made it harder."

She left him and walked along the turret flag-stones.

He turned his head. She was walking up and down, the cloak flowing about her. It was the one day of the year in which she was a wild gipsy. She had come up to the turret to think of her ragged clan, children of the open air, the wide spaces, whom no road on earth tethered, yet who owned more than the Georgios. And he was spoiling it. Soon they would be quarrelling, as they had quarrelled often of late, slashing each other with wild words, when really they were lovers quarrelling because they might not love.

Even as he thought of this, with bitter remorse, she came and stood beside him. Her face, pale through the darkness, was beside his.

"I am weary of love," she said, asperity in her tired voice. "I stood on this turret before you came, and every star of the Heavens was a joy to me. It is a tyranny, this love. This turret was a sacred place to me. Go down from it. Leave me here alone, to think of my people their dingy caravans resting under this sky, in almost even land on earth. Or their tents. And the fires lit casting shadows on the green turf. On this night my spirit always goes out to them, in greeting, in mournful greeting that I am not one of them, wandering wherever the tribe decides to go. Why have you followed me up here?"

"They are more to you, then, than I am?" he asked.

"Blessed be the sun!" she ejaculated, fiercely. "One's love for one's race is not a selfish thing."

"Burl, you are beginning to talk like a Georgio," derided Henri.

He had known that would fling her into a gipsy rage. It did.

The spectacle of her dancing about beside him, at this insult of being told she was talking like a Georgio, eased the pain at his heart. Two minutes later they were reconciled. Love, the savage eagle, chained and bound within them, was tired out also. They heard the drip of the night dews from rock wall to turret flagstones. They walked along the echoing flags, arm in arm, with tears of reconciliation on their faces. And with the gaiety of hearts turning ever to the sunshine of whatever joy they could find. Burl sang fragments of gipsy chants, and Henri sang in return old French folk-songs.

"She is going to buy cattle next week," Burl whispered to him, consolingly. We will finish work early. We shall have a whole half-day together. We will sing, and shout and laugh all the time."

"Yes," said Henri.

"In the gorge, with the sky above us," she told him.

"Yes. But the black trees, the black heather, the peat-coloured torrents," he lamented. "Browns and greys and blacks. They suffocate me."

"We will take one of the glasses from the lustres," she consoled him. "You can look at the trees and the hills, and they will be full of colour. You can think of Avignon. And I will sing you the songs my gipsy folk sing, who roam like the clouds, ragged, but free."

"Yes," he told her.

They leaned once more over the turret wall.

"Henri—" she gasped. "That light. What is it?"

He looked where she pointed into the darkness.

Over one hill slope, against the sky, where it seemed to touch the hill, was a red gleam through the mists.

"Perhaps it is Mars," he told her. "Mars, under which we plighted our troth."

Bitterness was creeping into his voice again.

Silence answered him.

"Henri," said Burl, breathless rapture in her tones. "It is a fire. It is a gipsy fire. Stay here. I am going to stand beside it, to talk with the gipsies. See. It is blazing up. The smoke. Can't you see it? Gipsies! I am going. Gipsies, And they are settling on that land where my father settled."

There was no holding her back.

"Take the lantern with you, then," he advised.

"What gipsy needs a lantern?" she gibed merrily.

She whirled past him.

He stood in the darkness, following her in imagination down the gorge, up the hill-slope, up to that fire now flaming its crimson splendour through the dark loneliness under the dark sky. Rain began to fall, a curtain of drizzle. He stood until the wetness struck through to his underclothes. The fire on the moor-top was a dull red blaze before which passed dark figures, puppet-small in the distance. Burl would be stood there, amongst them, laughing, greeting them, asking how long they were staying, talking in the gipsy tongue, hearing it with savage joy.

He turned on his heel, and went down from the turret. He made his way to the back of the house, past the kennels, where one of the wolf-hounds bared her teeth at him as he went by with the lantern. She had just littered. All a wolf-dun's fierceness was hers. He gave the kennel a wide berth. Her flaming eyes the gleamed at him out of blackness of the kennel.

Then he turned towards the door.

Passing the window of the kitchen, through its panes, slit-like in the black stone's mullions, he could see the old Medusa. The steam from the pan, where doubtless more doves were stewing, went up beside her. In the opposite chair old Luke was crunching away at barley sugar. He opened the door and went in. The lamp-glass was smashed. The lamp burned dimly. The fire was a red eye in the gloom of the chimney-corners.

"Henri, coom, cal with me," she said, plaintively. "Ger oop, Luke, an' let Henri ha' that chair. He's going to cal wi' me. Aren't ta, Henri?"

He bent his head, taking the chair old Luke grumblingly vacated.

He sat down, looking at her.

Her spare, long frame had scarce any flesh on it. The parchment-like skin was just stretched over the bones. But the spark of life in her eyes was fierce as ever. It glinted with her joy in his approach, at the prospect of his attention, his sitting by her, and "eating" with her. She had taken to wearing a black mutch, to keep her head and ears warm. It made her look more like an old eagless than ever. Last winter she had complained of the cold. Her blood was getting thin and poor. Old northerner though she was, the winters were beginning to be one long shivering agony, spent over the fire. She no longer drove off alone in the cart now. Luke always went with her to drive. And her bony frame could not stand the shaking about on the form on the cart. She sat on thick straw piled on the bottom of the cart.

"Ay. Sit thee down," she told him. "I'll soon be goan now, out o' your roads. Ninety and six. Ninety and seven. I'll soon be goan. An' tha'll ha' Eagles' Crag, an' sheep, an' cows, an't land fro' Brown Rigg to Hinbrough Lane Ends.

An' five farms. Nay, fowr, for I mun leave Luke summat Morn't I, Luke? One'll be enow for thee, Luke. For tha'rt dotin'."

Henri was staring at her in a stupefied way.

That she might leave him a goodly share of her land and farms he had expected. To hear that he would be the owner of four farms and all the lands caught his breath.

"Ay. That makes thy e'en shine," she laughed, feebly. "Na, be good. Sit by me, an' dunnot look like tha'rt goin' to rin fro' me every minnit. To dune, dune throo, to-day. To live wi' every bane a-ache, wi' nobbut one speed, an' that goin', is a weariness. Ay. A sore weariness. Be thee happy, mon? Old Jane Mowbray that likit thee not because o' the flesh, but because thee were like one she loved long ago— now i' th' groun'—where shoo's goin'—will soon be out o' thy road, an' Burl's road, ay, an' Luke's road. Luke'll sell his farm. He'll buy barley sugar, wi't brass. But you'll let him bide here wi' you, won't you, thet and Burl? I've left it in my will that tha gets a' —but he has to bide with you. Ninety an' seven. I've made my will. 'Twere lang enow to leave it."

Henri looked from old Jane to her son.

The crunching of the barley sugar had ceased. The old man was looking back at Henri. Out of the depths of those slinking eyes he caught, or fancied he caught, a look of positive hatred. But the next moment they were furtive, dull again. The crunching of the barley sugar awoke once more the dreary echoes,

"But thee mun sit an' cal wi' me," she reminded Henri, in a voice sharper with energy. "I've gan thee everything. Thee'll have yeth—rolling acres on it. Thee'll ha' heaven. Yan's no gude bowt t'other. Tha'd have had too much an' moil, a labourer all thy life, if I hadn't left thee yeth o' thy own—an' all tha'd ha' owned would ha' bin six foot o' groun' by three, to sleep in, clay-cowd. An' th' worms would ha' shared thats with thee. So dunnot grudge an old woman her fancy, to sit an' fill her e'en wi' thee before they're glassed ower wi' death—an' hear thee talk—as she once filled her e'en with another, who deceived her sore. But I've forgi'en him. I'll cross Jordon's icy floods, wi' him waitin' ont' other side. An' we'll both on us be young again, then. An' thee'll be welcome to Burl. But dunnot allus look like tha'rt goin' to rin away, when thee sits by me to ha' a cal. For I can alter my will. An' I can leave a' to Luke there."

Henri looked towards the old man once more.

A look of avarice had passed over his dull countenance. He had leaned forward. The firelight playing on his features gave it a momentary resemblance to the old woman's. It became keen, as though the tantalizing chance she held out of his owning five farms and all the land, if Henri did not please her, had given him a new lease of life. Henri looked from one to the other. If he had been sure that Burl would go away with him next day, he would have cared nothing about Eagles' Crag and the rolling acres. But since she would stay, since it had taken four years of bis life, and more of hers, it was some slight recompense to think that they, and not old Luke, would possess all.

He sat playing up to the old Medusa, and enjoying Luke's chagrin. Since last winter she had gone to bed at eight. The clock struck nine. They were still at "caling". Old Luke sat crunching barley sugar, sulking like a child. When she ordered him to bed, as the clock struck nine, his top lip stuck out, but he obeyed. His slinking footsteps woke the slinking echoes. Henri, looking at him in something like light-hearted amusement, caught again a look of hatred, knew that never again would Luke be willing to watch and warn them of the old woman's coming, if ever she went to town. Still, it did not matter now.

"Get off wi' thee," commanded old Jane. "Or have I to take my stick to thee?"

Her son slunk away, as she half-rose in her chair.

Even as he went up the stairs, the door through which Henri had recently come was thrown open. Burl rushed in. They heard her feet dancing along the passage. High above her head was lifted the tambourine. Her usually pale face was aglow. She stepped into the circle of fireglow, a gipsy, a wild gipsy, and as old Jane's dim eyes stared at her, and Henri's, with the surprise in them, the emerald ribbons of the tambourine swept the sanded floor.

Henri sprang up and turned up the lamp. Its light flared up in the smoked chimney-glass. Flames were coming out of it at the top from the jagged wick, cut hurriedly in the dim dawn, before they had gone out to sweep the shippen-floors of dung. The infection of this burst of wild gaiety, of youth still unextinguished, triumphant over the grim house, had fired Henri too. He almost flung the chairs out of the way. They had both forgotten the old woman. Burl, the pins rattling upon the flagged floor, shaken from her hair with the wild dancing, glanced at him from those eyes of darkness and sunlight. Round and round she whirled, and her voice lilted a song which went to the measure of her flying feet, to the strumming of her fingers which set the tambourine's bells ringing:

Children of the blowing winds
Blow they soft or loud,
Wandering, ever wandering,
Under sun and cloud.
Children of the forest's gloom,
Of the mountain's slope,
What rove ye a-gathering?
What your jocund hope?

House ye have none, save a tent
Stained with beating rains;
Never bide the journeying camps—
On, on, o'er the plains.
Silver plate and linen white
Are not yours to hold.
Whence comes then your royal mien,
Grace, and courage bold?

Sun and moon and stars are ours;
Every mountain's brow;
Life's a tent which all must fold,
When the sun drops low.
Wandering children, then we'll rest,
Whilst the camps move on.
Stars above us clouding mourn—
"Lo! A gipsy's gone."

Earth, too, is a wanderer old.
Lo, she left the sun,
Through the starry, un-walled skies

Wandering to run.
If we should come back to life
With its joy and pain—
Gipsies, we'll be gipsies still,
Gipsies carls again.

Faster and faster had twinkled Burl's feet. Wilder and wilder had pulsed the song. The sand, newly laid on the floor that noon, sputtered up, fine dust, about the flying and whirling gipsy. Her cloak lay, a heap, beside old Jane's chair. Henri was running round after her, touching at times the flying cloud of her hair, the emerald ribbons on the tambourine. The dance finished as wildly as it had begun. It was only as it finished, and Henri and Burl flung themselves, breathless, upon two of the chairs, that they noticed old Jane Mowbray.

She had risen from her chair in the chimney-corner.

She stood, pointing her stick at them, speechless fury on her face.

"And that's how you'll gan on when I'm laid i't groun'," she almost screamed at them, at length finding speech. "I've been in my dotage to think o' leaving Eagles' Crag to a gipsy an' a French toad. I'll leave my son everything. Everything. It's hissen, as soon as I can get that will altered. Tha's stayed on here, Henri, thinkin' o' gettin' a', so you two could laugh an' dance, when I'd gone. Th' brass would go thro' your fingers like watter. The land would go. Th' cattle'd go. Strangers would have Eagles' Crag. Luke shall have everything. Tha shall ha' naught, tha French toad."

She dropped into her chair.

Henri shook himself free from Burl's restraining clutch.

He crossed the sanded floor to where she sat, doddering, pathetic in the feebleness which had followed her jealous frenzy and hatred to have seen them so happy and forgetting her altogether. His face was livid.

"I'm leavin' Eagles' Crag to-morrow, soon as its daylight," he told her. "The wealth of the world would not pay me for living so long in its gloom."

Her mood changed.

"Noa, Henri, noa," she moaned.

Then she wheeled round in her chair.

"Thee'll not leave me, Burl?" she pleaded. The girl came towards her.

"Noa," she said slowly. She turned to Henri: "She be old," she told him.

Old Jane gripped Burl's dress.

"Bless thee," she said, quaveringly.

A tear dimmed the flashing fire which yet lingered in her sunken eyes. Then, maliciously, she looked triumph at Henri. If Burl stayed she knew he would stay. To-morrow would never come. Henri strode from the kitchen. As he went upstairs he stumbled against Luke, standing on the staircase. He was mumbling to himself: "Shoo'll leave everything to me." He slunk away, off to bed, as Henri burst into French oaths, oaths all the more fervid as he knew that he would not leave Eagles' Crag tomorrow, that old Jane, to the last flicker of the raising their hopes of them leaving them all, then, at every whim, dashing them to the ground. Would that he had never seen Eagles' Crag, he thought, standing by the window, and looking out on the quiet stars.

Across the moor-top was burning the fire of the gipsy camp. To and fro before it passed the gipsies, children of the wind and sunshine, owning nothing but life and the earth. He stood envying them with a dull ache of envy, the richest people in the world, hardy, independent of place or servitude, kow-towing to none, whilst Georgios the world over were constrained by their disease— crave for possessions to gather gear and money, seeing in those things security in old age, which gipsies feared not, being gipsies still.

Chapter Two

"The worldly hope men set their hearts upon
Turns ashes, or it prospers, and anon
Like snow upon the desert's dusty face,
Lighting a little hour or two, is gone."—KHAYYAM.

"I'm gannin', Burl," the old woman told Burl, who was setting loaves inside the fender, her head bent down so that she would not reveal the lightening of heart she felt at the prospect of a half-day with Henri. She nodded.

"An' thee'll get ower to Hinbrough Lane Ends, Henri," she commanded him, "an' gether them rents 'at are due."

Cognisant of their hidden joy, she dashed their delight from them at the last moment of departure. As she was taking horse and cart, and the other horse was just coming round from colic, Henri would have to make the journey afoot. The probability was that she would be back before he got back.

"Coom, tee my bonnet-strings ower," she said to Burl.

Burl, her heart turned to lead, sad and heavy went to do her bidding. It was difficult to keep her hands steady as she tied the bonnet-strings under the chin, with its sagging bags of wrinkle-netted skin. The bonnet-strings had been all right. Those sunken eyes had wanted to see the disappointment on her face. But it was a calm, if pale face, the old woman stared into.

"Thear!" she said, testily. "That'll do. That'll do."

She turned her gaze, its jealousy foiled of what it had hoped to see, upon Henri. He was kneeling on the dank flags in the chimney-corner, chopping firewood.

"Tha can leave that job till neet," she told him. "We'll take thee on in't cart as fur as Black Stane Farm. Tha'll only ha' four miles to walk then, an' eight back. If tha could be back at Black Stane by six, we could pike thee oop there an' save thy legs."

"I'll walk," said Henri, in a low, strangled voice.

Twelve miles of hill country to travel, to gather in the rents, a task which could have been done any day. Another day which he and Burl had planned to enjoy was gone.

"As tha pleases," the old Medusa told him. "They say them as has their own way lives't langest an' thrives't best. Coom on, Luke. If he doesn't want to ride wi' age an' elegance—thee being age, an' me being elegance—he can walk 'at way."

Her steps crunched on the sanded floor. Luke's slunk after her.

The additional feebleness which had been hers for the last two days, consequent on her outburst of frenzy at the sight of their love and youth still being alive, was gone this morning. Never had she looked so sprightly since Henri had come to Eagles' Crag. She was "laikin" with them as eagles play with their prey. She was almost erect this morning, for all her ninety-seven years. The spark of life in those red-lidded eyes was vigorous and keen with the delight of their torment. The thin, yellow neck craned up straightly from the three-tiered black cape. The bonnet shadowed the yellow, corrugated brow. The silk underskirt rustled as she walked towards the doorway, turning there to see if Henri would swallow the bitterness within him, and ride part of the way rather than walk sixteen miles through the wintry, northern landscape he hated. Indolence won.

"I thought tha'd gan wi' us," she told him. "Coom on, then. Get thy coit on. For November's noan a good month to be out in at neet fa', an' I want to get back soon."

As he struggled into the heavy top-coat, she flashed a look at Burl, as to say: "Sithee. He's gannin' wi' th' old woman again, an' leavin' th' young un." It was ridiculous as tragic.

Burl bent down over the loaves.

She was marking them with a knife, to let the witches out, as superstition had it, or, to make them rise the faster as science had it. She kept her back turned on the trio of them. She heard the old woman's lively step go down the passage, Luke's slinking one and Henri's reluctant one. When the door closed after them she was still bent over the loaves.

But before the cart jolted off, Henri driving, for old Jane had been scoffing at her son that he was getting in his dotage and none fit to drive, Burl ran out.

"You've left your fur," she told the old woman.

"Eh, thanks," said old Jane. "Reyk it ower here."

Burl stood on the side of the cart.

Her dark eyes were fixed on Henri's disconsolate face in an intense, eager way. He caught that look even through the November gloom, the darkness from the crag above.

Something dropped from the fur before the old woman got it.

"Well, get thy work done, Burl," she called, in lively tones, as the cart jolted away.

"Ay. I'll ha' a' done by you get back," answered Burl.

She watched the cart out of sight and turned back to the dark house. It was, she knew, quite probable that before the cart reached town, with the variability of old age, old Jane would have changed her mind about altering her will, that it might stand as it was. Then Luke would sulk. The sordidness of it all was like a blight.

Whilst the loaves rose in the tins, ready for the oven, she stood by the window. The fire of the gipsy encampment was burning on the moor-top. Her thoughts were of much the same trend as Henri's had been, as he had looked from his window, some nights past. Beggarly people, these of her race, but regal in comparison with Georgios.

"Hist, gipsy," sounded under the kitchen window, as she swept the dark kitchen, the brush dagging with the damp of the stones, as she waited for the bread to be done.

Burl flung the brush down.

She ran and looked through the misted panes.

A slouch hat, a sallow, handsome countenance rose to view.

"Hi, gipsy," she greeted him back.

She shut up the foot-square window-pane. The rush of cold air made the fire roar in the chimney.

"We have no dinner," said the Romany earl, simply.

He stood looking at her.

"That is a pity," Burl told him, coldly.

"You, a gipsy, have dinner," said the Romany earl.

"Yea. I have to earn it, as you see," Burl told him. Silence fell.

The draught from the window was burning more coal than need be.

"This house, you will one day own it," said the earl.

Burl's shoulders lifted, scornfully. She rejected the bribe of the gipsy prediction with gipsy scorn.

"The hen-house is twenty paces from where you stand, Jasper," she said. "But do not touch the old buff hen with the lame foot. She is too brave for the pot. She fought a hawk to take her chicken from its claws. For the rest—"

The window banged down.

Burl turned to her work.

She worked swiftly and thoroughly. Henri would soon be back. A few hours would be theirs, hours swift-flying and tragic all the time with the knowledge that they were flying, to be succeeded by hundreds of leaden-footed ones before they were together again, alone. Whilst the loaves cooled and cracked on the deal table, she went from one chill, gloomy room to another, sweeping up the clammy grey dust.

She went upstairs, made the old Medusa's bed, her own bed, which stood with but a yard of wooden floor between, Luke's bed, Henri's bed. That last she tossed and tossed again, lingering over the folding of the blankets. Her hand caressed the pillow where his head would rest, as well as it could rest in this gloomy eyrie. His hollowing cheeks, the eyes that had almost lost their gaiety, rose before her view. She sat on the cane-bottomed chair by the bedside and stared through the windows on the grey sky, the greyer hills. The Romany earl's bribing prophecy sounded to her ears again.

Even were it true, though every stick and stone of the land and farms should be theirs, Eagles' Crag had taken more of their lives than it could every give them back.

She went down to the kitchen. The loaves were almost done crackling. She carried them away to the dairy, set them on the stone bench. And looking through the window saw a form almost bending under the weight of poultry slung over its back. Jasper had indeed taken enough from the coop to ensure that the gipsy pot would not be empty for many a day. Through the thick greeny glass of the dairy window Jasper saw her face looking at him. It looked like a pale face seen through the deeps of a dim green vane. It had a look upon it like the look of someone drowning. He felt some compunction. But she was a gipsy, a gipsy living with Georgios. And the tribe would have had no dinner. She must bear the cost of gipsy fealty.

It was indeed, only as Burl saw the gipsy swing past with the dead poultry hanging heads down, that she realised that this filling of the gipsy pot could mean her being sent from Eagles' Crag. With the sang froid of gipsy hardihood she thrust the thought of being parted from Henri on account of a few old hens from her mind. If he managed to get back by three in the afternoon, there would be four hours between then and seven, which might bring who knew what? For did anyone know from day to day what might happen at Eagles' Crag. The fatalistic stoicism of gipsy and northerner staved off her anxiety. Here, at Eagles' Crag, one lived from slow hour to slow hour.

She went up to see how the old horse was going on. He was better, and rubbed his nose against her shoulder as her hand caressed his silky ears. Sitting down beside him in the straw, she laughed to see him eat thrice his usual ration of hay, sitting on her heels, hands clasped round her knees, then would toss him more hay, laughing and caressing him with her voice. The gipsies on the ridge of black moorland would be happy this day. The old horse in his stable should be happy too. And there were four hours from Henri returning to old Jane's fury when she came home and found that she and Henri had been together. Patting the horse, she left the stable, latching the door.

When Henri came through the grey fog of the afternoon, he saw her waiting for him.

"Henri—four hours!" she cried joyously. "She cannot get back till seven. Four hours of joy. We will go to roam under the sky, where this black roof does not shadow us. We will shout, and laugh, and sing, and—"

She broke off suddenly.

"And come back," said Henri, with bitter vehemence.

His clothes were sodden with the grey northern fog he so detested. They felt a ton weight. He had rushed the last two miles, and whilst the sight of Burl standing waiting for him had brought a moment's wild rapture to him, the very sight of Eagles' Crag waiting once more to enfold them in its gloom had snuffed it out. For was the old Medusa not gone to alter her will, to leave all to Luke, so that though they lived on years in this anguish of waiting, when she was gone they would both have only what they stood up in, and perhaps a hundred pounds in addition to the savings from his wages? True she might alter it again. That was quite likely.

There is nothing like a November fog for making what is bad seem worse, for glooming what is bright. Henri had been breathing that fog since ten in the morning. To be away from Eagles' Crag, roaming under the sky, as Burl had put it, was a temptation, tired as he was. But four more hours on top of the walking he had done felt beyond him.

"Yes. We shall always have to come back, whilst she lives," Burl told him. "You need not, though. But I must."

"Why you, either?" questioned Henri fiercely.

She looked from him to the gloomy rocks above, the gloomy rocks below, with the chimney-smoke curling up from the fire inside that gloomy kitchen.

"Who would live at Eagles' Crag with them but I?" she asked him, simply, austerely.

He stared at her, at the splendid fealty throbbing in that simple question.

"No one," he told her. "You stay, then, because none else would stay?"

She nodded, simply, the rare tears in her eyes.

"Poor old Jane," she said. "Poor old Luke. Picture them up here, without me. And do not ask me again why I stay. A Georgio would have left long ago. They depend on me much more than they know. Henri—they are both in their dotage. One day we also will be old. It will come to us also. We will creep about slowly. We will be like children. We will ache with the cold. We will say things many times over."

There is no revelation so wonderful as the revelation of tenderness in a fierce nature.

It is like the warmth of a fire bursting on the sight after frost and snow.

The strange nobility of the northern woman blended with the wild gay gipsy heart, touched Henri unaccountably.

"Come, we will have a happy afternoon," he told her. "But this fog. *C'est très mauvais.* Had we not best sit by the fire? Perhaps if we try hard, we could even sing in Eagles' Crag."

Burl stood pondering.

She turned to him, from her survey of the scene below, murky with deep winter gloom, with gipsy radiance on her face.

"We will go to the encampment," she told him. The gipsies are cooking dinner. We will eat with them. They will welcome us. You will breathe neither the fog, nor sit in Eagles' Crag."

"But yes," said Henri. "We will go and lock the place up, then. Let us waste no more time,"

Fifteen minutes later two figures made their way up the hillside slope towards the gipsy encampment. And as they clambered up the steep of the hill, holding on to a bush here, a heather-patch there, or by the rocks bedded in it, Henri bethought him of the old native who had said he had put his curse on Eagles' Crag and all in it. He had said Burl's mother was possibly Italian, since they had been known to eat macaroni.

"Your mother, Burl," he said, was she a northerner?"

"Yes," Burl told him. "Why?"

They sat on a grey rock, wet with the grey fog, to get their breath.

"You are a strange people," said Henri slowly. "You laugh at things the southerner would weep over. When we look to see you smile, you are weeping. It is the same with your weather. One gets up to a grey day. It turns out fine. On rejoices that it is fine, before breakfast. By noon it is St. Swithin's, and a flood. You have summers with winter strewn in them, and winters with days like summer." They sat on the rock for a little while, looking at the northern scenery through a piece of lustre glass, and pretending, like children, that they were in Avignon.

Then they went on up towards the gipsy camp.

The top of the tents were coming to sight now, like great brown mushrooms through the fogged air. The barking of dogs, giving warning of their approach, sounded down. The voices of children playing, the shrill clamour of the gipsies in their preparation of the coming feast, with laughter, and some heavy, thudding sounds, floated down to Henri and Burl as they scaled the last feet of the slope. Already the pungent scent of the wood-fire, and the savoury steam from the great pot swung over it, came to their nostrils.

"It smells good," Henri told Burl.

They stepped up, standing on the black moor-top, which immediately presented to them the swarming life of the encampment.

Feathers from the poultry were blown and blowing about the dark ling and heather. A dog was ravenously devouring the gizzards and entrails of the defunct birds, growling, and watching two other dogs, who slunk near, but dared come no farther. An old gipsy woman, bright kerchief on her head, was emptying slops from a dish into a hole scooped out from the soil. The children, six or seven of them, had stopped their noisy playing, and sauntered up to stare through the mist at Burl and Henri.

"Lovo," said one little gipsy to another, with a sly look, seeing in the visit of Georgios the hope of getting money.

Burl laughed and said, in Romani: "Tell Jasper that we have come to eat with him and Sophrono.

With a sigh that told of disappointment, the eldest of the gipsy children went off, his lithe little body swinging away towards Jasper's tent. As he went past, he kicked one of the hungry dogs sitting near the old grey dog with the gizzards and entrails. It scarce moved, as inured to ill-usage, nor did its greedy gaze shift from the feast the old grey dog was having. Burl and Henri walked slowly in the direction the gipsy boy had taken.

Two minutes later they were sitting in Jasper's rent, made like the rest from blankets, on a great pile of rushes, dead bracken, and springy heather-twigs. Upon another pile sat a very old gipsy woman. On an improvised couch which was probably a bed at night, lay Sophrono, her arm which hung languidly over the side pulling gently the long ears of a spaniel. She was a handsome gipsy whose unusual languor was explained by the fact that she was about to add another life to the already teeming life of the encampment. Even as she talked to Burl in Romani, at times her breath was caught by a twinge of pain. Jasper came in some twenty minutes later, and gave them welcome. The swart gipsy, as he had stooped to enter the tent, had flashed an anxious look towards Sophrono. Flushed, sweating from the boxing duel he had been having, he sat down on the edge of Sophrono's couch. There was neither tender greeting to her, nor caress. But as he sat, on the edge of the couch, with its ragged sheepskin hides, most likely trophies of purloined sheep, none would have needed to be told that as yet the rough, hard life of the camp had left the pair tender, if undemonstrative, lovers still.

"We should have been pleased for you to eat with us," said Jasper, "but Sophrono—"

"Yes," said Burl, "we will go shortly."

She accepted with equanimity this excluding of herself and Henri from the feast her gipsy impulse of generosity had provided. She talked with Jasper in the Romani tongue, and, as though the very speaking of the gipsy language brought to the surface her gipsy characteristics, certainly sitting in the dimness of that brown blanket tent perforated with the specks of light through the holes made by pin-thorns and kettle-prop in innumerable campings, and with only the light coming in through the low doorway, her dark eyes changing all the while, from a curious lustreless darkness to melancholy, or to the sheen of deep feeling she would have passed for a gipsy in all save that her skin had not the tawny olive of the Romanies.

"*Yoi comdas les*" said Burl, in answer to something Jasper asked of her.

Shortly afterwards she rose to go.

As they went down the slope she told Henri that Jasper had been asking why her mother had married her father.

Her answer had been that she had loved him. She was again all northerner. That gipsy self of hers might have been left behind in the tent.

"Henri," she told him, as they sat on the rock where they had rested on the way up, "Jasper did not ask us to the meal which I helped him to get. Yes. He came and stood before the window and said they had no dinner. I told him the coop was there."

"Th' *diable!*" ejaculated Henri.

But the expression of alarm was not due to the fact that Burl, quite forgetful of all but gipsy fealty, might find herself embroiled in battle with old Jane. Out of the heather just under the rock, a lean-faced old man had risen. It was the old native Henri had inquired the way to Eagles' Crag from, four years ago. He stood, staring up at them, anathema in his look. He seemed to be chewing his beard.

"Gipsy!" he managed to say at length.

He shook his clenched fist at Burl.

She sat still, on the rock, staring impassively back at him through the mist.

Then, to Henri's astonishment, she slid down from the rock standing with her feet on the same patch of heather on which the old man stood.

"It was not my fault that your son ran after me," she told him. "He must have had a screw loose to kill himself because I could not love him. Yet I am sorry now."

She gazed at him with mournful intentness.

"Thee—thee didn't say that afore, when they come up to tell thee he ligged stiff an' cowd," he raved. "Thee didn't say thee were sorry then. Thee laughed."

He stood staring at her.

Then his eyes lit up with fierce vindictiveness. His gaze went to Henri, then back to her;

"He's taught thee what 'tis, then, to love? That's why thou'rt sorry now?" he asked. Spluttering with vindictive laughter, he went down the slope. The mists swallowed him from their sight.

"He will tell old Jane," said Burl.

"About the poultry?"

"Yes. He has been hanging about all morning. That would be him I saw through the mists, soon after Jasper had taken them. No one comes up here. He saw Jasper take the hens. He will tell her."

They went down the slope, climbed up the gorge, and stood at the head of it. Then slowly they went back to Eagles' Crag. Burl mended up the fire. After some minutes its swithering heat and brightness banished the gloomy shadows as far as the circle of its light could reach. Burl sat down within its red glow. Her hair was wet with the mist they had come through. Shower of heavy rain had come on as they stood at the head of the gorge. She knelt on the fender, shaking her hair in front of her, to dry it.

Henri glanced at the clock.

Only two of the precious hours of the four remained.

And those two they could spend in endearments, in caresses which would make the savage eagle of love grow more weary and wild at delays in its nesting and fulfilment—or, they could be tame Georgios, talking of the weather, what would happen when old Jane came back and found the coop robbed, and what they must say to placate her. Henri glanced at Burl.

Her hair was almost dried.

She tossed it back from the strongly marked brow, the brow which along with the full, dark eyes, now composed, almost dreamy as she stared into the fire, gave her countenance the only differentiation from a northern face. With her hair tossed back thus, its glossy sheen like a raven's burnished purple-black wing in the fire-glow, the nobility of look which he had noticed often appeared in her on the eve of any crisis, was upon her now. It was a look which invariably affected awing the lover in him into taking a back seat, making him willing to sit there and contemplate her. It was never when she was in her gipsy moods.

He sat, pondering her, wondering as he had often wondered, when that look shone out in her, if he would have cared for her at all had she not been a light-hearted gipsy. But it was when she was all northern, with that aloofness, almost austerity, almost that look which said: "I am of the storms, and know it, born for their withstanding, or for their doom, in the end," when she did not stir pulse or heart, and was even too strong for his mind's caressing;

when she seemed like one born to be alone, desolate, wild and proud, that she seemed most wonderful, most herself.

She looked from the fire to his face.

"Henri," she told him, like one coming back to him from a long way, "when I am dead, I will have a funeral pyre."

From what primeval deeps she spoke he could only wonder, as she turned her face, with that desire for a funeral pyre, upon it, towards him.

"I would like it on a wild sea-shore," she told him. "With the dark, stormy waves rolling in, crested with flying foam. And the petrels wheeling round in the sea-mist. And the rocks green-black in the gloom. And my ashes to blow in the sea-spume, far, very far, to some shore where—"

She stopped.

" 'Where?' " prompted Henri.

"There. I do not know. It is gone now," she told him, as returning from a vision.

"Where I would be, too, I hope?" Henri enquired.

But she was neither gipsy, nor visionary, in her reply.

"I expect so. But you are not an unmixed blessing," came her answer, with northern phlegmatism.

"Ditto," Henri told her.

They laughed together. Then, as though the surly echoes of Eagles' Crag, repeating that merry, youthful laughter of theirs recalled to them on what swift wings the precious moments were going by, both pairs of eyes gazed involuntarily at the dial of the old clock. A cinder fell on the hearthstone. They heard the cattle moving lowing in their stalls on the other side the wall.

"It is time to milk now," Henri said.

"Yes. We will get it done. Then perhaps there will be half an hour before they come," Burl told him.

She went to get the lamps, lit them, and they went off into the cow-shed. They should have milked before the light had gone. They were burning oil unnecessarily. Burl sat milking in one stall, Henri in another. Their voices floated to each other over the partitions. The swish of the milk going into the pails, and the soft wurthering of the winds outside were the only sounds, saving for the cattle moving to stand over.

"Henri," called Burl. "There was something in what she said. We should laugh and dance and sing all the day, don't you think, if we had thousands and thousands of francs?"

"But yes," came back Henri's gay voice. "Or we would have electric milkers. You could strum on your tambourine to my singing of 'Avignon', and the cows might dance to it."

Then he gave an exclamation of consternation.

There was the sound of a clanking pail handle, a sounding thwack—

The pail half-full of milk had gone over. Burl left her milking to come and view the catastrophe. Henri was laid on his back, the stool having been kicked from under him. His legs were in the air. He was swearing vehemently. She dragged him to his feet. Their merry laughter rolled through the shed, sonorous, hearty—the bottled laughter of long and dreary weeks. Then, from the other stall came the sound of another pail going over, kicked by an impatient cow, her udders painful with the milk. Henri and Burl stared at each other. It was almost unbelievable. Two buckets of milk—

Burl's peal of laughter sounded first.

"It is nothing to laugh at," she said, in the next breath. "Two pails—"

She burst out again.

Henri joined her. When one ceased laughing, the other started again. Then, with laughter-lit hearts, still bursting out again from time to time, they returned more soberly to the milking.

"Six o'clock," said Henri. "The *bon Dieu*! What shall we say. Poultry gone. Gallons of milk spilled. And she will ask me for the rents I did not go on to get. We are truly in for it. Let us finish and have some little time over the fire."

By six-thirty the milk was sieved, and standing in the kits, ready for morning. The coops, all but the one from which Jasper had taken dinner for the tribe, were fastened. There was but the old buff hen with her lame foot stood on the perch, as they shone the lantern into that last. She blinked at them looking rather wise for a hen; The sight of her perched there—the only one Jasper had spared—

set them off laughing again. But their laughter had in it something like a note of hysteria. Well to laugh when the old Medusa was away, when Eagles' Crag scarce seemed Eagles' Crag without that ancient and terrible eagless, without old Luke cowering and slinking and cringing, the many echoes waking, as responsive to their two gloomy personalities. But she would soon be back.

Tick-tick, said the old clock, as they sat over the fire. Tick-tick, they will soon be back, it said for Henri. Tick-tick, she will never send me away. Tick-tock, she will alter her will before the spring. Tick-tock, what matters a few more years, since one can still laugh. Tick-tock, the cart will be coming on the path over the ravine now. Tick-tick. If the cart would only topple over.

And for Burl.

She sat back in her chair, looking into the red fire. Four happy hours. They were ended now. When would the next be? How swiftly they had gone! Why did happy hours go so swiftly? The sad ones should go swiftly. The happy ones should go slow. In childhood the happy hours had gone slowly. How long the days had seemed, how full. Why should they go ever swifter, swifter, swifter, if one was happy at all, when grown-up? Even when one was sad, too. Since her twenty-first birthday much faster. Was that how it was to the old? Was it time ever going faster as life diminished? For old Jane was it going very swift? Did she want to stop them, the swift days bearing her as they were to the timeless eternity? She shivered.

"Henri," she told him suddenly, "what an awful thing it must be to be old!"

"How?" he asked, in surprise. "If one has lived, *chérie*? How awful? The sheaves are gathered in. The leaves fall. The flowers fade. Friends depart. Who would live on, alone, amongst all new faces, weary and ready for sleep? Age is as beautiful as youth, *chérie*. Death and the close of things as wonderful as birth and the opening of life. I do not understand why you should think old age awful."

"Yes. If one has lived," said Burl. "Perhaps that is so. But, she had not lived, only here at Eagles' Crag, lonely and disappointed. "

97

He looked at her.

"*Oui*," he said, at last. "*C'est vrai*. But what is this to us?"'

Burl looked into the fire.

Like most intense people she had the unhappy knack of being able to see from the point of view of the suffering. Never had she been able to say at the sight of suffering: "What is this to me?"

"Be good to her, Henri," she said, gently. "You can make her very happy. She believes the spirit of one she loved in youth is in you. Let it make up for the wrong that spirit did her seventy years ago. She merely loves to have you near her."

Then she turned her face towards him.

"I shall not be jealous," she said, whimsically.

"Hush," said Henri, the answering smile dying out of his eyes as she gave him that whimsical look.

They listened.

The cart was coming along the path beyond the rocks over the house.

Holiday was over.

"Yes, if you will kiss me," said Henri.

The eagless was returning. Eagles' Crag was once more becoming a dungeon of gloom. The very shadows in the chimney-corners grew ghoulish once more. The wind in its higher notes had a thin screech. The deeper notes moaned. The uncurtained windows looking on the black night outside looked blacker. The silence had a dolorous sombre depth in it. They heard her rating Luke, heard the sound of the old man scraping his boots on the scraper. And rushing together, now that the old eagless was returned, a guard of eternal watchfulness, for one brief moment before the door opened—let warm mouth kiss warm mouth. The eagle of love flapped its wild wings, crying at that farewell caress for who knew how long?

When old Jane came in, Luke at her heels, Luke with a jubilant hilarity in his face, she found them standing on each side the fire-jaumbs.

"When did ta get back?" she asked Henri. "Where's them rents? Clap 'em on't table."

"I never went," said Henri.

She glanced at him in almost choking fury.

Then the storm burst.

"An' thee, Luke," she yelled at her son, "get out an' fasten a' oop."

Luke trudged off.

The slinking echoes of his steps seemed to follow him along.

She turned to Henri and Burl.

Chapter Three

"Tha never went for rents?" echoed the old woman, as the heavy door slammed after her son.

Burl was lighting the lamp, much as though the storm of which they had had one burst, would feel less terrible if they could see each other.

"'I never went," repeated Henri.

His tall figure, dark against the fireglow, seemed taller from his being tipped up on his toes. He stood on the rugless flagstones of the hearth, dark with the dampness that gathered under the floors in winter time, as though his toes were digging into the stone. Burl flashed one nervous look at him, and looked away again. The Frenchman's face was full of suppressed rage. There had been the white heat of chained lightning in his voice as he had answered the old Medusa. But tall as he was he was less in stature than the old woman, her form straightened out with the anger at his deception, with that jealousy that he had come back to be with Burl.

Burl turned up the lamp-wick.

Even in the feeble light the lamp threw over the scene, Jane Mowbray's face, with that raging frenzy upon its yellow age, was something to shudder back from. The fatigue of the journey to town, the shaking in the cart as it had bumped up and down the hill-roads, the wrath which had sent her forth on that journey, and her distaste at giving pleasure to Luke, to spite Henri, had brought her through the doorway a stooping, palsied old woman, ready for her bowl of bread and milk, and weary to lie down.

A skeleton with chamois stretched over it for skin, dressed and held together by galvanism, could scarce have looked more terrible. By sheer electric force of that terrific will

100

she was standing on her feet at all. Dark shadows, which gave to those inflamed eyes, in this, dim light, almost the appearance of holes, out of which the eyeballs blamed, had been left by the day's fatigue. As that fierce gaze turned on the Frenchman, her scrawny hand attempted futilely to untie her bonnet-strings. Palsied by weariness and rage she could not untie them. To the tragedy of her rage against the lovers was added the pathos of her exceeding age.

"Let me take your bonnet off," beseeched Burl, leaving the chair into which she had tremblingly seated herself, after putting on the lamp-glass.

"Thee!" ejaculated old Jane, in a voice of such venomous hatred the pronoun went through the air like a burning missile. She stood grinning at Burl. The grin was so like the grin on the face of a skeleton, Burl retreated and sunk down upon the chair she had left, in despair and horror.

She flashed one imploring look at Henri, begging him in that look, with all the fervour of her being not to add fuel to the fire. He took not the least notice. She might not have been there.

Like two demon spirits, the old woman and the young man confronted each other—-Henri mad and desperate with all his youthful blood at Luke's having got all— at Avignon going farther and farther away—and the old woman in this frenzy of ire that he and Burl had been together all the time she had been "cutting her nose off to spite her face".

"Yes. I came back to be with her," said Henri, "You know we love each other."

"Stop!" ejaculated old Jane, the command coming from her yellow throat with a jagged sound.

"I came back to be with her," repeated Henri. "Yes. We had one *très bon* day. Did we not, Burl?"

The impetuous Frenchman was getting some of his own back. He also was on the rising tide of anger, fierce and deep and strong. Whilst old Jane's anger had all the characteristics of the North, a stormy flood of ire, gathering with greater force, and battering her even as it gathered within her, the Frenchman's was characterized by the cold gaiety of the Latin races, something even more diabolical, a light-hearted childish joy, almost inhuman. He was of the people who had sung whilst the heads had dropped in the baskets*

"Ah, but yes," said Henri, in that soft glee of rage. "Sit down, my dear old *grandmère*. French for grandmother, you know, old Jane. Or should I say my great grandmother? Yes. For you are old enough to be so. Let me tell you, then, *ma chère* great grandmother, that Burl and I have kissed each other scores of times whilst you thought you were spiting us. Are not her lips more rosy? And how we have laughed. These old rafters have rung. We are young, you see. *Ma foi!* What would you have? We are young. It is good to be young. And one is only young once. And you are very old—"

An incoherent splutter came from old Jane's lips.

She tottered slowly to the table, and stood leaning against it. Burl made a movement to go to her. But the old eagless flung her a look so murderous in its ire that despite northern blood and gipsy blood, she shrank back.

"Do not hearken to him," said Burl, compassion in her look and voice. "He is only telling you this to plague you. An' sit down, do, afore you fa'."

"Fa'," screeched old Jane. "I'll noan fa'. Out tha goes fro' Eagles' Crag, Henri. Gather thy traps up. They're noan wuth ten shillings. An' I were only 'plaguin' thee about leaving all to Luke. I meant to alter it again, sohowbeit. Now it shill stan'. Ay. It shall stan'. Get thy things piked up. I'll show thee whether tha shall laugh at me because tha thowt I mun see thee about the place, hear thy foot-fa'—because tha'rt like he wot when we were young. Old, am I? Thy granny, am I? Tha'rt him, I tell thee. The speerit o' him entered thee as tha came up to Eagles' Crag. It had creepit out o' the churchyard, an' waited till tha came up to Eagles' Crag, an' entered into thee, Tha'rt him. I gan him another chance—in thee, fakin' it as he'd come back because he were sorry. Maist like he came back to plague me to't end. He had thrown his chance away, ageon. Now, I'll chuck him out, in thee, out into't pitch-dark neet, like the darkness he piked me out into, afore, nigh on seventy years gone. But shoo'll stay here."

She pointed her skinny forefinger at Burl.

Dementia, the dementia of age, had sounded in her voice, as she had spoken, even as it was now stamped on her skeleton-like countenance. Rage and pride and grief and wounded vanity, and hate, had passed like burning shadows over that yellow face. Her head, shaking to and fro in the palsy of feebleness, still more the rusty black bonnet, which shook with it, and gave to her something of the ridiculous look of an automatic figure.

Burl looked at her—then at Henri.

She rose from the chair and walked over to Henri.

The very way she walked across to him should have been a warning. The tenderness she felt for the old woman whom he was so flinging into madness, through her foolish fancy, brought to his side a gipsy, her dark eyes full of hate.

"Say another word to plague her," she told him, hands on her hips, and her dark eyes stating full into his, "an' I'll plague thee, till shoo's cowd an' beyond thy plagueing. I'll ne'er kiss thee more, if tha says one more word. For thee'rt only wild because she's left a' to Luke. Not because she stands between us. Thee'rt a demon, too."

The Frenchman stared at Burl.

Her taunt, instead of calming him, enraged him.

There was all the sting of love that is not intellectually blind in her last three sentences.

Burl's eyes, still fixed on him, retreated, with her. She went and sat down in her chair, waiting to see if he would still further deride the old woman, after that threat.

She sat like one turned into stone, as his gay voice, ignoring her threat, ran on.

"I'll pick up my things and go," said Henri, gaily. "*Ma chère grandmère* so bids me. *Ma foi!* My grandmother who sees in me the spirit of her old lover bids me leave her. A little rouge, *ma chère grandmère*, would much improve your appearance. Your lips are so thin and blue. And your hand, stroking my face in the dead o' night when first I came here—*ma foi*—it gave me what you English call the pip, is it not so? The pity. The spectral eagle which occasionally visits your habitation gives you nothing like the feeling I got as I felt your hand stroking my brow. You should look in the glass, *ma chère grandmère.* Then you would not expect that I should love you—"

His voice, gaily running on, ceased suddenly, For the old woman standing by the table had tottered. Burl reached her just in time. She placed her in her chair.

Old Jane's eyes, glassed almost as in death, gazed across at Henri.

"The same fiend," she said, almost in a whisper. "The same fiend. If I were not sure tha were him, afore—I am now."

Henri walked over to the chair in the opposite corner.

The demon which had felt to be driving him on, was laid. He saw the old woman's death-like countenance—those eyes glassed over, a look of burning agony under their glazed uncanniness. He saw Burl bending over her, every line of that pale countenance a line of grief from the affection of a heart which must have been tormented beyond endurance almost by their raging against each equally loved.

"*Voila!* I believe she is right," muttered Henri. "I believe as I came up the gorge that night, some black demon soul entered my body."

Burl took no notice of him.

She was talking to the old woman.

"Let him depart to perdition," she was telling her. "Whether be'st' one or t'other—hissel' or th' other faithless devil. Let him get gone. I'll stay wi' you. What does it matter, when I'm here? I'll sit an' cal wi' you. You can leave Eagles' Crag to Luke, an' all you have. I bide wi' you because you need me. Let him go. Men be butterflees. Fro' flower to flower they flit. 'Tis their nature. When the colour has gone fro' the posy, they toss it away. I saw that as he talked to you, scoffin' your old age. I want no more of him. I'll bide wi' you here, at Eagles' Crag. You'll live years an' years an' years yet, an' never one too many for me."

"No. Don't let him go," moaned the old woman. "No. I'm gettin' old an' peevish. An' I couldn't do without Henri sittin' to cal wi' me. An' never to hear his foot-fa'. But tha'rt a devil, Henri."

She laughed, feebly, and turned her gaze to where the Frenchman was sitting.

His now melancholy face was turned upon the two women.

"Did you mean you were willing that I should go, Burl?" he added.

"Ay. Get gone," she told him, fiercely.

"Noa, noa," said the old woman. "Take no heed on her. Shoo doesn't mean it.

Henri rose to his feet.

"If Burl wishes me to go," he said, in a stricken tone.

"Oh, tha'll go if she wants thee to go?" said old woman.

Burl left her side.

She stood up, facing Henri.

"Nay, stop, Henri. Don't go," she said. "I'm askin' thee to stop."

The gipsy eyes, lustreless and mysterious, looked at him.

She was asking him to stop because old Jane wished her to ask him.

Love was dead for him then.

He had slain it as he had jested at the old woman's folly and strange notion that he was the lover of her youth returned. Love which had been dying, dying of this dark house, with its mouldy air, was dead, as they had felt it dying latterly. Or, if it was not quite dead, it would die. Burl had declared that if he went on riling the old woman he should have no loving word, no loving kiss, to keep love alive. He had gone on. Some demon, had driven him on. If he left Eagles' Crag he had left years of his life there, wasted, blighted. He would stay. There might still be Avignon—and the old woman's possessions turned into francs.

"I'll stay,' said Henri.

"Th' Eagle!"

It was Luke's voice, hoarse with excitement, blown to them on the gust of the wind.

"Th' Eagle," he bellowed, running with all his speed to get into the house. Then they heard the rattle of stones and his blubbering panic.

"He's fa'en," said the old woman. "Th' great loon. Would that th' Eagle'd catty him off. Go an' help un oop, Burl. Henri'll sit an' cal wi' me. Dang th' Eagle."

Burl went out. The night had closed in dark and misty. She had rushed out without lantern.

"Luke," she called, over and over.

But no sound reached her in reply.

At length she stumbled against his prostrate form. The old man was laid moaning.

"Are you hurt, Luke?" she inquired.

"Th' Eagle!" moaned Luke.

Burl raised him to his feet. They stood in the misted darkness. Burl looked up at the sky.

"Whear?" she asked. "There's naught but mist an' darkness. Where did you see th' Eagle, Luke?"

"Thear! Thear! A great shadow-eagle," blubbered Luke. "It went reight ower my yed. Reight over thear—"

He pointed into the darkness.

There was nothing to be seen. Only the roar of the torrent to be heard.

"Come along in, Luke," Burl told the old man. "There's naught to be feared on at Eagles' Crag nobbut them at live thear."

Her youthful voice had a sound of bitterness.

"No. Tha'rt reight," said old Luke, recovering somewhat. "But I saw it. It went ower thear—"

Burl looked again to satisfy him.

Then she stood, staring.

Old Luke had pointed towards the gipsy encampment as the direction over which the spectral eagle had gone.

A great indistinct shadow did appear to be moving over the dim slope of the moorside. "It's thear," said the old man. "Tha's sin it now."

The bellowing was coming back into his tone.

"Shut up, Luke," she told him, sharply. "I can't see for thy din."

He chuckled feebly, evidently gaining courage from being stood by one not afraid. "It's smoke an' mist," Buri told him."It's naught. Come along in."

Then she stopped and looked again.

Through the indistinctness of the night, lit by the gipsy fire, a great moving shadow-shape was certainly moving.

She saw against the fire a figure, evidently building it up. Wood was being piled upon it. The fire flared up suddenly.

Then—

High above the camp, through the murky air, went the moving shadow. Its pinions became distinct.

"It's red," yelled Luke, suddenly. "It's red. Sitha! It's wings are red."

And indeed, for one fleeting moment, the shape of a great eagle, its wings touched as by the fires of a setting sun, appeared to go through the mists above the encampment. Then all was dark again.

"It's red. It's red. Th' Eagle is red," moaned Luke, as she led him back towards the house. And over and over, he muttered the legend of Eagles' Crag, as they went.

"When the Eagle red shall fly,
Eagles' Crag to earth shall lie."

"Well, it's not laid to earth yet," Burl told him "Tha'rt goin' through't door-hole, Luke. So th' house is stannin' yet."

"Ay. But it's a sign. A sign," muttered the old man. "An' what's good o' her having left it me in her will, if it's goin' to lie low to't yeth?"

"What's that about th' Eagle being red," said old Jane, when they got inside.

"It were red," said old Luke. "Red as it were dipped in blood."

"Get to bed wi' thee," said old Jane.

"No. Let me stay oop," begged the old man. "I'll be hearkening for't rocks fa'ing on't roof."

"Get to bed wi' thee, or I'll belt thee," commanded his mother.

"Can I have a leet, then?" he whimpered.

"Ay. Take him a leet, Burl," the old woman told Burl.

"An what's good o' your havin' left me Eagles' Crag, when th' Eagle's gone ower it—red, which means it's to fa' to't ground?" asked Luke,

The old woman whipped round in her chair.

"Tha'll noan get Eagles' Crag," she told him. "I were mad at Henri when I altered my will. I'm changing it back. We'me friends again, Henri an' me. Aren't we, Henri?"

Burl looked at Henri.

His chair was pulled up near the old woman's.

A light-hearted devilry was on his face. He had been making her laugh. She was looking almost sprightly in the gladness of his being staying on, and that they were friends again.

"But yes, we are friends," said the Frenchman gaily.

A feverish glittering shone from his eyes. His face was deathly pale, but smiling. Burl stood looking at him uneasily.

Luke was staring at him also. The Frenchman was vividly aware of the hatred boiling in the old man. And he enjoyed the joke that the old woman had told him in return for a gay *bon mot* brought from a mind racked with the agony that love between him and Burl was dead at last—dead, a brave eagle that would beat its wild wings for life no more, never any more. Old Jane had just told him that she had never altered her will at all. She had left Luke outside. He had believed that she had altered it. But she had not done so. All was his still, unless she lied. But even so, he would soon be in her favour again. But Burl—

He lifted his gaze to where she stood, in gipsy scorn at his playing up to the poor old doting woman.

"Come on, Luke," she told the old man. "Tha can ha' two cannels. An' t' house'll noan fa'. There's no such good luck."

Luke moved towards the stairs, following her. Then he said, turning back, his gaze upon the Frenchman: "Whilst you're bin away, instead o' lookin' after things, th' hen coop had been robbed."

"What?" yelled his mother.

"That's how they'll gan on when you're gone," said old Luke. "There's only one hen in't end coop."

Old Jane stared at him.

"Get th' lantern, Henri," she said. "Thee tak' un oop to bed, Burl."

Burl lit the old man up the stairs.

When she came down, she listened for old Jane and Henri returning. They came. Old Jane sat down in her chair.

"It's noan thy fault, lad," she told Henri.

She looked at Burl.

"It's them thievin' gipsy folk o' thine," she said. "They go t-morn. I'll ha' them driven off."

"No," pleaded Burl.

The appeal was almost a torn sob.

"Yigh. They'll be goan in't mornin'! Henri'll go an' tell't police. Won't ta, Henri?"

Burl's gaze went to his face.

He nodded.

Burl rushed towards old Jane.

"You'll have them driven away, where I can never see their fire going up—my people—for the sake of a few old hens?" she asked.

"Ay. I'll have thy thieving people driven off," old Jane told her.

"Honester folk than Georgios," said Burl.

Grief and savage anger made the words almost incoherent.

Never to see the fire of the encampment going up. Old folk and young driven off like so much vermin by the Georgios, who lied more, and did more robbery, though of a more subtle order, in one month, than gipsies in their whole lives.

"An' gan off to bed," old Jane told her. "Henri an' me is sittin' up cal-in'. There's a good fire. We'll sit by it."

Burl stood in the doorway looking back at them.

"I would Eagles' Crag would fall, an' bury us' all," she said.

"Well, thy can save thy wind. It won't. It'll be here in't morn. But them thievin' gypsies will have gone."

Burl stood leaning against the doorway.

"I hate you. I wish you were dead," she said, in a fierce, low breath. "My people, to be driven away, never to see their fire, for the sake of a few lousy old hens. I hate you, old Jane. I wish you were dead."

The old woman laughed.

"Get off to bed wi' thee, treacherous gipsy trash," she said. "I care naught whether tha hates me or not, so long as Henri likes me."

"An' I know tha'd be thick wi' me again," said the old woman to Henri. "I fetched a bottle o' that French wine tha likes. We'll break it. And drink to when tha owns Eagles' Crag."

Burl, half-way up the stairs, heard that. Contemptuously, she went up the stairs.

She heard Luke talking in his room.

Going softly along, she peeped in at him, through the doorway of his room.

He was knelt by the bedside praying. The two lighted candles threw their glow on his grey head. He was praying to his God. The pagan woman looking in at the doorway envied him. Truly one could do with a God to pray to at Eagles' Crag. But her father had always said: "There is the sun. That is the source of life. Without it everything were dead. When I look at the sun, I think of God. Everyone has a different God. Even the Georgios, everyone of them, has a different God." And with no God she had been left.

She stood listening to old Luke.

"Give me Eagles' Crag, oh Lord," he was praying. "An' a't land fro' Brown Rigg to Hingbrough Lane Ends. Put it into her heart to leave the will as it stan's. An' make her die afore she has time to change it. Or if there's some bit shoe leaves away fro' me, make her leave it Burl, an' nobo'ry else. Take her soin, oh Lord, so's I've time to enjoy it, for soin I'll be three score an' ten, an' my days a burden. Don't let that French devil get round her, Lord. For shoo's belted me shameful, an' I've a reet to a' shoo has. An' ll give to'art the buildin' o' the new chapel, Lord, if tha'll nobbut see I get everything."

Old Luke's eyes were turned up now.

Hurl could see the whites of them, and the ecstasy on his face. She turned away, shivering. Even when the Georgios prayed, they were asking for money and goods, like so many creditors sueing at a bank. Better the sun for God. She crept quietly away and going into the dark room she shared with old Jane, stood by the window looking out for what might be the last time on the fire on the moor-tops. It streamed up through the gloom, the only colour in the darkness all about. .

She stood very still, her face close to the pane. Surely, on the winds, came the sound of the gipsies singing the

Romany folk-songs, how old no one knew, for all their admixture with the Georgio ballads. She stood. It was like hearing the blown music of a broken chant. Perhaps she was imagining it, she mused. Perhaps her spirit was going out to them so keenly, in grief that they were soon to be driven away, that she could hear them, was standing in spirit with them, unseen, beside that tent touched with the fire's flickering glow and shadows. She pictured the scene of their going, old folk and young, driven off the bit of rough land, through the November murk and cold.

A passionate flame of resentment was in her heart.

She lay down with it still burning there.

As she was falling off to sleep, she heard downstairs Henri singing "Avignon". She had never grudged any attention he gave to old Jane. But that he should sing "Avignon"—which was sacred to them both—to please the one who divided them from its dream. Yes. He was worse than old Luke, asking his God for all the land from Brown Rigg to Hingbrough Lane Ends. She could hear the clink of their glasses, too, touching, in some toast after Henri's singing.

She pondered, and the truth burst on her. With ironic devilry Henri was drinking to Avignon and the sunlit farm lands of his dream farm purchased with the francs Eagles' Crag would bring. Old Jane had brought the wine for that toast. She was drinking her own death, for only by her death could Henri have his dream farm in Avignon.

She sat up in bed, shuddering at the devil in him which the old woman evoked. Then she recalled that in to-morrow's blush dawn, like vermin, her people would be driven from the moor, that never again would her heart leap up to see their fire burning there, to bring her joy in this rock—shadowed wilderness. With a gipsy laugh, she turned her face down to the pillow and slept, after wondering if old Luke was yet on his knees waiting for the Lord's answer to his prayer.

Chapter Four

Henri moved in his chair, feeling chill and wooden-limbed. Half-opening his eyes, he saw the lamp burning. Then, despite cold and stiffness, he-slumbered again. The fire shuttered down in the grate. Once more he stirred, his sleep-misted gaze falling on the lamp. And the old woman, she was sitting there still. The clock struck, a great many times. He tried to count the strokes, but lost count. *Voila!* Surely it was time to go to bed. Then he slept again. Once more the chilliness of the air awoke him.

"Froid comme la morte!" he ejaculated. His gaze, more wide awake, saw the lamp once more. Tick-tick, said the big clock, like an upended dark coffin. He turned to look at tl>e old woman. She was there still. He pondered whether to awaken her. *Mais non!* This had been a great occasion to the old beldame. The wine they had drunk. A great *bon mot* for Burl to come down in the morning and find them both sitting there—that though she could plague him by keeping to her word never to have any word of love for him or any token of it till the old woman was dead, since he had over-ridden her desire that he say nothing back to her—they were still friends and Avignon made secure again. And to have the laugh at the old man, who would be wild to know he still stood first in her favour.

Mais non! He would not awaken her. To do so would be like crying *peccavi*. If the old beldame going on for a hundred could sit the night out for love of his company, he also would sit it out, till daybreak, if needs be. That wine. The taste of it. French wine from the Bourdeaux vineyards. Was there any left in the bottle still? One more glass, if there was. Then one little promenade outside to blow the wine-fumes from his brain. The old woman was so fast asleep she would not miss him. When she awoke he would be sitting there, superbly patient. One glass, one promenade, then he would mend up the fire, and read until the old woman awoke, going over the old farming journals, as he read them stocking a farm in Avignon, hearing in fancy French chanticleers crow in the morning over the fertile fields of that warm land.

One *petite tres bon glass*—

He turned towards the table, stretching out his hand for the bottle. *Ces froid!* He shivered. And the stillness, the deathly stillness. The place felt cold and silent as a morgue. The old woman sat as silent as though she were dead.

He looked at her sitting in the chimney-corner, where the shadows hung heavily about her.

Diable! But how stiffly she sat on her chair, amongst the black shadows. And how pale her face. Did very old people, then, sleep with eyes partially opened? Then he turned his attention to the bottle.

The fumes of the wine still reeked in his brain. Silly little flashes of gay thoughts ran in and out of it, *bon mots*, and anon melancholy, which he hoped one little glass would banish quite away, dark melancholy, for it was a mad agony that he and Burl should be estranged. *Ces l'amour!* It had kept him in this morgue of a place four winters. Next winter he would still be here. And the next. And the next after that. Love would be dead by then, perished of no loving look or word from Burl. But there would be Avignon, and the thousands of francs.

Glug-glug—

The remainder of the wine in the bottle went into the glass.

Henri drained it all into the glass.

He stood up, holding it in his hand, and looked at the old woman. *Ma foi!* But with what grave comicness she sat in her chair, so silent and pale, as though it were the last sleep she had fallen into. He walked towards her, glass in hand, and bent over her. She was sound asleep. No breath which he could hear came from her lips. *Tiens!* But this corner she sat in felt icy. He left it, casting a glance at the uncurtained windows, showing the black night outside, the lamp reflected in the wide blackness.

He set the wine to his lips, sipped it slowly, felt it trickle down his throat, touching tongue and palate. The warm sweetness of it stole through his senses. When he had half-emptied the glass he set it on the table. He would keep that for the old woman when she awoke. A good *bon mot* that had been, to have got her to drink to Avignon. No Frenchwoman, he ruminated, however old, however illiterate, however doting, would haw drunk to Avignon. Her suspicious wit would have been too keen. She would have suspected that he wanted her out of the way. *Voila!* But the old woman was indeed a silent companion. And this deathly stillness of midnight; this cold; those windows looking blankly out into the black waste of the lone night. Yes. He would awaken her.

Crossing to the table he took up the glass, still half-full of wine.

Then he stood, staring, noticing for the time that there were two glasses still standing beside the bottle. Whence the third glass? He looked at the one in his hand. Yes. One, two, three. Three glasses with the one he held in his hand. There had been but two when he had fallen asleep. Perhaps the old woman had brought out another after he had fallen asleep, forgetting there were two on the table.

The wine he had drank was now beginning to make him quite gay.

He stood surveying the old woman in the chimney-corner.

"Hear you not my chanticleers crowing from Avignon?" he asked her, standing on the hearthstone damp with the winter rains. "My chanticleers. Hear them."

And with the old woman staring across at him, he imitated the chanticleers he would purchase with the money of her farms, turned into francs. After one very loud "cock-a-doodle-do", he looked at her, surprised that it had not awakened her.

"*Ma foi!* You sleep on, with my chanticleers calling in morning?" he asked her. "Come, then, we will see if the turkeys will awaken you."

He came back from the dream-farm in Avignon, where the turkeys had talked, and stared at her once more. He took two steps towards her.

"Late hours, *ma chère grandmère*," Henri told her, shaking his finger at her, "are not good for you. You are missing your beauty sleep. All to stay up with your faithless old lover who crept from the churchyard and entered my body as I came up to Eagles' Crag. And truly sometimes I have felt you were right. But now I am not he, but Henri. Come, you are too old to sit the night out. Awaken, now, and go to bed. Taste now a little more wine—"

Henri, in gay mood, mixed with a fitful sudden pity for the old woman, had crossed once more to the chimney-corner.

He reached her, leaned the glass gently against her lips, and bent over her, waiting for her to open her eyes properly, a *bon mot* ready on his tongue.

There was the sound of something trickling into the glass.

"*Tiens!* But you should not put wine back," he jested, gaily.

Then, with an unearthly yell, he stood back from her. Blood was trickling from her mouth corners. In the ghastly silence which followed the echoes of Eagles' Crag repeating that yell of terror, he stood, trying to take his gaze from the old woman. Two lines of red were going down from mouth to chin. Those cold eyes looked back at him with fixed and stony gaze. He backed, further, further. Something clanked under his feet. He stared down stupidly, backed again, and then saw the pool of blood by her chair, even as he had just grasped the fact that the cold clanking thing his foot had clattered over was a sword. It was red. And the blood—

Paralysed with horror, he stumbled to a chair.

He sat, trying not to look at the figure in the chimney-corner. He was trying to grasp the fact that old Jane had been murdered, murdered whilst he had slept there, but a few yards from her. But even as he tried to realize it, he was conscious all the time of those two lines of red going down from her mouth-corners, of her stony stare at him from the black shadows, at the smile upon her face.

"Burl!" broke across his mind.

And with the thought came his recollection of her going along the mouldy hall, taking down the sword, and going to the old woman's room with it. They had waited for her to die. They had wished her dead. And last night Burl, standing in the doorway, fiercely pale, in her grief-stricken agony that by the noon of this day the gipsy tribe would have been driven away—

Her face came before his mind's eye, its pallor, its lightning blaze of anger.

"Burl!" he groaned.

He crossed over to the chimney-corner.

With shuddering touch he laid his hand on the old woman's arm.

It was cold, icy cold.

The wild, irrational hope that she might not be dead, died at the coldness of the flesh he touched.

He backed from the stony gaze which seemed to deride him—fixed, eternal.

"*Mon Dieu!*" gasped Henri. "*Mon Dieu!* And I have sat here, whilst she was murdered."

"'Murdered'," repeated the air about him. From outside, from the black night, came the sound of the dogs barking. Was someone creeping away under this black sky? Was it not Burl? *Mon Dieu!*, no, it could not be Burl. They had sat with the door unfastened, he and the old woman. *Pauvre agée femme.* Someone could have come in. Why were the dogs barking so? Someone was outside there, in this black night. *Mon Dieu!*, yes. The blackest night ever. If so, he should rouse the house. After all, he had been sitting with her. It would seem strange that he could have slept—

Then, for the first time the terrible thought, that he could be suspected of the deed, struck him. He stood staring across at the old woman.

"*Mon Dieu!*" he ejaculated, in a whisper.

It seemed to him, that as he stared across at her, she smiled back, pleased at his dreadful plight.

Clay-cold, he collapsed upon a chair.

Cold drops gathered on his brow. They ran down his clammy flesh. The coldness of death spread through him.

"*Ma foi!*" he heard his own whisper. Then; "*Non,* it may have been Burl."

"*Non, non,*" he heard his own response to the dreadful thought, that desire to be clear of suspicion at the price of her guilt. "*Non, non.* Better that it were! *Non.* Not Burl."

And as though the shadows round the old woman's chair had answered, came the most dreadful thought: "But you may have done it. You drank much wine. Can you recall all the evening?

He sat down, trying to think.

It was impossible.

If the old woman had gone to sleep before him—

"*Non, non,*" he whispered.

Then, from outside, came the sound of footsteps. They were Burl's. She was out, then. Yes. Otherwise would not his yell have aroused her? Burl— yes, it was Burl. She had done this. She would be hung. Avignon—ah, where was Avignon now? The old woman, she was sitting there smiling. She was delighted at their despair. Yes. She was delighted, vindictive dead as alive, hating them for their love, saying still, though she was dead: "I stand between you still. And it is now for ever." He sat staring at the old woman.

"You are mistaken," he told her, as though she could hear. "We shall love when we have followed you. Do you hear? When we have followed you."

"Henri," breathed Burl, standing by his side.

She had come in, without his hearing, as he had been swept away by the agony of this end to all things. She saw him standing by old Jane's chair. He was shaking his fist at her.

"What is the matter?" she asked. "Do you quarrel with her when she sleeps, after sitting all night to keep in her good graces?"

He turned from the old woman at these words of scorn.

The proud aloofness of her look changed to terror, reflecting the look on his face.

"What is it?" she asked. "Beloved—what is the matter?"

"I woke to find her dead," he said.

"Dead?"

Her incredulous question was a breath.

He bent his head.

"You lie," she told him fiercely.

She strode over to the old woman's chair.

"*Ma foi!*" he groaned. "You have walked in it."

But she was staring into the old woman's face, fierce love in every line of her face, in her attitude, breathless, poignant.

"Dead," Henri heard. "Dead. And but a few hours ago I told her I hated her. Dead.

Like one in the grip of some hideous nightmare, he saw Burl shaking the old woman, as though she dared her to be dead, unable to hear her.

"Now you have walked in it again," he moaned.

He saw the old woman sit back in her chair.

"Walked in what?" Burl questioned him.

He pointed.

"There, in the blood," he told her, shudderingly.

"Blood. Where?" she asked, dully.

The white agony of her face loomed on him from the shadows. Her wild, dilated eyes burned in her face. Grief that the old woman was beyond the reach of anything she could say, was stamped in her looks.

"There," he almost screamed. "There. You have walked in it."

She looked down, saw the pool of blood by the chair, sickened—then rushed at him as about to tear him to pieces.

"Fiend!" she ejaculated. "Fiend. You, you have murdered her?"

She followed him as he backed, and at every step he saw red footmarks on the sanded floor.

Then the fascination of seeing them ended. They stood staring at each other. Burl was sobbing.

"You!" she grieved, in a low, teeth-caught whisper, "You, beloved, you!"

"*Non, non,*" he said.

"But all the night, sitting here, and now—"

He saw the horror in her eyes.

"Yes. I awoke. She was dead," he told her, simply.

Then, for the first time, he looked at her closely.

The dampness of the outdoor world was on her dress. The night dew was on her hair.

The agony of her suspicion, withal it was fading from her face, leaving only an emotionless despair, had stung her to the depths.

"And you—where have you been?" he inquired.

"I?"

She stared at him.

"Yes."

"I must have walked in my sleep. I found myself standing down the gorge."

Silence hung heavy on the kitchen.

"Yes?" said Henri.

She stared at him uncomprehending the meaning of his question. Then a wild agony swept ha face.

"You think—?" she asked, and shrank bat from him.

Silence fell again.

Then her words came, scarcely breathed.

"Is it possible? Is it possible? I fell asleep hating her. I fell asleep hating her."

In a world turned to black horror they stared at each other.

"Henri," she appealed, suddenly, like a frightened child.

He sprang to her.

They stood, each folded in the other's chill embrace.

"But, *non*, you could not have done this," he told her.

"Nor you," she replied faintly.

"No. Neither of us," he said. "But we must go. If I stay here much longer—"

"Yes," she told him. "But why did you shake your fist when she was dead?"

He answered her in a voice changed out of recognition almost.

"Because she hates us, even when she is dead," he told her. "Because she is glad to stand between."

A cinder fell on the hearth.

They jumped, and looked towards the chair where the old woman was sitting. Now that the first unreality of the awful happening was passing, they spoke in whispers. And the figure sitting amongst the shadow's of the chimney-corner, its living delight in their torment remembered, became imbued again with its own personality. And its personality seemed all the more vigorous, in that, despite its own awful cessation, it seemed now to be fixed, in that slow, malicious smile, those stony, chill eyes, sitting there stiffly, as laughing at this utter ending of their warm, human dream.

The stillness of the kitchen grew suddenly more awful.

They stood, holding each other, chillily, and looking into each other's horror-haunted eyes.

"The clock has stopped," Burl whispered.

Henri tottered suddenly from her weak hold.

He sat down heavily. His gaze fell on the dead fire, its ashes, its burnt-out cinders.

"Yes. All has stopped," he said. "Dead time. Dead love. Dead life. All has stopped. She has kept us waiting all this time. She stands between us for all time. It is her revenge."

"Henri," said Burl, beseechingly.

She reached his side, drew his head against her breast.

.But his gaze stared over to the old woman.

"She is smiling at us," he told her, in a low, uneven whisper. "See the ghastly smile. She sits there for all time, dividing us more dead than she did alive. She has taken all from us. Nothing is left. And—yet—to die. Life which remains will be a charnel house, in which love sits—dead."

"Hush, hush," Burl told him, in despairing agony. "No. Love is not dead. That is left."

But no faith sounded in her voice.

"You are cold as ice," he told her. "Ice. *Mon Dieu!* Yes. All is dead."

"The fire is out," she told him.

"Yes. All is dead. Even the fire," he raved on, mournfully. "The clock—why did that stop also?"

She stood staring at him in bewilderment.

"Come," she told him, resolutely, at length.

"Where?" he asked.

"From here," she answered him. "Come. One of us must have done this. We shall die for it. Come, we will live first. They shall take us when we have lived."

From the stupor into which he had fallen, he gazed upon her face.

In this hour of doom, the revelation of her titanic and fierce desire to drink the cup of love in one swift gulping draught ere life was ended, amazed him.

While the urge within him was just to get away from Eagles' Crag, from the old woman sitting there smiling that ghastly smile of triumph amidst the black shadows.

"Yes. Away, away, away!" he murmured over and over. "To die. But to die away from this place."

He saw her looking at him with tender compassion.

"To die is nothing," she told him, "if one has lived."

Silence fell again.

"Old Luke," he said, suddenly, grasping her arm with wild hope.

She shook her head.

"Yes. But she had told him she would alter her will—" he began.

She shook her head again.

"But if you like I will go up to see if he is in bed asleep—"

"Yes. Go. Go."

He sat, head bowed on his hands, whilst she went upstairs.

How long he had sat, occasionally staring across at the dread figure in the chimney-corner, he could not have told. It seemed an eternity. Then she stood beside him once more. She shook her head slowly from side to side. Even before she spoke, the hope that the old man had done this—that life and love remained to them, away from Eagles' Crag—died as he saw her face.

"He is fast asleep," she said.

The horror-haunted silence closed round them again.

"See!" he cried, starting up, wildly."The lamp is going out."

She stared at the lamp.

"And must we go, and leave him here, and go like rats, to awaken and find her like this?" she asked.

He scarcely heard her.

"The lamp is going out!" he almost screamed, "Away, away, away. We cannot be here in the dark with her."

A moment later they stood outside.

The great black night was over their heads.

"Stay there," Burl told Henri.

He was leaning against a tree, a faint relief touching his spirit as the chill midnight winds blew upon him.

He clutched at her.

"Old Luke will go," she told him. "The dumb beasts must be fed. We cannot leave them to starve."

He heard her open the coop doors and throw corn in to the poultry. They cluttered down from their perches as the rays of the lantern, the rattling of the corn, came to them. After what seemed interminable time she came back from feeding the horses and cattle.

"Now we will go," she told him.

Silently, chill hand in chill hand, they through the darkness, clambering up to the above the rock.. The loud clattering of stones loosened by their feet echoed through the stillness of the night. A deathly stillness brooded over everything. It was as if they walked in a world where lifelessness had fallen all about them. The grasses made no slightest whisper. The black trees they passed were unmoving. The winter fields empty of cattle stretched blackly beyond the hedge whose grass they moved over, up to the black sky. Their breaths travelled out into the blackness beyond the lantern's rays like faint smoke. They spoke no word, until Henri, starting, pointed at a shadow which loomed through the gloom.

"What is that?" he whispered, in terror.

Burl's cold hand tightened on his.

"One of the rocks on the hillside," she whispered back to him, soothingly.

"Yes, yes," he told her.

They went on again.

"And—that—over there?" he questioned in a fearful breath.

"A tree, beloved."

"Yes, yes," he murmured.

His hand, which had been ice as they had left Eagles' Crag, was burning now.

The world was phantasmagoria. His steps tottered. Had Burl not been as physically strong as he was, withal a woman, he would have collapsed by the roadside. As though this weakness of his gave her additional strength, she upheld him. They dragged along slowly through the silent night, the lantern-rays falling before them on heavy, motionless grass, on the hedge of hawthorns to the left, on the pitchy vacuum of the ravine below.

"Away, away," he said, once. Then: "Can we go no faster," quite unconscious that it was his lagging steps which retarded their speed from Eagles' Crag.

She gave no answer.

And he forgot to repeat the question, walking on, occasionally sighing: "Away, away—"

When his steps went too near the ravine, she steered them back to the middle of the road.

Something fluttered through the air, glimmering ghostly in the lantern-rays, a first flake of winter snow. Faster and faster came the flakes. They danced about the lantern, fell on the top of it. The road was soon white.

The black sky leaned down to the hills and fields, clad in that shining whiteness.

"Snow," said Henri. "Snow. Ice. Hail. Rain. Winter after winter. In Avignon—"

He laughed wildly, his laughter echoing through the night, as the thought of far Avignon came to him, the gay town amongst the vine-clad hills—and his dream—of Burl, in sabots, with the baby in her arms, calling him to dinner. The dream was dead, too.

"Have we far to go, yet?" he asked, wearily.

"Not far, beloved," she told him.

They walked on.

She raised the lantern once, to shine its light to see the gap in the wall they must pass through, to go up the hill, where the crags stood, great looming shapes as black as the night.

Her grip on Henri never relaxed.

When his steps went too near the ravine she dragged him by sheer force back towards the middle of the road.

But the lantern-rays falling on her face revealed its stony misery, its bitter despair. Tears hung on her lashes. The coldness of the air had turned them into ice. They hung there like beads. And out from them her eyes stared fixedly, almost as fixedly as old Jane's, who sat dead in the midnight house, the rats scampering about her motionless, rigid fingers.

They stared into a world of night and loneliness.

The road ran through it, a road of night and loneliness, in a wide world of night and loneliness. And at the end of it was death.

A few days, a few weeks, at most—

Each hour an agony.

And the cup of love, an agony also—since Henri would fail her. She knew it. In that black hour in which she upheld him with lonely strength and the tenderness which had blossomed in this night of doom, she knew it. He was not of the North. As his avarice had partially brought this upon them, so his lack of any element of granite would leave her, when the time came, alone. Nay, was she not alone now, as she steered him through the night?

"How far yet?" he asked, almost with a peevish whine, which her spirit cringed to hear from him.

She guided him through the gap in the wall.

"Not far," she told him.

They went up the hill, towards the crags, towering blackly into the black night.

She blew out the lantern.

Its light shining through the night might he seen.

She was taking him to the cave amongst the rocks which would be their home until—the swift end came.

Chapter Five

The light of a fire made from leaves, twigs, and tree branches, flickered over the rough walls of the cave, one of those recesses amongst the rocks of which any long country walk in northern England almost reveals several as having possibly, in ancient times, sheltered hermit, sheep-stealer, or highwayman. Some six feet by ten, upon its uneven earth floor, were pools of rain in which was the crimson glow, the leap and flicker of the fire, saving in the pool which stood at the end, farthest from the fire. This was in inky gloom. Over it brooded great black shadows, standing unmoving, like silent ghosts. Shaggy grass grew long over the rock door. Beyond the glow of the fire it hung down like a coarse blackened thatch.

Trailing bushes of blackberry, which the fugitives had disturbed as little as might be in entering, also stood black against that rosy glow. The black leaves, large and stiff with frost, yet clung to the brambles, late as the year was. There were even a few berries, withered and ill to eat, as northern custom holds, after October—when the witches have kissed them—clinging to the ragged bramble trails. For, though the cave was set high on the hillside, so surrounded by huge rock was it, these in some measure stayed the full force of the savage, sweeping winds. Before the doorway,, rock which almost obscured the opening, served as a protection against the fire-glow shining down the now whited hillside. The wind muttered softly, blowing amongst the rocks, rushes, dead bracken and black heather over which would soon gleam a dawn sky.

Beside the fire, on leaves which past month of winds and stones had drifted in through the opening in the rocks, lay the two lovers, locked in each other's arms.

Upon both their faces was the rapturous expression and content which told that they were one flesh at last. Love, the wild eagle, was with them in this bleak solitude. It beat its pinioned wings no longer. It had fled with them from Eagles' Crag, and pinnacled on the highest point of mortal ecstasy, stared fearlessly at the sun of life. Only love and lovers had entered this cave. Death and doom might lurk in wait even now amongst the crags and heather. But their shadows had not entered here.

Henri was asleep.

His head, pillowed on Burl's breast, rose fell with her breathing, lifting gently as on the swell and ebb of a wave—the mysterious wave of living breath. Her arms, like rounded, sunset-flushed ivory, held him closely and securely, that even in sleep he might know they were near together.

Her unpinned tresses flung backwards from her had moved softly on the couch of leaves in the faint wind blowing in from the outer world. So long they were, their black silken beauty roamed over the pillow of leaves, and trailed over into the edge of the rain-pool lit up with the flickering fire.

She lay, staring upwards at the roof of the cave, her eyes filled with a look of almost unearthly happiness—withal it was happiness doomed to rapid extinction, a meteor, not a calm-abiding star.

Across the projecting roughnesses and bulges in that rock-roof were countless swaying webs of dead spiders. Some of these, wind-blown, had trailed the rough rock walls. Great moths, too, hung in them. Grey lichens covered some of the stone. In the warm glow of the fire they looked like pink moss a-wander over the grey and black walls. Vivid patches of green, bright as verdigris, streamed out on those portions of the walls where cloud-bursts of year after year had poured in through the openings, and washed down the walls like torrents.

From the earth, along the wall-sides, grew shepherd's purse, sorrel, two feet high, with its wire-like stems tufted with its red seeds, and great clumps of coltsfoot leaves grown to prodigious size in this sheltered cave—

coltsfoot which old-time country folk smoke to ease chest complaints. There were wonderful feathery grasses, too, which swaying in this gentlest of moot winds, soft as a sigh, as though the very elements pitied these two who loved under the shadows of the wings of death, were like silver-specked foam-flowers swung on stems of fire.

But, strangest sight of all, was a primrose—a pale yellow star which had shone twice that year, Bedded in the ledge of rock which stood above the couch of leaves, and reflected in the rain-pool into which trailed Burl's hair, it seemed to smile down on them with something beautiful but untimely in its portent. Rapt in the transcendental glory of the fulfilment of their long-retarded love, Burl lay staring upwards, through a chink in the rock-roof.

Set round with the blue of the now serene night sky— such blue as only leans down over a white and silent world, snow-capped and wonderful— she could see a star.

Snowflakes no longer sizzled into the fire, as when they had first lit it.

The uncultured woman lay staring up at the star, her spirit greeting it, even as to her simple fancy, it greeted her back. Imagination and philosophy were things beyond her ken. All that she knew of tenderness and fierceness, instincts and rough experience of life had taught her. Yet it is a widening of both emotional and intellectual vision to love and be loved in return. With Henri clasped in her arms she looked up at this star, shining down between the rock-crevices, until its surpassing beauty and wonder made it swim in tears sprung from her deepest being.

Thoughts, like white birds, passed to and fro across her spirit's sky, ignorant and crude though it was. Perhaps the nearest approach to a clear thought in her pagan mind was: "That star up there is alive. It has its own form of life. From it to the grass in this cave, all is alive. There are no vacuums. The air is ripples of life. Henri and I belong to the same life. Love made us. Love is therefore God. Henri is God also. I am God. The grass is God. The star is God."

Whilst her emotional expansion and the thoughts arising from it was nebulous rather than clear under its vagueness, as stars within star-mist and radiance, these thoughts were beating. They filled her pagan eyes with tears at this hitherto undiscovered country. It is peculiar to all women, from the simplest to the most complex, if love has no spiritual significance, to be scarce an experience at all. Thus she lay dreaming, though the dream was rather emotional than intellectual, afraid to go to sleep for one moment, since to do so was to lose the consciousness of this great epoch in her life and Henri's. Her life, ever active, had needed always instinct rather than thought—swift instinct.

In this hour she more nearly approached intellect, its vast and mighty realm, than might have been thought possible. She stood close to its frontiers and heard in the darkness which barred her from that great land—a darkness only consequent on lack of education—the beating pinions of great thoughts and wonderful dreams and creative impulses journeying close to her, just past her, into that land where giants of the world and of the ages have travelled. She stopped at its frontier. The greatness of those thoughts stirring within her alarmed her. They sunk back into her breast, silently, and could not journey into the mighty realm of intellect. But so near as the greatest of all human emotions can swing one beyond the barriers of crude, hard, uncultured life so near as she could go—this epoch in her life, this hour of unparalleled happiness had borne her, yea, even though it was happiness gulped in the race between Love and Death.

Then she came back and found that she was staring up at a star. The fire was dying down. It needed more leaves and tree branches. Reaching to the pile of brushwood Henri had gathered, gathered at her bidding, since she had made him gather it to rouse him from thoughts of the horror they had fled from—she threw on the fire several handfuls of dry leaves. The cave became flushed with rosy light. Then she threw on twigs. They crackled and spluttered. Sparks flew up from them She lay listening to the lively, cheerful sound of them, and looking down at the profile of her lover's face, pressed close against her breast. Whilst Henri had drunk this cup of love to dispel thoughts of their approaching doom, Burl had drunk it with the eagerness for life, its refulgent blaze, the experience of it, joy, to take with her into the still land of nothingness.

For years his head had wearied to lie here.

For years she had wearied to have it rest here.

With resolute, iron will she shut out all thought of the menace hanging over them. There was only so much of life left to live. This little that was left was Love's alone— nothing to do with all life before, nothing to do with whatever followed after. And that Love was crowned not with roses but a cypress-wreath; came to them not with gaiety and laughter, but with a sombre and awful solemnity on his brows, affrighted her not at all. So much the less time there was to love in, so much the more must they hurry to drink in a short time the cup which others sipped slowly, and which was not emptied, in quiet, humdrum life, even when slow Death came with his lethe-cup. Though she could not have expressed her thoughts in these words, these were her thoughts, as she lay, from time to time, throwing leaves and twigs on the fire, till the dawn came up.

As the night in its snow-swathed beauty and soft blowing wind had been wonderful, so came the morning, in deep, hushed silence, "on silver-sandalled feet". Even the wind which had arisen and blown so gently during the night was now hushed. And in this great stillness which hung over a white world came a dawn rarely exquisite for the depths of winter.

It was as though very Nature, the insensate and cruel, the careless of what happens to the individual, bent over the cave so like the first home of her first human children, and murmured pityingly: "But so many days, children of mine who warm yourselves at my fires. Then you will go hence. I will be kind. Earth's beauty shall answer the beauty of your evanescent dream."

Burl and Henri sat on the couch of leaves, watching this dawn come up.

Against the snow which pathed whitely the space between the cave door and the great rock which had stayed the fireshine from flooding down the hillside was the trellised beauty of the blackberry brambles, its dark leaves outlined against whitened rock and earth. Frost and snow glistened on their edges and weavings. The far-off barking of a dog from one of the farms across the valley came faintly to their ears. Ice-drops melted by the fire, on the ledges above the cave, dripped with clear, cold sound. To the left a few pale stars were scattering, like silver sheep fleeing before the sun-shepherd' s golden rod. To the right were bars of amber and banks of purple, amethyst streakings and fire-gleamings, and saffron isles set round with green lakes of sky.

The eyes of the two lovers turned from the survey of this dawn which was different from any dawn they had known.

"The sun rises in our love," said their eyes, wistfully gazing each on each, on beloved features growing more distinct in the growing light.

"Shall we sleep by the fire this night, when this day which is opening has closed?" was their unspoken question. It rose in each heart at the same time. With a sigh, they looked out once more on the dawn, hand clasping hand closely, with the passionate desire to touch each other, to feel the tremor of love's first ecstasies of touch, even as they stared out on this dawn.

Slowly, as the sun came up across the valley, Burl withdrew her hand from Henri's. Slowly she raised her arms above her head, greeting its coming. From what primeval emotion that gesture of hers, that solemn salutation, came, Henri could not tell. The same look was in her eyes, on her face, as when in the darkness of Eagles' Crag she had expressed her desire for a funeral pyre on some Weak sea-shore lashed with the ocean-mists and tolling breakers.

'Blessed be the sun," she said in rapt, solemn tones, "We have lived. We have lived."

Her long arms dropped slowly to her sides after that salutation. There lay across her face that strange, wild, desolate look which Henri had often felt marked her out as one born to live alone, by some law of the universe, to be cast-off from crowd-life.

But to that look which he had so often beheld — that look aloof and sad and proud, was added a look he had never seen on her face before. It was though she defied the grimmest and blackest night of any death to blot out the memory of their joy. It was as though she cried out to the elements:

"I am no longer alone. I have broken the decree of the gods who gave me loneliness as a heritage. Now let their doom fall on me."

"Beloved," she breathed, laying her hand again on his.

"Yes?"

"I shall go this evening, to the gipsy camp," she told him.

"No."

His voice, sharp, with fear and amazement, was matched by his expression.

"You will need clothes. Jasper, or some of the others, must let you have some," she told him. "You can get away. You can get to one of the ports. From there you can sail to France. You can live in Avignon. There are my savings. You can have those. For years I have saved the shillings each week I got in Eagles' Crag. I have forty pounds—"

Henri gazed at, her in wonder.

"And—leave you here?" he asked.

She nodded, and stared from him to the of the landscape now brightening under the sun-rays.

"To face doom?" he asked.

She nodded again.

The almost flint-like practicality of the North was in her answer.

"Why should two perish—as we might—where I one would suffice? And why should that one not be I?"

"But, *ma foi*, it may be I who—" he paused.

"Who killed her," finished Burl. "Since we can never know that—since as you told me by the fire, last night, that you have rages which blot out memory, and since I also may have killed her in my sleep, we shall never know. It might be held that we had conspired together. Then both of us go where no sun shines. To go where no sun shines, no birds sing, no morning breaks the long night. That is death. Why should two go where one would suffice? It is wicked waste."

"*C'est vrai,*" Henri answered. "But I cannot leave you now."

She turned her face towards him.

Its wild strange beauty, stamped with that distant look which seemed to look beyond him, had upon it a question.

"One does not love and leave one's mate," he said.

"I believe," said Burl, slowly, "that it was I who killed her. I come of a gipsy race. I fell asleep hating her. Our race loves and hates fiercely. The Georgios are paler of face and paler of heart than our sallow, despised wandering tribes. I believe you are entirely innocent. Why then, should you stay and dance at the end of a rope?"

Henri shuddered even as she spoke the last words, He had fled in horror from Eagles' Crag, to get away from the sight of the old woman, smiling her ghastly fixed smile, and the lamp going out No thought of escaping the consequence of so dreadful a deed had been the urge which had made him fly.

But now the dread spectacle of so ignominious an end loomed up, dark and grim.

"But I—I hated her also," said Henri. "And we had had much wine. It might be—"

"Beloved, what does it matter which?" inquired Burl. "The thing is why should two lives be lost where one would do?"

He sat staring at her in stupefaction.

This North. Its economy was so fixed a quality that it could look at anything from a point of view of waste and base the most momentous of decisions on whether anything could be saved, the mere fact of saving waste making that decision not only obligatory but almost a religious duty.

"I am an extravagant mortal," he told her, with tenderness not without a little irony. "Both of us go, or none."

But none the less the grim spectacle of dancing on the end of a rope was now obtruded between them and the ceasing of the horror, which the love 0f the flight now gone had temporarily brought. It was not the fear of the old Medusa, sitting dead in her chair, in the lone house, under the midnight sty but the fear of death for himself which now haunted him.

"We may be days here. We will not think of it," he told Burl. But even as he spoke the words he knew that this awakened fear would never sleep now, until their doom was sealed.

"It will only be days," Burl told him. "We have brought no money. Even had we done so, to have gone to buy food would have been impossible, You will not, then, try to get to France—"

"*Non, non,*" he told her, passionately. "I shall stay with you."

'Then I must go back to Eagles' Crag to get food," she told him. "I would like many days here. The fire at night. To sleep by it. To love until we have had, if not enough, enough to be happy in remembering "

"The dead are dead," said Henri, sombrely. "They sleep in the cold dust and eternal darkness. No memories of kisses or embraces journey beyond to that patch of nothingness. *Tiens!* It is just as well. Otherwise the earth would be haunted—at least, by those who had died under forty. No, Burl. Nothing of all this which we have experienced travels beyond the grave, for there is no beyond. All ends there. And your Georgios who are Christians—they also leave human love on this side of the grave. That, the greatest of all human passion dies with the body they say. It is the most unique blasphemy that they should sanctify marriage and confine it to earth only. But religion is not logical any more than love. When we die, Burl, nothing of all this we have experienced, no memory of this cave, this fire, the wonder and glory of all we feel for each other, will go with us. Death is the end of that and every human experience. Hence the preciousness of life."

She gave a piteous sigh.

Henri was book read.

She was not.

In the imminence of the threat of death, foiled life and youth, eager for the continuance of it for their meeting elsewhere, for passionate and affectionate living on some other sphere, had cried out for some great beyond. This was the end, then. For the Georgios who were Christians left human love outside the range of heavenly attributes. She had no desire, therefore, for the cold Heaven where she and Henri might not desire to kiss, as they kissed here on earth. And Henri had studied. He would have known if life went on. It was even as her father had said. The sun was the source of life. One died and could not feel its warmth. One was then dead. And death was the end.

All through the day, until the sun sank, they sat together on the couch of leaves, saving when Henri walked restlessly about the cave, trying, but vainly, to throw from his mind the terrifying spectacle of imminent death. Burdened by imagination, he went over and over every horrible detail of the agonies to be, from the waiting in a wretched cell to the last grim phase, when quicklime would be thrown on his mutilated body, with his tongue thrust out betwixt his teeth, his neck wealed and empurpled by the strangling rope. The sweetness of life, even life without Burl, and shadowed ever by the recollection of her departure hence, became all the more a precious thing to hold on to, as he thought of exit.

Pacing, he would turn to look at her, sitting passively on the couch of leaves, her hair pinned up once more, and looking in the dim light of the cave like a heavy black crown. The calmness of her face, saving when she cast an anxious glance in his direction, irritated him. Then he would sit down beside her, and they would endeavour to forget the doom awaiting them, in kisses, every one of which now reminded them that it was one less they would take. The darkening of the cave as the sun dropped like a great fiery ball in the grey sky, the rising of the wind, which was puttering the snow on the hillside into fantastic snow-shapes of white mist, which went by to the wail of the gathering storm like ghosts, had become a gloom neither fire nor passionate loving could banish.

Hunger, too, had assailed them.

Since the night of their flight they had not broken their fast. The icy water of a stream the had drunk from went into stomachs empty of food. When Henri had last sat down on the couch of leaves, the gurgling of it, after his drinking, had sounded emptily through the cave. And as the darkness gathered, the wind blowing more loudly than its wont amongst the blackberry bramble round the door of the cave made him start. They had not gathered a big pile of brushwood this day for the night fire. The fire burnt low. The cave was full of shadows and blackness, like the black starkness of the end which awaited them.

"The cattle will be starving, too," said Burl. "Poor dumb beasts."

Silence fell once more. The cave grew darker. The fire was but a few red embers. The wind blew shrilly through the crannies of the rocks.

"Yes. But what can we do?" came Henri's answer, after a long interval.

The stars shone in the sky they looked out upon, cold, far-off, unfeeling.

They shivered with cold. Their bodies huddled together for very warmth to defeat the shuddering of the blood as the cold increased with the darkness.

"Beloved," said Burl, gently releasing herself from his embrace, "I am going to end this misery."

She rose, a tall dark form against the starshine and snow of the cave door.

Henri clutched at her.

"Not yet," he said, in a hollow voice.

Even whilst to-morrow, like the day that had gone, without food, became an agony to look forward to, he clutched at her desperately.

"I am going to bring food back," she told him. "And to feed the cattle."

"Going—going there!" he gasped, in horror.

She dragged her garments from his clutch.

"Either that, or we sit here and starve," she told him. "Besides, the cattle, they will be stamping in their stalls. Why should they suffer?"

"And I—I have to remain here, alone, till you return?" he questioned. "Perhaps I shall wait and wait, and you will not return. No. Stay here with me. Do not go. It will soon be morning. Morning. *Mon Dieu!*"

For a time he would not give in to the idea of her returning to Eagles' Crag. To wait in the cave, alone, wondering if she would return, seemed more unbearable than that they should sit together in the cold gloom, enduring the ravenings of hunger.

But at length he let her go.

"Keep the fire in," she told him, and before departing piled it up with the whole of the brushwood that was left, and waited until its cheery light streamed over the cave before leaving him.

"But one moment, yes, but one,' said Henri, several times.

And again, she would turn in the doorway and come back to him,

With agonized lips they kissed each other once more.

Their shadows kissed on the rough walls of the cave.

Then once more they would tear themselves asunder, Burl to go back to the horror-haunted eyrie on the heights, to bring food—food without which even love was of no avail, Henri to wait by the fire for her return.

"No. I cannot be left here. I will go," he had volunteered once.

But, even as he had spoken, fear had gripped him lest she should answer; "Yes. I will wait. You go."

She had not done so.

Their home a cave, it was yet the absolute reversal of the old primeval position of man and woman. But to Burl, descendant of a race in which the hardest burdens were borne by the women, there was nothing strange in this. Moreover, she knew that it would be better for her to go than to trust to Henri. To get food he would have to enter Eagles' Crag. The probability was that he would come away without it. The brief joy which could have been theirs, withal snatched on the brink of the grave, was going to be briefer than she had counted on. Determination that for a few days yet they would stay in the cave, eat and sleep, and gaze on each other, before the end, made her steps steady as she finally left Henri.

He had called to her, and half-way down the hillside, she looked back at him, waved her hand, but did not turn back, only motioned to him to go within. He could see her against starshine and snow. She walked erect—walking towards the horror of Eagles' Crag. Her form grew ever smaller amongst the scattered rocks which glistened under the cold light of the stars. She would be an eternity. Yes. An eternity. Even if she returned swiftly, it would be an eternity. And, down there amongst the rocks, forms might be lurking to spring out on her.

Tensely, he listened. But there was only the small sounds of the wintry night, the sliding of snow from some rock-top, with a cold, shuttering sound upon the ground, the blowing of the wind over the snowy wastes, the soughing song of some winter tree's boughs set amongst the rocks, the rusty sound of the bramble leaves, their stiff edges blowing against each other, and the drip of the ice-drops from the ledges above the cave door as the warmth of the fire struck up to them.

In the silence, else, he sat by the fire, nerves on edge, listening to every least sound, each moment like an hour, lengthened by this agony of tension.

Chapter Six

Snow piled high and drifted in deep drifts in the road above the ravine. It was empty, save of snow and wind, and the night sky bending over it. The trees to the right were snow-blown into all kinds of fantastic shapes against the blue of the starlit heavens. In all the earth it seemed that there were only the sound of her own lonely steps, crunching over the snow. Her skirts trailed along through it, sweeping its white waste. Her breath, hurried with the speed she went at, was a sighing murmur. She was almost running, now that she had got down the hillside, beyond Henri's sight. Such rocks as the winds had swept bare of their snow-covering, stood out inkily black in the whiteness of the landscape, as she went by. She tried to think of what she must bring back with her, and which way to return to the cave in order to most easily get the fuelling they would require. For the few bushes surrounding the cave they had now used.

The unlighted lantern swung in her frozen hand.

A few flakes of snow fell upon her arm, bare to the elbow through the opening in her cloak. She did not feel them. The stars shone down coldly. She scarce knew that they shone.

Eagles' Crag was looming up in her mind, not the entire horror it was to Henri, but something more terrible—a dark thought of grief, bitter and agonized grief.

The snow would be whitening the frames of the window-panes. The wind would be blowing the white ashes in the grate over the desolate hearthstone. The cows would be bellowing in the dark sheds, in an agony of torture with the milk in their heavy udders, half-mad and kicking the walls. The dark snowed-up coops would hold the cackling poultry which should have been fed at four. The horses would be champing at their mangers, chewing the wood.

And in the chimney-corner, in the unlighted gloom, by the dead fire with its white blowing ashes, old Jane would be sitting, stiff now as a board.

And old Luke, poor demented old man, where was he?

She knew he would have gone, fled at the sight of his mother, sitting in the dawn, dead, no more able to scold or threaten to belt him—silent, quite silent now, silent for ever.

Heavy sighs broke from her pale lips and fell upon the night air.

She had hailed the Eagle of Eagles' Crag, and this was what it had brought. Doom and disaster she had dared it to bring, so it brought love. It had brought death, desolation, and love, a purgatorial agony. But it had brought love. It had answered. She walked on, never wishing that Henri had never come to Eagles' Crag, even as this grief for the rack and ruin waiting for her at that place burst over her like a flood, with which her fierce, strong spirit wrestled, gathering together the thoughts it broke across—thoughts still of Henri, waiting by the cave fire for her return; thoughts of the things she must take back with her to make their last few days together as little oft physical torment as might be. Ah, but was it not all torment?

She walked through the wild waste of the cold and lonely landscape, swinging the lantern whose light had been lifted up to hail the spectral eagle. That also was burnt out. The oil was gone. Was it not all a torment, even this loving? But so many hungry kisses to snatch, so many hungry looks to appease, so many hungry embraces to satisfy—and still this greatest torment of all, to know that love could never be satisfied, that the more it was fed, the more it grew, an insatiate thing, a passion so great that she knew that for her part, had they lived to be doddering old people-it would have been a cup still unemptied, still with its mellow, though milder and gentler sweetness, when they went down the valley to that nothingness Henri said death was, with nothing beyond.

She stayed her steps, once, when nearing Eagle's Crag, and looked down on the cold gloom of the ravine. The tops of the trees, dark where the snow was blown from them, made it look as though a dark river wound along its hollow, where the winds were beating. And away, across it, were twinkling lights on the hills across. They looked like tiny golden stars. Each one was the light of a farmstead.

She went on again.

Just over Eagles' Crag, she paused again.

She stood staring down.

The snow was on the rocks above it.

Just under the rocks were the turrets where she and Henri had walked—how long ago? Distant time it seemed. They had thought themselves very wretched beings then. Looking back on that time, how happy it seemed they had been, compared with this dark and dreadful now. For then they had had hope.

She stood under the wide starry sky, struggling with sobs bursting up from her being.

Oh, that they were walking along those turret flagstones now, looking on these stars, mourning that they were separated from love's fulfilment, till old Jane died. Now——

She stood, choking with heavy sobs, and then started towards the place where the gipsy encampment had been. She only noticed now that it was all dark. No fire went up on the moor-edge. Silence and the night's dimness reigned there. The gipsies were gone.

She stood, pondering, even as with frozen hand she dashed the tear-spray from her eyes.

Gone. Yes. The gipsies were gone. The fire was not burning. No tents stood, dim shapes against its glow and smoke. Why was this? Had the camp merely moved on, following its nomad instincts for eternal moving? Or had some prowling gipsy, paying another visit to the coops, looked in through the window and seen the dead woman sitting there? If this latter was the case, the camp would indeed have moved swiftly, since, a persecuted race, the gipsies would fear that they might be made scapegoats for the deeds of Georgios, She stood staring towards the moor-top.

She could see the white flatness of it, the sparkling faint cloud of the snow, under the sky, from this height which looked across and down on it.

They were gone, those wandering children.

And with them had gone Henri's chance of escape, of getting to the ports and away to Avignon.

That which had felt an untold agony but a short time ago—that that moor-top should not have their fire going up into the sky, gave her now a wild and passionate though transient joy. The gipsies were gone. Henri would have to stay. This end which had come to all things would be the end for him also. He would not live, happy in Avignon, with some other woman, and the farm he had dreamed of. She had offered to Henri the chance of escape, of Avignon, of life without her. And tonight had meant to visit the gipsy camp and plan for his escape. The snow-covered empty moor-top across denied her this. If he had done this bloody deed, he would die for it, and she with him. If she had done it, he would die with her. Neither life would go on without the other. The passionate meteor of their ill-fated love would reach its height and fall down, extinguished only by death.

Standing looking across at the empty moor-top, something more nearly like calmness fell on the turmoil of her spirit than it had known since she had walked in, awakened by the torrent's water around her feet, to find Henri shaking his fist at the corpse of one to whom her last words had been words of bitter anger.

There was no need for the sacrifice she had spurred herself to make.

As they had shared ill-fated love, so they would share ill-fated death.

These were the last days of their life—for her and Henri together.

When they were parted, to await death, that would be the real end, the falling of the curtain of night.

Better, too, than any slow death for the one that would be left. Into Something or Nothingness to journey together. If into Nothingness, to be Nothing together. If to Something, to be conscious that they were together. But whatever happened, that it should be the same for both.

Slowly, she moved from the last bit of road above the rocks above Eagles' Crag and took the path up which she and Henri had clambered not many hours since as time was counted, but yet more long than all her life seemed to have been, for those few hours had held more of human pain and more of human joy than all she had ever known.

As she went down the path, the loud racket of the farm stock stamping, cackling, mowing and bellowing, came to her, telling its own tragic tale.

Old Luke had fled, as she had surmised he would.

The frantic animals were going mad, in coop and stall and mistal.

The kicking of horses' hoofs against the door of the stable came thunderingly loud on the silence of the night. The bellowing of the cows went through it like the deep notes of a chorus of trumpets.

Tears ran down her cheeks in the darkness as she stood listening.

She went down the rest of the path towards the house. It loomed, a black cloud through the starlit night. The stampeding of the cattle was now pandemonium in her ears. She went nearer to the threshold of the door from which she and Henri had rushed into the night, not long ago. Its eyriness gripped her. Within its dark and lonely gloom sat the old woman, stiff now as a board. She must creep past that terrible and silent form to get provender for the cattle.

Even as she opened the door, it seemed to her that upon the chill, dark air was borne that faint smell putrefaction sickly with death's odour.

The black gloom of the low roof weighed on her crushingly.

The chink of the lantern's loose wires against the side of the glass felt to echo through the place, now indeed a black vault.

Without Henri's imaginative terror, her simpler, more pagan nature shuddered back and away from what she might see on lighting the lamp which was standing on the kitchen table. It was the pagan's violent repugnance to the sight of death, from the sheer ugliness of it, from the hopeless nihilism it represented.

Slowly she advanced into the kitchen.

The wind was blowing in the chimney. Then it would stop. All would be dead still, till that mournful sound started again. The door she had forgotten to latch blew to with the wind. Every echo in the place awoke. She stood still, listening to them.

The smell of death—its first decaying processes —oozed to her from that silent figure whose shape she could see against the frosted windows, glittering in the light of the stars outside.

Should she light the lamp?

Yes. Best light it. Otherwise she might touch that grisly form—

Long shudders ran through her at the very thought.

Yes. She must light the lamp.

Standing upon the fender she reached up to the mantelpiece, found the matches, and then, with blood feeling to run thickly and heavily in her veins, struck one.

It broke off.

She struck another.

Its feeble splutter of light just shone on the blackness about that figure sitting by the window.

Then she gave a little cry of horror.

Something grey and stealthy had run from where the old woman was sitting. It bumped against the lantern she had set on the flagstones, giving a squeak. A rat! A rat! Rats dined on dead people, she had heard. No. She could not light the lamp. Best creep past that awful figure, without knowing what it looked like, what changes had stolen over it through the long, black night and the dawn and noon, till this night which now kindly obscured its dread looks.

Trembling in every limb, she stood with the matchbox in hand.

From outside came the pandemonium of the animals in their sheds.

Resolutely, she struck another match and walked towards the table.

The hollow roaring of the wind was in the chimney again.

Her hand touched the chill and frosted lamp-glass. She took if off, laying it on the table. Then, striking another match, she turned up the wick and lit it. There was no oil in the lamp. But the dim light of the wick would be enough.

She turned.

Then stood staring, paralysed beyond the ability to make the smallest sound.

Over the ghastly countenance was a white sere-cloth.

It had fallen to the shape of the dead lineaments. And it was moving—

Yes. It was moving, heaving, as though the dead face beneath it moved, stirring the cloth.

With a cry that came between her clenched teeth, Burl rushed suddenly to the lamp. She lifted it from the table and carried it to that dead face.

The next moment, a fearful shriek echoed through Eagles' Crag.

The sere-cloth was covered with death lice.

A heaving, ghastly multitude, the cloth was alive with them.

Staggering to the table with the lamp, Burl blew out the light. Her breath, faint, and almost as expiring in horror, had to blow many times. She rushed out into the darkness of the night, only knowing that each step took her farther from that horror in the chimney-corner. She pulled herself up the path by the bushes, the heather, the rock projections, and at last stood above the house. The stamping of the famishing cattle came up to her through the night. She listened to them for a moment. Then, turning, her hands pressed against her ears to shut out their pandemonium, fled once more through the night, on and up to the cave. As she went through the gap leading to the cave, someone barred her progress.

"Summat to do?" inquired a voice.

The rays of a lantern fell on her face.

Her eyes, wide with horror, stared into the countenance of the old native whose son had made away with himself for love of her.

She shook her head mutely.

"Oh, I thowt summat were happen up," said the old man. "Goin' up there?"

He motioned towards the hill.

"No—yes—" she said, through her stiff, pale lips. "I'll walk agate wi' thee, then. I'm goin' up thear," he told her.

The thought of Henri waiting for her, in the cave, roused her from the shock she had received. The old man had followed her through the gap. Their footsteps went over the snowy ground.

"Cowd an' late for thee to be out," said the old man.

"We've lost a sheep," she told him.

"Well, I've naught to do. I'll help thee find it," came the answer.

With despairing look she stared into the darkness. How should she shake old Jabez off?

"I were up at Eagles' Crag an hour sin'," said the old man. "The cattle sounded like they'd a' gone mad. I thowt there were happen summat to do—"

"Nay," she told him.

He was keeping close to her, his step side by side with her step.

With swift, desperate courage, she pushed at him suddenly and unexpectedly as they passed a rock. His feet slid from under him on the ice-surfaced snow. His lantern flew from his grasp, and being only a candle lantern, its light guttered out. It rolled down the hillside.

She ran, on and up to the cave, bursting in on Henri. The dull red glare of the fire lit the cave. He gave one glance at her face. The silence of the cave had become ominous. The wind's wuthering outside had a note of doom.

"Shall we go, or wait?" she asked.

The crackling of the dying embers sounded through the cave, before his answer came.

"Wait," he said, merely.

They sat down on the couch of leaves, arms about each other, kissing with pale, sad mouths, as the cave filled slowly with shadows and finally became quite black, the last embers expired. They did not move, or make any exclamation, even when they heard footsteps coming towards the cave. They clung closely to each other in these last moments they might have together on earth or throughout eternity.

Then, as the footsteps paused outside the door, they arose, standing together, then pale faces turned towards their pursuers.

Chapter Seven

Burl walked slowly round her cell. She had been here, in this narrow space, so long she had lost count of the weeks. Along the stone corridors she could hear the echoes of the wardresses' feet. It was evening once more. They were departing from their rounds of seeing that all prisoners were behind the locked doors. After those echoes died away all was silence, stony silence, so deep, so terrible she had to bite her lips to prevent a fierce wail bursting from them.

With a faint moan she sank down on her plank bed and stared across at the wall. Her gait journeyed slowly upwards to the tiny grid of barred window. A moonbeam was dancing on the wall She sat staring at it. Moonlight would be shining on the gorge, on the torrent, on the rocks. Far away she saw it all. But most bitter torment to think of, was the moorland breeze. This air felt heavy as the stone walls encompassing it. Breeze! Space! Sky! Sun! Stars! People outside this stone city partitioned off to hold so many living human beings, had all those things and did not even give thanks. Ah, if they knew what it was to be cut off from them, to live as in a great piece of stone honeycombed into cells, to feel no breeze lift the hair or stroke the cheek, to see no sky but a hand's breadth grey or blue, to scarcely know if the sun shone, saving that when it did the shadow of the gridded window fell on the grey wall opposite.

And to hear only the echo of one's steps, of one's sigh. She recalled old Jane saying that every time one sighed one lost a drop of blood. That was a lie. She had proved it. Had it been true, she would have sighed every drop of blood she had away by this.

But worst of all the silence, the terrible silence, the silence which seemed to be a living thing here; to ooze from the high walls, from the flags of the floor, until one got afraid of the sound of one's own feet, until one felt one must beat upon the wall and call through it to any other pacing on the other side of it, though one did not know them: "Speak to me. Speak. Let me hear a human voice. Speak to me, and I will speak back." But that was against the rules. All was rules here. One got up by rule the morning and laid down on the plank bed by rule at night. One was not a human being any longer. A rule pulled you and you rose up and found it was morning again. A rule said you must lie down. You laid down. You watched the shadows gather on the cell wall, and creep up, like a grey tide creeping up, growing darker an darker. Then it was night, night once again.

"Ah, but whatever anyone had done at me I could not put them in such a place!" was Burl's fierce thought. "I might kill them. I would not entomb them alive where the very echoes turn to stone."

Then she sat, in despair, thought fading into incoherency, growing blank like the stone wall of he cell. She forgot very existence. One felt to grow like stone here. One's heart grew like stone. One's mind grew like stone. The breath on one's lips grew heavy and cold. One scarce knew indeed if one breathed. And on each side was a heavy silence, cold and still, unless one heard pacing footsteps, which did not go on long, as a human being remembered it was against the rules. One was not only treated as not like a human being. One grew less like a human being. The very pulse of the heart beat more heavily and coldly and slowly, as though stone were growing around it and stifling its pulse. But the silence, ah, that was the most cruel thing of all.

And outside people were hearing rain fall on grass, and window-panes, and roads. They were speaking to each other very carelessly, not valuing that they could hear a human voice speak back to them. They had never known what it was to be shut off in a stone coffin with silence all about They could get up from where they sat in one room and walk into another. They could go out and see the stars over their head. They would say of any cramping circumstance: "It is as bad as being in prison." That was because they did not know what prison was like. Prison was Silence and Stone and Rules. Not about one ate or wore, for outside were people who wore rags and ate crusts. But they were not being driven mad by Silence and Stone and Rules.

She sat staring at the cold, grey wall.

The moonbeam had gone from it.

Even the moonbeam went soon, from a prison wall.

It just peeped in through the gridded window and fled. All beautiful things fled from here. Humanity fled from humanity, as it sat waiting, surrounded by Silence and Stone and Rules. One grew either fierce and almost mad, or turned half into Stone, so that one would not know one was surrounded by Silence and Stone and Rules which were also Stone.

She felt her own nature changing.

What nature would not change, surrounded by Silence and Stone—unless it were stone to begin with?

She had sometimes to beat down in herself wild, almost overmastering impulses to rush to the cell door, and beat upon it, and yell against the Silence and the Stone.

Even as she sat down, with bowed head, and listless droop of body-away in this great stone catacomb some living being gave way to impulse she wrestled with.

Someone was screaming.

The sound went echoing along the great stone place.

As though the sound had liberated in some other the same impulse, another scream arose from farther away. Then another.

There were the sounds of hurrying feet, of the wardresses coming to restore—order.

Burl walked slowly across from the plank bed to the door. Silence had fallen again on the great, grey stone catacomb. Order had been restored.

All the craving for space, for movement, of her gipsy forbears rose in her like a tide, and took her nearer to that door.

Then she walked back from it, till she stood against the wall.

She sprang rather than ran towards the door.

The full force of her fists beating upon the sounded their blows. She beat upon it till her knuckles were red to the bone.

A wardress looked in on her.

She saw a pallid gipsy face, its eyes fathomless tarns of utter misery.

"What do you want?" she asked, officially.

"To be hung," shrieked Burl. "To be hung. So that I will not know I am in this Stone Hell."

"Have you any complaints? You can send them to the Prison Governor?" she was asked.

The gipsy walked fiercely backwards and forwards over the cell floor before replying.

"Yes. I complain that I was not hung instead of being brought into this place," she raved fiercely. I am turning to stone in this Stone Hell. Get me hung and have done with it. I would say I had committed anything to get out of this Stone Hell."

The wardress walked away, after saying: "You can send in your complaint to the Governor to-morrow."

Burl sank upon her plank bed.

Henri, what was he feeling, surrounded by the same Stone, Silence and Rules? She had received no news of him. Away in another grey catacomb, what was he feeling? The thought broke the icy stoniness which had followed on her wild outburst. She lay weeping, thinking of what he was enduring, forgetting her own misery. Then, through the darkness, she lay, licking her bleeding knuckles. She slept a little before dawn. She awoke from a dream in which she was with Henri, in which they were close together, wandering under a blue, wide sky in an unfamiliar land.

She sat up with savage joy in her heart, joy which melted the stone of the despair and hopelessness which had gathered around it, during these eternal weeks.

She was sitting up on the plank bed.

Dawn was creeping wanly upon the walls.

Her outstretched arms touched their cold stone. She was back in a world of Stone. She was back in the Stone Hell. It was the dawn of another day streaming blankly over this Stone Catacomb. She lay down and turned her face to the wall, watching the tide of dawn creeping up over it, Henri would be watching this same dawntide creep up over the walls of his Stone Hell also. She watched it, trying to imagine that they were watching it together. Hard dry sobs jagged her throat. Dreams died, in this Stone Hell. Nothing could live here. Not even humanity. She was glad she would soon leave it. To be living and conscious amidst this Stone and Silence was worse than being dead. Henri had said there was nothing beyond. That death was the end of all. She perceived that there were agonies worse than simply ceasing to be. They were, to be alive in this Stone Hell. And outside, not far away, people were looking up at these walls and saying: "A prison!" They merely thought of it as a place where one was kept safely. They had never visualized it as a place where Humanity lived, pressed in upon by Silence and Stone, till they grew like it, or broke. Or broke. And Henri—

Somehow she knew that Henri would be very much changed when next she saw him.

How much she little dreamed.

Chapter Eight

Henri lay on his plank bed, staring up into the darkness of the night which filled his cell. For days he had eaten little, for nights slept little. The darkness of the cell reminded him of the blackness of death waiting for him, or for Burl, or for both of them. The narrowness, too, of the cell, for days had been a potent reminder of the narrow space he might soon occupy. Materialist through and through, no faintest hope tinged the black sky stretching before him. Death was the end of life, its experience, its sensations, its memories. The horrible and brutal details of the violent and enforced exit were lived over again and again. Already he had been hung a hundred times. Already he had walked with pinioned arms, in a cold dawn looking over high prison walls. Already, the priest, black-robed and solemn-faced had commended his soul to God.

He had laughed wildly and shrilly at the mockery it all was—to push a human being into eternal darkness as expiation for another human being having been pushed into darkness, and whilst murdering to justify murder, to drag the Deity into the business in a paltry attempt to hallow it.

But the worst agony of all had been to think of the quicklime which would be surrounding his body, the way his tongue would be thrust out, lolling hideously, the way his face would be contorted, and the great purple weal round his neck. He thought perpetually of this insult to his body—the body that had enjoyed the sunshine, breathed air, laughed, warmed at the taste of wine, toiled in the fields, been held in a woman's aims,

Had he been a dog dangerous to human society, he would have been shot. Being a human being he must lie in gaol for weary week after weary week, till very reason foundered, till morale rotted; on a set day to be taken into a crowded court, his brain supposedly fit to fight against the brains of those eager to convict him, who had been living during all these weeks normal lives. The bitter injustice of it all rankled in him. He lay, his face staring upwards, trying to picture the day that was ever drawing nearer. Finally, as the first beams of dawn stole through the gridded window he fell into exhausted sleep.

His weary mind, released from its torment, dreamed.

He was in Avignon.

No thought of Eagles' Crag, nor the agonies his going there had brought upon him, darkened the fairness of that dream. Burl was not in it. He was in Avignon, at the farm with the rich-coloured shingles on the roof. Doves cooed on it, perching thereon, their lustrous tints burnished still farther ta the sun. It was a warm, still day. The poplars beside the farm were motionless. He was sitting lax, looking out on waving, shimmering meadow-lands, all his. Goat-bells were tinkling away in the distance. The path wound through acres of wheat, its green ears ripening and hardening whilst he sat there. A dog came trotting along the path, and coming to him, laid its muzzle between his hands. He stared across over the wheat to the meadows. They were going to haymake next week.

"Henri!" called a voice from the doorway.

He turned, lazily, and let his gaze travel over her.

She was the *petite femme* he had dreamed of before Burl had come into his existence.

She was gay and vivacious and small and *charmante*, all the things Burl was not. She answered the lightness of heart which had been thrust away from him in this dolorous and heavy North, where life was a cold-coloured pewter pot holding the bitter fennel of struggle, of eternal toil and fight against weariness and the hard weather. As she came down the path she scarcely seemed to touch the ground with her small feet. She came towards him, sat on the little seat beside him, and he was surrounded by an atmosphere of love which was all laughter, all sunshine, all innocent beauty.

"But yes," he told her, gaily. "We will go to the city after the hay is in. You shall have the new dress—."

He awoke.

He was sitting up on the plank bed.

The cell door was opening,

The warder brought in his breakfast, set it down silently, after a cold, official glance at him.

It was only a dream. Only a dream. He was not in Avignon. He was in an English gaol, waiting trial on a charge of murder, *Diable!* Why had the gay little dream come to him here? The agony added to the untold agony he had gone through in the past weeks, unnerved him beyond measure.

The warder came in and took away the breakfast he had not tasted. The heavy door clanged to. With desperate despair he walked to and fro in the cell.

The sound of his pacing eventually brought the warder..

"Non, non! I have no complaint to make about the food," he told the warder.

The heavy door clanged to once more.

He continued to pace the cell.

Life, how it pulled at one.

He paced about from end to end of the cell. Backwards, forwards, backwards, forwards, many paces. Turn. Swing round on the heels. Backwards forwards, turn, swing on the heels.

The warder brought in his dinner.

"*Non.* I have no complaint to make about the food," he said. "Leave it. I will try to eat."

The heavy door clanged to once more.

He paced to and fro.

He only ceased pacing when sheer exhaustion compelled him to. Then, lying down on the plank bed, he stared upwards at the window, set high in the dizzy wall. A burst of afternoon sunshine came through it. It cast a golden square of light on the grey wall. A bird went past, its wings beating across that radiant patch of sunshine.

Ah, why had he not thought of it before.

He stared wildly at those wings of the bird beating across the glow of the sunshine on the wall.

Burl must have killed the old woman.

He had only to swear it.

Who knew?

Old Jane might have left him all.

Freedom could be his, and Avignon, and the *petite femme*, if that was so. In any case, life could remain.

"*Non, non,*" he moaned, in great distress.

But when the warder again opened the door and brought in tea, he found a remarkable change in Henri. He had made himself as spruce as he could. He had eaten the dinner.

"*Merci,*" he said as the warder set it down. "And could I have more sugar for the tea? And—coffee—could I have coffee instead of tea?"

The warder stared at him in amazement, "You may have anything in reason," he said.

"Very well. I will have coffee. And cigarettes? I would like the Egyptian ones."

"You may have them," the warder told him.

"Thank you. It is good to be able to get everything one wants in the world, and be hung afterwards," Henri told him.

The warder grinned and withdrew, closing the door.

It was only after he had got many yards away from it that he began to fully appreciate the subtle irony of the Frenchman's epigram.

Chapter Nine

For fourteen days the Eagles' Crag murder trial had come up in the court.

It was now drawing to its close, judge and jurymen, and even the most morbid of the fashionable crowd which had almost fought to witness the spectacle of two people being tried for their lives, were getting tired of it. There was now a distinct note of hurry stealing into the proceedings.

It was nearing tea-time on a sultry June day. Women were furtively dabbing their faces with powder-sachets from vanity bags, the heat of the court-room having made rivulets run down their morning make-up. Men stirred restlessly in their seats, wishing it had been permitted that they could smoke.

Henri and Burl stood in the dock.

But though standing quite near each other, they stood worlds asunder.

Henri's gaze was fixed on the face of the Judge. Burl's was staring away into space.

For days be had been fighting for his own life.

She had not fought at all.

What indeed was there to fight for, in a world where love and faith had perished?

On the fourth day of the trial the fact that old Jane had left Henri everything had gone against him, since he would have a motive in her departure, But the fact that he had not been certain about this, that he had thought it possible for her to have altered her will in Luke's favour, had been in his favour.

Burl was again being cross-examined.

"You have not denied that your lover may have seen you once, in your sleep, take a sword from the wall, and go to deceased's room, as to murder her?" inquired the prosecuting counsel.

"I have not denied it."

"You think it possible? You have wished her dead that you might marry this man when he had inherited all she left him?"

"It is quite possible."

"It was you who said, after the murder: 'Come, Let us go'?"

"Yes."

"And who had the brutal hardihood to go back to Eagles' Crag after the murder?"

"I went back because I could not bear to think—"

"Answer 'yes' or 'no'. We do not want to know why you went back or what you could not bear to think—"

"Yes. It was I who went back."

"It was also you who spoke of going to the gipsy camp and getting clothes that you might leave the country?"

"Yes."

"Do you still say that you are not guilty?"

Her gaze turned upon Henri.

From his pallid face to the whiteness of his knuckles, as he gripped the dock-rail, that look enfolded him. It noted all the anguish of his fear, all his desire to hear that he was free, even at the price of her death.

She drooped her head slowly.

As though the summing-up had been too much for her, she murmured, without lifting her head:

"I plead guilty."

A sensation ran through the crowded court.

She only heard one sound—Henri's intense sigh of relief. She moved slightly as he almost lurched against the dock-rail.

"Gentlemen of the jury," said the Judge, "you will now make your decision."

The jurymen trooped out.

Henri stood by the dock-rail.

He did not look at Burl.

She did not look at him.

After what seemed an eternity the jurymen came back.

"We find Burl Furber guilty of the murder of Jane Mowbray."

Shortly after, the awful words sounded through the court.

"To be hanged by the neck until you are dead."

She swayed a little.

She stood staring before her.

A sunbeam was gleaming over the wall at which she stared.

"To be hanged by the neck until you are dead."

The words rang over again in her brain. Down in the court a commotion arose. A countryman was standing up and would not be quiet. She looked at him vaguely. Then with a violent start recognized old Luke, who all these weeks had been no one knew where.

"Noa," he shouted over the tumult. "T'weren't Burl. T'weren't her. T'were the Lord. He answered my prayer an' told me to do it."

The prosecuting counsel sat down.

Another commotion arose.

"I saw him do it," came from a swart gipsy.

She dully realized that Jasper was there in court, Jasper who had robbed the coop. The mystery of the third wineglass was cleared, as he told how he had gone into Eagles' Crag, after looking through the window, seeing a drunken man and an old woman asleep, a bottle of wine on the table. He had taken a glass from the cupboard, drank, and been about to go away. The old woman had awakened and told him that they would be driven off on the morrow. He had looked in through the window once more, as he passed it, in returning towards the encampment.

He had seen the old man strike her with the sword. Terror had seized him. The camp had moved in the night. He had meant to speak all along, but had not done so, fearful that having been into Eagles' Crag he might be suspect himself. And, besides which, Burl was half a Georgio.

The trial was over.

Jasper came and spoke to Burl.

"How is Sophrono?" she asked.

"She died, through our moving," said Jasper.

He turned away with a heavy sigh.

The words acquitting the lovers were spoken.

The court emptied.

They went out into the free air.

A crowd was gathered outside. Would they go away separately or together? To save his neck the Frenchman had assisted in the conviction of an innocent woman. Slowly Burl moved towards Henri. She felt dizzy with the air and the sun, with the sight of the sky.

"Blessed be the sun," she said in a low breath, teaching his side. "It shines for us at last."

With a deep and profound amazement Henri looked on her face.

She had forgiven him.

He had hurled her towards death, to have life.

She had forgiven him.

Her suffering eyes said: "Let us be a little happy. Let us forget. Nothing matters since we are together."

"Yes. Where shall we go?" he asked, pale with remorse.

"We shall have to go back to Eagles' Crag," she told him, in surprise.

"*Tiens!* There?" he asked, shudderingly.

"Yes. You will have to get all the deeds and papers, and sell everything, won't you? Think— we shall soon be in Avignon."

"Yes," he told her.

They moved away, and were soon speeding towards the train which took them North. They would reach Eagles' Crag by midnight.

"Are you ill?" she asked Henri, from the dimness of the taxi.

"Not very well, " he admitted.

She took his hand in hers.

It was burning.

She drew his head down on her shoulder.

"Soon you will leave the North you have always hated," she told him. "Sleep. Soon we will be at the station. We will only be one more week at Eagles' Crag. Then, away."

"Yes. Away, away," he murmured.

But he could not sleep.

He felt ill, very ill, and wondered how he would manage to get up to Eagles' Crag from the station.

Only a few more days amongst its gloomy and tragic memories— then away, away. Avignon and sunlight like golden wine at last.

Chapter Ten

Summer walked in the gorge, by the torrent. So gently and softly fell the voice of the waters on the warm and scented air it seemed that it could never thunder round black rocks with a roar like the sea's. Great ferns, some of them three feet in length, had uncurled, frond by frond. Tiny ones hung in the crevices of great rocks, tossing with the gentle breath of the waters, moving to their flow, so delicate, so airy they looked like maidenhair.

This great North, rugged and savage, which produced the strong heather, the great oak, produced also some of the most frail and delicate of beauties in flower and herbage and leaf. There were gossamer webs stretched from one lady's-mantle leaf to another, not far from the torrent's course, with its mighty rocks, where the lichens and mosses, now out of the water, turned golden and green and red in air and sunlight. In the still, brown pools between the rocks minnows darted. The water's course close to the banks of the moor-sides was green with the reflected glory of new bracken. Whin was in flower. Blue bugle was out. Waterhaven swung its flesh-coloured bells in their fawny cups. Birds went across the sky on swift wing, carrying food to their yet unflown young. The air was alive with their goings and comings.

From the lichened rocks to the sky over which the birds went in their never-ending task of feeding birds which next year would go across this same sky, all was a-quiver and astir with life. Beauty unfurled a great banner, emblazoned with life—life of the soil, life of the water, life of the air. The sun rose and rolled through the heavens, streaming his light and warmth on all living things. In the long midsummer evenings the air was full of bird wings. Grouse and plover and curlews cried from the moors. Shrewd mice peeped from the long grasses. The sandpiper's voice went through the still golden hush of the days, thin and fine as a dream of a sound. Bees hung and swung on great clover flowers. Larks went up and sung their joy, fading out of sight as they had vanished through the doorways of the sun, then with a shrill, pulsing rapture dropped to mate and nest on the ground'

Henri sat in a chair by the fire, the chair turned sideways so that he could look out of the bedroom window.

The weeks had gone by.

He was still here, in Eagles' Crag, everything delayed by his illness. Despite the summer-time, its gloom yet depressed his spirits. For though outside the sun shone gloriously, the overhanging rocks prevented the rooms getting the benefit the increased light.

He sat listening to a fly buzzing in the window.

Then he heard Burl's feet on the stairs.

Night and day she had tended him. Her footsteps lagged as she came up the stairs once more.

She came and stood beside him, handing him the long envelope, watching him open it.

He almost leaped out of his chair after reading its enclosure.

"Sixty thousand francs," he said. "Sixty-thousand. Everything has brought its full value. We can leave, now, so soon as I am strong enough to go. Adieu, then, to the North. Never again the barbarious winter, the damp autumn, in which one lives as in wet hay. Come, smile, *chérie*. Soon, away to the warm lands."

He stared into Burl's face.

"You do not smile?" he questioned her.

She moved a little way off and stood looking out on the moor-slopes, the sky leaning down over the gorge.

"Never to see the heather swinging again," she sighed, her words almost a sob. "Never the mists. Never the curlews going through the sky's great wet greyness, like ships over a grey sea. Never to look up and see a plover's breast shining down white as she goes over the moor-top. Always to be where all is calm, and sunny, and pretty—

never wild and grim, and—grand. It is a great deal you ask me to leave.

"Never to be chilled to the bone by fogs, cold as distilled from ice," mocked Henri. "Never to feel the weight of the hills pressing one's very soul. Never the black heather. Never the cold grey skies. Never to wear the heavy clothes. Would we could fly to Avignon this moment, away from this North."

She came from the window.

"How can you love all that dreary wildness out there in winter?" he asked, pointing through the window.

"There is something the matter with those who do not love wild scenery," she told him.

The pain of being torn from the North she had loved was in her tone and words.

"*Tiens!*" he exclaimed. "There is something the matter with those who love rocks black with rain, trees bare more than half the year, winds that sweep and swirl so that one can scarce stand up against them. *Oui.* They must be savages.

"Those who are not a little savage, however deep down, are not much—" she told him, fiercely. "Henri, I will never be able to bear it. There are moods in which black heather and wet winds and the misted sky answer something in me. I shall go mad where there are no hills to see. Everything flat—"

"The breadth and width of the sky, nothing shutting it out," said Henri, eagerly.

"And our summer," she said. "There are none like them. They steal slowly upon us. Who can want summer all the time? They steal slowly away, the leaves slowly changing, falling—"

"*Oui,*" mocked Henri. "The summer is over by the middle of July. The leaves have all grown dark. The shadow of winter is approaching. The sun is withdrawing his warmth. It is all like a box of wet hay—yellow and rotting. The mists are everywhere, after August. That is English autumn."

He turned amused eyes on her silence.

"You will then stay here, in the North, rather than go where no heather grows, no grey skies hang, no wild water

162

dashes as though it were through from a weeping earth?" he inquired.

She eyed him steadily.

Once before he had thrown out a tentative suggestion that she might prefer to remain and not accompany him to Avignon. She had treated it then as a sick fear.

"That is an insult," she told him, "to suggest that I would remain behind. Where you go, I shall go. Yea. Though I never see a sprig of leather or a northern sky to my life's end."

She stood, her dark eyes regarding him sombrely, steadily out of her pale face.

"But, *chérie*—" he exclaimed.

The next moment she was kneeling by his chair. The fireelow flickered over both faces.

"I got the fear that you wished to leave me here," she said simply.

"This Eagles' Crag is making us both—not quite ourselves," he told her. "The sooner we get away from it the better. Last night I dreamed of the old woman. *Mon Dieu*. It was a terrible dream."

"Tell me of it," she asked.

"*Non, non,*" he denied. "It was too terrible."

Nor would he do so.

They had tea.

After which Burl went out to attend to the farm work.

Henri went back to bed at eight.

She took him supper, and then, as he slept, went downstairs and out into the beauty of the midsummer evening. She walked down the gorge, leaping from rock to rock. To leave it all, was the cry of her heart. Then— why, yes, that was love or love was nothing at all. To leave everything. To give up everything. If she could not do that, she was counting a bit of moorland soil, a rock or two, the hills and the moor-fowl, more than Henri. He could not endure this bleak, wild North which was as the breath of her being. Here he would pine. There in the land without these black hills, these moorland wastes, these towering crags and boulders, she would pine.

She could have lived on at Eagles' Crag all her life. Where, in all the wide world, would she find another spot so grandly beautiful as this gorge? From early childhood those moorland slopes had been familiar to her eyes. Those great rocks had been her tables, on whose tops she had sat, playing with imaginary playfellows, since she had no real ones. This torrent's roaring in winter had been great music to her, all the music she had ever known. Henri wished to go where there was music. Where would she find music like this torrent had made for her? Vines grew in the land to which they were going.

Everything smiled there, Henri had told her. Meadowlands, vineyards, sky, winds, all smiled. But who wished to live in a land where everything smiled and shone all the time? Mild, radiant, warm; but what of the beauty one would miss in grey mists and rolling clouds, rugged black moorland, land which looked as though it must have been as it was from the beginning of the earth; land which said in its rough wild outlines: "Untameable as the elements."

She sat on a rock in the torrent's midstream.

A star was shining down in the evening pools.

For an hour she roamed along the gorge, bidding silent farewell to every beauty it held, touching ferns and grasses, the whin and the blowing heather.

Then slowly, with grief growing more subdued, she walked back to Eagles' Crag.

The light shone from Henri's window.

She fastened up the coops before going into the house,

The last curlews were wheeling about the now dimming sky. The sunset hung over the darkening moors as they had hung from time immemorial, She drew deep breaths of the pure, wild air, Then passed into the house.

She lit the lamp, from whose glass she had once fumbled, sick with dread.

Its light streamed over the huge kitchen.

It fell upon the wall where hung the Daguerreotype picture of old Jane's lover, dead half a hundred years ago. She looked at it several times. He was certainly like Henri. But Henri had seemed less like that picture since they had come back to Eagles' Crag alone, without old Jane sitting there, without old Luke slinking about. Could it be, she wondered, that there were such things as spirits entering the bodies of the living? Certainly Henri had been almost devilish at times, when old Jane was alive. Could it be that seeking a body to live in again, spirits could take possession of a living body. If it could be so, since old Jane was dead, possibly Henri was Henri again.

She shivered.

But Henri was less like now—

"Burl!"

The tone in which Henri called her made her run up the stairs.

"What is it?" she asked, bursting into the room.

"She has been."

"Who?"

"The old Medusa!" he exclaimed.

"Henri, she is dead," she told him.

"Yes. But it was still the same Medusa. She has been. I awoke. She was standing, bending over me. *Mon Dieu!* Her hands, icy cold, were touching my brow. She must not have found him. She came back to me. *Mon Dieu!* Shall I never be free of her?"

"Beloved, you have been dreaming," she told him.

"*Non, non.* She was there."

She sat down on the bedside and tried to laugh. "Henri, you said the dead were dead. You said they slept in the cold dust, the eternal darkness," she told him.

"Would that they did," he told her.

There was a look of ghastly terror upon him.

"She is here with us, in Eagles' Crag yet," he told her in shuddering tones. "She has not found him. Or she seeks him still in me. *Mon Dieu!* We must leave to-morrow."

"Yes. But I still think you have been dreaming," she told him.

"*Non.* She was there. See how dimly the fire burns. See how the light splutters as though a shadow had gone over it, cold and dismal, I shall not sleep all night."

Burl turned and looked at the fire.

Then at the light.

Was it imagination? They did indeed seem to burn dimly as though a chill blast of cold wind laden with mist had gone over them.

"You must sleep here in this room for to-night," he told her wildly.

"Yes. Of course. I will sleep before the fire," she answered him.

Shortly afterwards she spread blankets and bedding before the fire. The soft muttering of the summer wind over the hills and rocks and moors sounded from outside. The window-sashes rattled. The glow of the great fire roaring in the chimney made radiance and shadows on the great ceiling.

"Do not go to sleep," Henri asked from time to time.

"No. I am still awake," Burl told him.

She was still awake at morning, weary from her vigil.

"I must have been dreaming," said Henri, in the broad and cheerful light of day.

"You must," Burl told him.

He sat up in bed.

She took up his breakfast.

When she entered the room he was looking through the window.

He was humming "Avignon".

Half-way through the song, he stopped.

"*Diable!*" he ejaculated. "That was her step along the landing. Listen."

Burl listened.

There was only silence.

"I heard nothing," she told him.

He turned on her with a fury so terrible she gazed at him appalled. For a moment it seemed to her that from his eyes looked not Henri, but one possessed.

The next moment he fell sobbing against her shoulder.

"Do you think you could go to town, and get all settled up, if I drove you in the cart?" she asked.

"Yes, yes."

"We will go after dinner."

"*Non.* But we will go before."

"Very well, then."

"But if she goes also to Avignon with us?" he asked, with horror in his eyes.

Burl felt a coldness steal through her breast.

"Come, get dressed. Come down. We will soon be off," she told him.

Later, as they sat on the cart, Burl driving, he asked, in melancholy tones: "Do you think she comes because she still wishes us to be apart? Do you think if I left you—?"

Burl sat up on the seat, the reins tight in her hands.

"If she comes to scare you into leaving me," she told him, fiercely, "she will come till she grows weary. She will tire before me. Do not mention leaving me again. When you leave here, I shall leave. Where you go, I shall go. We shall soon be away from Eagles' Crag. We shall see if she comes after us."

Henri gave no answer.

She cast a look at him.

Her look told him that if it was possible he could think of leaving her, after their stormy and wild loving had been crowned by her surrender, he was thinking vainly. His glance shifted from hers. He sat staring down into the ravine, with its tree-tops green and bright, their leaves shining in the sunshine, stirring in the wind. The song of birds came up to them. Here and there, a white-blossomed tree broke like foam on a green sea amongst the other trees. They could see the green patches of the bracken on the moorland across.

A blue sky, looking as though a brush dipped in the silver of dawn had been dragged over it, leaned down to the moor-top. The scent of clover, blobbed with morning dew and warm with the sun, came up to them from the other side the cart. They were passing the gap in the wall where they had fled up to the cave. Both glances went towards it, then turned away and met.

Burl's, fierce, tenacious, northern in its significance, swept Henri's face.

"You leave me now," it said quite plainly.

He sat looking before him, apparently looking at the road before them.

The old horse jogged along.

Then he sat looking down at the cart.

The spell of Eagles' Crag was upon him again.

He was pondering if he got away from Eagles' Crag, and left Burl, if the old woman would be satisfied. But even as the thought was in his mind, the question arose how to get away from Burl. There would be the sixty thousand francs, and the farm in Avignon. Taking Burl with him, would the old woman follow them?

Then, such was the morning's beauty and brightness, the thoughts passed from his mind. He knew, as the cart rattled over the town pavements, that his nerves had suffered from the terrific strain of living in Eagles' Crag. Would that they were not going back there this night. Would that they were far away.

"Away," Burl heard him murmur.

She laid her hand on his.

"In a few days we shall have left Eagles' Crag," she told him. "I shall be glad also."

And looking into her face he saw its worn look, the shadows the dreary years had left, the sad darkness of her eyes, the wistfulness of them, looking also towards Avignon, though she must We heather and bracken and grey skies and hills behind, never to look on them again whilst she lived; leaving in return for all these things which had been her one joy at Eagles' Crag until he came —merely him, Henri.

Two hours later the cart was going back along the road over the ravine.

"See!" exclaimed Henri.

Burl turned her head.

"See how like an eagle that looks," he said.

They stared at a great cloud going over the sky.

"It is a cloud," Burl told him.

Then she stopped driving, the reins falling iron her hands.

The cloud had gone.

One moment it had been there.

Now the sky was empty.

Swift as they knew clouds could travel—-

Fear was in both their eyes.

"We shall have to go back and wait till the business is quite settled," Burl told Henri. "But two days now."

"And two nights," he answered. "Could we not stay elsewhere? Need we go back to Eagles' Crag—"

"The new tenant comes in two days. Then we can go," she told him.

Chapter Eleven

Thunder rolled round the great rocks. The hills stood black almost, under a brassy sky. Streaming vapours filled the gorge, right up to the moor-top. Across the sky's lurid and wild light, in which the trees had somewhat of the strange colour which is seen when a sun eclipse is on, travelled swift clouds, like battalions of epic warriors, with black spears and wildly-careering, wind-driven horses. Cattle had moved from upper to lower ends of fields. Poultry huddled together behind walls, with the instincts of their kind.

An occasional shaft of lightning went like a flash over black rock, dark moor, or streams that sounded also to have a hoarse and stormy note in s gloom which had ridden down so swiftly et a bright summer's day. Then the thunder would roll again, like a mighty organ pealing against the rocks and the echoes reverberating on and away along the hills. The moor-tops fetched, looking almost as black as in winter against the livid and angry sky that bent down overt it, so louring that it seemed at each moment as though the thunder clouds must burst. But so no drop of thunder-rain had fallen. So thick the gloom, there was no colour of flower, however bright, but looked hung over with the grey mist of the storm, almost dense as November fog. Within Eagles' Crag it was dark as midnight, though the clock stood but at eight.

When Burl had gone out to bed the horses down, and give them their feed, she had looked up at the house, with the rocks towering above it in this gloom which seemed deeper over it than anywhere. Despite her love of the wild North, she had felt, withal its stupendous grandeur, something like fear. The rocks towered up into the clouds like great slabs and pinnacles of iron. The torrent's voice had a sullen roar she never before heard in it in summer.

The sky stretched over the streaming vapours which clotted the hill-slopes with a vast of dolorous gloom which looked as though it could never brighten. Hades itself could have looked no more grimly gloomy. And Eagles' Crag, shadowed by those rocks, was ebony-like under them. Its chimneys were dark as rocks above. Its roof—an overhanging beetling gloom, which made it seem as though the place scowled—scowled back at the menacing sky, the vapour-filled gorge, at the black torrent, a demon's wild eyrie defying the fury of the oncoming storm.

The thought of the eagle they had seen, returning from the town, was in her mind. Had it indeed been an eagle? Or only a swift-scudding cloud? Or, nerve-racked by all the traditions of this old lace, its ancient gloom, its weird legend, had the spectral eagle been all imagination, born of their superstition, and the wild effects of moorland mist and moonlight, all the time? Could people live in places like these, wild and remote from social intercourse, with no exchange of thoughts from other minds, no pouring out of their own thoughts, in return, and be quite normal-minded? She doubted it.

Old Jane had been absolutely unlettered. Old Luke the same. She herself was well-nigh without culture. Henri was a creature of almost super-sensitive imagination. Might they not all have imagined the eagle, a spectral thing which swept and hovered over Eagles' Crag as a portent of coming evil? Even as Henri, shattered by his incarceration in prison, following on the dreadful night in which he had found the old woman dead, coupled to the savage intensity of her fancy for him, her fixed idea that he was the lover of her youth come from the churchyard and entered into his body, might have imagined that again she had stood bending over him, her fancy still unobliterated by death, which supposedly ended all emotions?

So thinking, Burl hurried into the house.

Henri had lit the lamp an hour ago.

But so huge was the kitchen its rays scarce travelled beyond the top of the table. The walls were dim. The corners were black shadows.

"What a night," said Henri. "I wonder if this storm will last long?"

He stooped to the coal-box which stood in the ingle-nook, and picking it up, tipped more coals on the fire. The flames went roaring up the chimney.

"Suppose we stay up all night?" he asked of Burl.

"We shall be very tired," she told him.

"Yes. But I do not want to dream again," he told her.

"It was certainly a dream," she answered. "Yes. We will sit up if you like."

"After this night, but one more night here," he said.

There was an eagerness, keen as pain, in his voice.

He sat down by the fire.

"Yes. The new tenant comes the day after to-morrow," she told him. "We can leave by noon. I will get all packed up by to-morrow. You can help me."

"Pack?" he questioned.

"Yes?" she questioned his question.

"What do you wish to take?" he asked.

"I would take the heather with the wind blowing over it, if I could," she told him, with whimsical sadness. "But I cannot."

"*Tiens!* I am glad of it," he replied.

He went to stand by the window and looked out on the lowering sky, the gloomy landscape.

"One can very well imagine the ancient Britons," he said, ruefully, his back turned to Burl, "when looking out on a scene like this. Wild folk should live in such places, not civilized beings. Yes. One can imagine ancient Britons—"

He came back to the fire.

Over the string across the mantelpiece hung a whole row of socks. They had bought four pairs when in town. There also hung his old socks.

"I will do some darning," said Burl.

"No. Talk to me," he said. "Cal with me, as the old Medusa—"

He broke off, and stared wildly at her.

*What demon possesses me?" he asked, almost in a frenzy, to call her 'old Medusa', when she is dead?"

"It is not very kind," said Burl.

'No. I am aware of it," Henri admitted. "Burl, do you believe that before I came here I had a very kind, warm heart?"

She looked at him in wonder.

"Yes. Yes. I am sure you had," she said, earnestly.

His own tone had been so earnest, so unlike his usual half-jesting tones, that all the earnestness in her answered that simple question of his.

"So soon as I entered Eagles' Crag—even before, as I stood outside in the gloom—I changed," he told her. "Why? Why? Why? Unless she was right and some spirit did enter into me—"

"Henri," said Burl, with loving firmness, "we are going to play dominoes. Get the box out of the table drawer."

"But yes," he told her, with almost childish delight in his tones, "we will play for money, shall we?"

"No. I shall not play for money," Burl told him. "This is just to pass the time on. I shall not encourage your love of gain, always gain."

She had spoken lightly.

To her amazement he fell into almost a frenzy of rage.

"We will play for money or not at all," he finished up with. "Sit down. Do as I tell you. We will play for two francs. I will deal."

The shuffling of the dominoes over the table followed on his command.

"Henri—" began Burl.

She had been about to reproach him for the way he had spoken, to remind him that he was not absolutely likely to get all his own way on every point.

"Sit down," he thundered.

She stood staring at him in sheer amazement.

"Sit down, can't you?" he almost yelled.

She opened her mouth, fierce words on her lips. But she never spoke them. Staring out of his eyes, stamped on his face, was the same look as in the eyes of the Daguerreotype on the wall—nay, surely they were the same eyes, not eyes with just the same look. His very features had changed. It was as though they wore the stamp of another personality.

"Very well. I will sit down," she said, with what dignity she could command.

Then he laughed, in sheer light-hearted gaiety. The look passed from his eyes, from his features. He looked like Henri again.

"There. A dozen. My lead," he told her gaily.

The first game Henri won.

He scooped the couple of shillings she had lost towards him. He laughed, and Burl laughed with him.

Once more he dealt out the dominoes.

"Four francs—we will play for four francs this time," he said.

"But, Henri—"

"Four francs, I tell you. *Tiens!* What is the good of playing if one does not play for money? Four francs! Then we will double it to eight. Why are you looking at me like that?

"Because I do not care to play for money. Nor shall I do so," Burl told him.

"You will not?" he asked. "Why?

"Because I do not care to."

"You will play whether you care to or not, because I tell you to," he said.

She stood staring at him.

"That I shall not," she told him, with quiet stubbornness. "You have no right over me to make me do anything I do not choose to do."

With one sweep of his hand he swept the dominoes off the table. They flew wildly in all directions. In the silence which followed they stood looking at each other.

Suddenly, he laughed.

"Forgive me, *chérie,*" he said. And began to pick up the dominoes.

The look that had been again on his face, faded. He sat down by the fire after placing the dominoes in the box. Burl sat down also, and took a pair of socks from the line across the mantelpiece. The brief disquietude she had felt passed away, the uncanny feeling that the strange change in his looks and features had been from his own looks and features to those of the man in the daguerreotype. It was indeed time they left Eagles' Crag, she thought, as she darned away at the socks. The clock struck the half-hour.

Immediately it had struck, the house was shaken by a thunder-clap which made them think the bolt must have fallen just above the house. From flagstones to roof, the great building felt to rock. Then across the darkness which was now grown so dark outside that the trees were one blackness, the moors inky hedges driven against a sky of brass, the lightning forked across the dismal gathering night.

For hours the storm raged in the black night. They sat watching it. The thunder would roll, its echoes sounding back from the rocks, peal after peal, so that above the roof it sounded as though the gods of the storm were having the crags for instruments to beat out savage and barbaric harmonies. The black sky outside would open.

It was then as they looked into abysses of livid flame and sheets of fire. The lowing of the terrified cattle came from the stalls.

Some great thunderclap more terrible than usual would sound. It was as though tons of stones were being shuttered down on the rocks. Eagles' Crag would shake, as to its foundations. Then the echoes would die into silence. Tick-tick, they heard the clock. And Henri's voice talking of the farm in Avignon, would run on, until the next thunder-clap drowned it.

They had supper, sitting by the windows, looking out on that scene of storm, a picture in black of night illuminated with lightning's finger. He was Henri again. The fear that had taken hold of Burl as he had become so like the Daguerreotype on the wall—the Daguerreotype of old Jane's lover, a likeness she had noticed as she had come down from the turret and seen him by the rays of her lantern, years ago, on the first night of his arrival at Eagles' Crag, was gone.

They banked up the fire once more.

Sleep came slowly down on their eyes, pressing ever more heavily, despite their determination to keep awake, as the night wore on.

The great fire threw its glow on the hearthstone.

In the chimney-corner where old Jane had been wont to sit the shadows hung black. By common consent they had pushed the chair she had used to sit in into the corner. It stood there, with the tragic look any empty chair has when its erstwhile owner lies on the ground.

A wind-driven storm of rain had followed on the thunder and lightning. All round the house was the raving sound of the heavy rain beaten by the wind-storm. Rain blew down the wide chimney into the fire. It ran down the windows black with the night outside, which held the reflection of the lamp, and those two sleeping figures, their faces rosy with the fireglow and sleep, their expressions soft with the contentment of the thoughts they had fallen to sleep with, that when one more night was gone they would have left Eagles' Crag, gone from whatever eyrie spell it held, beyond the shadow of its walls, to happiness and prosperity and life and love, their heritage.

"Henri," breathed Burl, sitting up, wide awake.

She stared across at him.

What was it that had awakened her?

The Frenchman was sitting in the chair, head propped up on his hand, legs outstretched across the hearthstone—red in the glow of the yet great fire.

The rattling of the window-frames, the tick of the clock, the wind and rain outside, alone broke the stillness.

But between him and Burl what was that shadow which seemed to be stood by him, looking at him?

Her eyes, wide with fear, stared at it.

What was it?

She tried to speak to him, but her breath froze before it could part her lips.

And it was not growing less distinct as she looked, but more distinct. From being a thin, scarcely imagined shadow, which might be a smoke-cloud blown down the chimney by the wind, and curling away into nothingness, it was taking a more opaque outline.

With blood turned to ice in her veins, Burl sat stiffly on her chair, realizing with awful horror that she was looking at old Jane. The tallness of the unstooping figure was more pronounced than when she had been alive, even when anger had straightened it. Its lineaments were not in the flesh of this world. Yet they were growing ever more distinct. The great kitchen was growing more dim as though the force of the old woman's personality was reducing the material solidity of material things into the dust-atoms of which they were built and which time would claim as mere transient dust compared with the inextinguishable matter of the spirit. The form of Henri himself was growing dim along with the furniture and even the lamp s flame. And as it darkened and dimmed, until it looked no more than a shape made out of rather heavy cloud, Burl, her hair rising slowly on her head, without the power to warn or awaken him, saw on each side of him two shapes which began to glow, like incandescence on the darkening and dimming room.

She realized them as emanations arising from his sleeping form. On one side were radiant and warm-tinted colours, violet and rose and green, all mingling exquisitely. On the other were darker and more sombre shades, shot through with crimson, which gave to the other shades the look of a stormy cloud lit by the last blood-red glares of the departing sun. Slowly she saw the dark and sombre shades travel over the brighter and warmer and beautiful tintings.

She saw old Jane's face contort into something like laughter.

She stretched out her fleshless arms to this emanation of Henri—Henri dark and cruel and wild—Henri, who with demonic *bon mots* had often frenzied her last days. Slowly her face turned from him to Burl.

Upon it was the old expression, the expression ridiculous as tragic, the expression it had often worn as she had looked across at Burl as to say: "Henry's cal-in' with me" Or "He's gannin' with the old woman again an' leavin't young 'un."

Then with frozen will as frozen breath, Burl saw the old woman go nearer to that emanation which had blotted out the Henri all warmth and gaiety and beauty.

She knew somehow that if that fleshless old woman touched him, he would wake no more.

"Henri," she screamed.

Henri sat up in his chair, staring wildly.

The figure of old Jane went past Burl's chair. It flashed upon her a look of terrific jealousy, hate, and triumphant vengefulness. It said, with a swiftness no mortal thought could weave itself upon mortal countenance: "You've got Eagles' Crag. But Henri'll gan wi' me. He'll gan wi' th' old woman. He's him."

"*Diable!* Why did you awaken me?" grunted Henri.

Burl hesitated.

Then, recalling the already overstrung condition he was in, she said, with a great effort: "I got nervous, listening to the wind and rain outside."

And as she spoke, her gaze went towards the Daguerreotype on the wall.

It had no expression.

Its expression was on Henri's face, in his eyes, his features, savage-wild that she had awakened him for so trifling a cause.

The next moment it was gone.

They sat and watched the dawn come up across the moor-tops.

Chapter Twelve

On the morrow, at ten, the new tenant of Eagles' Crag was to arrive. All day they had worked, getting all ready. Evening of their last night in Eagles' Crag found them tired. The excitement of being about to depart at noon on the morrow was upon them.

"I am going to the station to get our tickets," Henri told Burl.

"Shall I go with you?" she inquired.

"No. I'll be back soon," he told her.

It was not until he had gone that a vague uneasiness fell on her spirits. He had departed hurriedly. And as he had stood in the doorway, upon his face had been a melancholy, lingering look, almost like—yes. After he had gone she realized that it was a farewell look.

Putting on her outdoor things, she locked up the place, and hurried after him. He had been gone ten minutes. Burl, standing on the highest place she could find, she saw him going down the road. Gone without her.

She ran down from the height she had stood on to survey the road, and clambered down into the ravine. Going along through the trees, she could get to town before him.

It was childish to think he could go without her, leave her here, at Eagles' Crag. But the agony of it.

She went along between the trees that arched over her head in their summer greenery. The wind was rustling pleasantly in the leaves. It was the most desolate sound she had heard in her life. She hated the leaves for singing in the wind when she was so wretchedly miserable.

Henri was leaving her.

No. He thought he was leaving her.

She was passing the ravine whose top just fronted the road where the gap was, leading to their cave. Her cheeks burned with fierce pride. Leave her, after that. Her trembling limbs went on again, steadied by a determined will. Leave her, here in this North, to think of that night in the cave, for ever. Leave her, with nothing but the sky, the heather, the blowing winds, all of which would bring memories, so that she would see and hear them, her heart feeling grey as the sky, her mind crying with the wind's wail over the heather. But he would see whether he could leave her like this, so easily. Frenchwomen, perhaps. But not northern women. And not gipsies.

She rushed along through the trees, falling sometimes as her feet caught in the brushwood. Then she would run on again. Old Jane—yes—was to get away from the fear that the old spectre would follow them, which was taking him from her. But a living woman, with blood in her veins, was stronger than the ghost of an old one laid amongst the churchyard dankness wrapped in blanket of dust.

With cheeks pale with dread, looking almost like a ghost herself, she rushed on through the trees. The birds hopped from one bough to another. Rabbits sat playing on one grassy patch of evening bank. Velvety shadows from trees fell on the amber glimmering made by the trees on spaces of grass. Splinters of golden light touched turf edges and glinted through the interspaces of the foliage. The stream clattered around its pebbles and stones. Swift as an arrow goes from the bow she went in pursuit of Henri.

She reached his side as he was coming out of a shop where he had been buying clothing. They stood staring at each other.

Upon his face she read his disappointment, then guile.

Smarting of heart, her own guile endeavoured to match it.

"I came down to get a few things I require," she told him. "Did you get the tickets?"

"*Non.* I was so long in the shop. There was not time. We will leave it till morning."

"Yes."

She knew he had got but one ticket.

She must not sleep this night.

He would be gone else, in the morning.

As they walked back, along the road over the ravine, her gaze went towards the cave. She saw again the rough walls, the leaping fire-glow, the couch of leaves, their two forms lay looking up at the stats, thinking of the wonder and beauty of life.

And he would leave her.

Would he?

Not unless he killed her first.

The thought sprang to her mind as out of the glowering dusk. It caught her breath as it came, caught it savagely. They walked on.

Chapter Thirteen

Yes, I was leaving you. You were right in thinking so," said Henri.

It was midnight.

"Why?"

Her apparent calmness surprised him agreeably.

"*Tiens!* Eagles' Crag has been too terrible. I wish to go alone and forget it as though I had never lived here," he told her. "To take you with me—"

He paused.

"Yes. You have not a nature that can surmount storm," she told him. "You are shallow, Henri. That is why you do not like our North in the wild winter. Those who do not love a place in winter do not love people when storm comes. They love only in the sunshine and the peace.

"Yes. I am very shallow. Not worthy of you," he told her.

"You will do," she told him, tenaciously.

"*Tiens!* You would be very unhappy with me."

"I know it. People are born to have some measure of unhappiness. It would not sunder us."

He looked at her recklessly.

"I have got but one ticket," he told her.

'You will get another in the morning " she answered.

"*Non.* Not unless you buy your own," he retorted.

A blaze of withering scorn went over her face for a moment. Then she recovered.

"Old Jane left me a hundred. I will buy it from that. And my trousseau. Your Frenchwomen always buy themselves trousseaux, don't they? I will buy mine."

Their eyes challenging and challenged looked deep into each other's.

"I have told you you will not be happy with me," said Henri.

"I have told you few people ever are. I can stand unhappiness. It will be nothing new."

Upon her face came that strange wild look.

She tossed her hair back from her brow. When it swept back like that—

It was no longer the lover who spoke now.

"Burl—I shall never forget Eagles' Crag if I take you with me. Let me go. Let us part peacefully. We have loved—and go our ways. We have had that."

"Had?"

The past tense of the phrase had an electrical effect on her.

"That which you would remember with pleasure I should remember with agony—if you go," she told him. "But you are not going, Henri. You cannot."

Her last words were a wail.

"Let us have supper," he asked.

As yet they had not dined, late as the hour was.

"I shall always remember the cave, *chérie*," he said, tenderly.

Her eyes became black tarns, sunless and wild.

"Do not drive me mad. If you must go, do drive me mad by speaking of that—since you go," she told him.

They ate to the tick-tick of the old clock.

She brightened during the meal. The pallor that had tinctured her cheek was less deathly.

"I have made over Eagles' Crag to you," he told her. "The new tenant can lease it, or you can stay on here."

"You have done that?" she inquired.

"Yes."

"I shall like living here when you have gone," she remarked, with no tremor of voice, no reproach of look. "In another eighty years or so I will look like old Jane. And the Daguerreotype on the wall will remind me of you."

He gave no answer.

That she was taking it so passively was a tremendous surprise.

She heard his feet go up the stairs.

She dragged from its corner the chair where old Jane had sat for seventy years almost, in the lonely gloom of

Eagles' Crag, spiritually a pauper. She sat in it, as trying to think of the years in which she might so sit—alone.

All through the night she sat silently.

As his footsteps stealthily creeping down the stairs to escape her sounded, she stood up.

He started in seeing her there.

"*Adieu, chérie,*" he said, with remorseful tenderness.

His eyes were wild with desire to get away.

She saw them.

Even as he saw the gipsy dress she had put on, to remind him he was leaving a gipsy, that in the firelit cave they had broken a tile together.

She gave no answer for a while.

Then—

"*Adieu,* Henri," she said.

"*Adieu.*"

Dawn was coming over the hills.

He noticed that she had stacked up the fire with great logs of wood, as they had had it in the cave. The fire made that same sound, wood crackling and blazing.

The gipsy fires in her were smouldering.

He saw it in her eyes.

Without offering to him her hand, she turned to the door.

"*Adieu,*" he said once more.

"*Adieu,*" she answered, a chill monosyllable.

The next moment he flung wide the door and rushed out into the dawn.

"*Adieu,*" cried his heart, deliriously to the black rocks jutting up in the pale light. "Adieu, wild, dark land of mist and moors, *adieu*, wild, fierce woman. A gay little *femme* waits me—"

And in the delight of his heart that Burl had not made it more difficult for him to go, he hummed "Avignon".

Chapter Fourteen

He saw her.

She was standing on the stone above the gorge, above the torrent, by whose waters, touched with the breaking sunrise, he was going.

"*Adieu!*" he called once more.

For answer, she raised her tambourine above her head, and tapped it to a mockery of bell-music which travelled to him. Her face, pale in the dawnlight, was surrounded by the waving curtain of her flowing hair. Her cloak waved in the wind. Her white arm gleamed against the gloom of Eagles' Crag, which was behind her, Eagles' Crag where she would stay for ever—alone.

She was dancing on that stone above the gorge. He stopped staring up at her.

She was dancing him the gipsy dance she had danced in the cave, before she had thrown herself into his arms, the wind their priest, the stars their witnesses.

Dancing, whilst he left her, whilst her heart broke, as he knew it was breaking.

Awe, the awe the North had ever thrown on him, seized him, held him a captive for a moment, to that figure up there with the last night stars over its head.

"Henri—remember only this—" she called.

He paused still.

Tiens! She was going to call some endearment after him to remember.

He waited.

"It was you who murdered her," she called, gipsy laughter in her voice. "Not old Luke. He only said he had done it to save me. It was you, Henri. You. Now forget Eagles' Crag if you can."

Henri stood.

What dark recollection went over his mind?

If what she said were true he would never get away from the memory of Eagles' Crag. If she lied—

The next moment he was running back.

With a flourish of the tambourine she ran.

He followed her.

Two minutes later they faced each other.

"I do not know if it is true," he said, thickly, but I am going to kill you."

She laughed and ran round the table, still beating on the tambourine, tirra-lirra, tirra-lirra, her voice mockingly singing the dulcet words as she stared at him, defying him.

She ran as to avoid him.

The next moment the full force the sword he had taken from the hall went through cloak, through breast, through heart.

The tambourine clattered to the floor, its bells jingling on.

"*Mon Dieu!*" gasped Henri.

He was kneeling beside her, where she had fallen on the hearth. Her hair streamed over the hearthstone. It gave her a look of being floating, her hair lifted and flung outwards by the tide. It was flung back from her brow, lending to her countenance that strange, wild nobility. There was laughter in her eyes, gipsy laughter. And over it and their darkness a film was spreading. She was quite dead. Little crimson bubbles of blood were on her lips.

He rose to his feet.

The look in those eyes, under the film of death, was of ineffable love.

It struck him with agony, swift and mortal as the blow he had dealt her.

He staggered to the table.

The lamp was still burning.

From under it poked a note.

He held it in his shaking hands.

"Beloved," it ran, "I knew you would do this. Go now to Avignon. No living gipsy is ever left."

A cry of anguish rang through Eagles' Crag.

Then a moment's silence, and a groan.

All was still again. Silence hung over the walls, over the roof, over the floors. The clock ticked on through it.

Then something fell from the fire, clattered beside those two still figures.

It was Burl's torch, lighting her funeral pyre—Eagles' Crag.

A sea-wind blowing from across the hills fanned the burning building. Sky, gorge, and moor-slopes were lit up with it.

Across the red sky went a great eagle, circling away, its wings lit up with the glare.

The molten rocks above Eagles' Crag, loosened from their soil, pressed slowly downwards. There was a thundering sound, which the hills threw back, a shower of sparks, flashes of flame, and down over the gorge went part of Eagles' Crag; the walls burst open as the roof went under that thundering force of rocks. The sheets of flame played in that opening. The sea-wind blew and fanned them. They spread like the wings of a great eagle shaped in fire. Slowly the house trembled. Another great pile of rocks moved downwards, and fell.

As though it leaped, Eagles' Crag was moving forwards.

It toppled over the gorge.

The dawn shone down on a heap of stones. From the reddened moor-slopes, alight with fire, came the cry of the curlews.

They rose over the burning heather.

They circled the sky, their wailings journeying through it.

The eagle was gone from the sky.

Eagles' Crag was laid low to the earth.

Of such fire is that which men call love.

The End